Praise for the
Cupcake Bakery Mysteries

"[McKinlay's] characters are delicious."
—*New York Times* bestselling author Sheila Connolly

"All the ingredients for a winning read."
—Cleo Coyle, *New York Times* bestselling author
of the Coffeehouse Mysteries

"McKinlay bakes a sweet read!"
—Krista Davis, *New York Times* bestselling author
of the Domestic Diva Mysteries

"A tender cozy full of warm and likable characters and a
refreshingly sympathetic murder victim. . . . Readers will
look forward to more of McKinlay's tasty concoctions."
—*Publishers Weekly* (starred review)

"Good plotting and carefully placed clues make this an en-
joyable, light mystery, made a little sweeter with recipes for
the cupcakes Mel's team creates." —The Mystery Reader

D0054546

For Batter or Worse

Jenn McKinlay

BERKLEY PRIME CRIME
New York

BERKLEY PRIME CRIME
Published by Berkley
An imprint of Penguin Random House LLC
penguinrandomhouse.com

ISBN: 9780593333372

First Edition: May 2021

Printed in the United States of America
1 3 5 7 9 10 8 6 4 2

For the Hub, Chris Hansen Orf, there aren't enough words to express how grateful I am for you. When my world fell apart and I was buried in grief, you held me together with infinite kindness, patience, understanding, and love. You truly are my best friend, my soul mate, and my one true love.

For
Batter
or Worse

One

"Wow, I just realized you're going to be a DeLaura and I'm not," Angie Harper said.

"Maybe." Melanie Cooper opened the door for her friend as they exited their co-owned bakery, Fairy Tale Cupcakes, and walked to Mel's car.

Well, Mel walked, Angie waddled. At thirty-two weeks, pregnant and being slight in stature, Angie carried her baby high and tight, looking like she'd strapped a basketball to her midsection.

"You're not going to take the DeLaura family name?" Angie asked. She sounded shocked. Mel was marrying Angie's older brother Joe DeLaura, who was smack in the middle of her seven older brothers.

"I haven't decided," Mel said. "We're a few weeks out yet, so I have time."

"Not if the brothers find out," Angie said. "You know they'll have something to say about it. What about Joe, what does he think?"

"He said I can do whatever I want," Mel said.

"Good," Angie said.

"What made you decide to take Tate's name?" Mel asked. She was genuinely curious as to why her normally independent-minded friend had gone traditional on the name thing.

Angie hugged her belly. "I surprised myself with that one, too, but I wanted to feel like I was becoming someone new. Also, Tate offered to become a DeLaura, so I felt like if it wasn't a big deal for him, it didn't need to be one for me. Also, there are enough DeLauras already. Besides, we've agreed that all of our kids will have De-Laura as a middle name, so that was enough for me."

"I imagine Joe and I will come up with something similar," Mel said. She opened the passenger-side door so Angie could slide into the front seat. "Maybe we—"

"Haven't you had that baby yet, Harper?"

Uh-oh. Mel glanced up and saw Olivia Puckett bearing down on them with her usual no-nonsense stride. A rival bakery owner, Olivia always wore a blue chef's coat and had her curly gray hair contained in an unruly topknot. She was not known for her tact or her diplomacy, and when she and Angie bumped into each other, it was usually with the force of two similarly charged magnets. They repelled each other.

"Not yet," Angie replied. She smiled at Olivia. "And how are you today?"

Olivia stumbled. She blinked. She frowned. "You look like you're having twins."

Mel hissed a breath. Didn't Olivia know not to comment on a pregnant woman's belly? This was going to get ugly. She glanced around the street, looking for help. There was no one. It was still early in the day for any tourists to be roaming Old Town Scottsdale. She reached for the phone in her purse. Marty Zelaznik, their main employee, was actually dating Olivia, and Mel figured it was his responsibility to rein her in. Not that Mel was afraid of Olivia. She glanced at the other woman's muscled forearms. Okay, she was a little afraid.

"Not twins," Angie said. She continued smiling and shrugged. "Just a big, bouncy, healthy baby."

Mel gave her a side eye. Was Angie okay? Had she spiked a fever? Usually, about now, the insults would be volleying back and forth between these women like a badminton birdie. Mel glanced at her friend's eyes. Were her pupils dilated?

Olivia's mouth twisted up as tight as her topknot. "Well, you should be grateful. Elephants gestate for twenty-three months."

"Twenty-two months, actually," Angie said. Then she leaned in and said in a conspiratorial whisper, "You wouldn't believe the number of people who have shared that factoid with me."

"Yeah, well . . ." Olivia looked flummoxed. "It's almost two years."

"Crazy, right?" Angie shook her head in wonder.

Olivia turned to Mel. "What's wrong with her?"

Mel shrugged. "Search me."

Angie reached over and patted Olivia's arm. "Have I ever told you how flattering that shade of blue is on you? You're really very pretty, you know."

3

Olivia started to back away. She glanced at Mel with wide eyes. "You should take her to the emergency room."

Then she hurried down the sidewalk as if she were afraid that Angie's sudden bout of niceness might be contagious. As soon as she was out of earshot, Mel burst out laughing. She turned to Angie and asked, "Is that your new way to drive her bananas?"

Angie looked puzzled. "I have no idea what you mean. I adore Olivia."

With that, she slid into the passenger seat, moving her legs so that Mel could shut the door after her. They were on their way to visit their former employee and friend Oscar Ruiz, known to all as Oz, at the Sun Dial Resort, where he was the master pastry chef. Mel and Joe were having their small wedding reception there, and Oz was baking the cupcakes, naturally, but now she wondered if perhaps Olivia wasn't right. Maybe she should take Angie to see her obstetrician on the way. Of all the symptoms she'd read about pregnancy, a personality transplant wasn't one of them.

Mel circled the car and got into the driver's seat. She glanced at Angie and said, "Feeling dehydrated at all?"

"No, I had a huge glass of water before we left the bakery."

"And you've been taking your vitamins."

"Faithfully."

"Huh."

Angie glanced at her as Mel started the car and left her parking spot to merge onto the street.

"What?" Angie asked.

"Nothing."

"Nope, I know you like I know my own eyebrows," Angie said. "That 'huh' wasn't nothing."

"I'm just surprised, that's all," Mel said.

"Surprised by what?"

"Your reaction to Olivia," Mel said. "You know she was trying to insult you."

Angie shrugged. She hugged her belly and said, "Whatever. I don't have time for that. Besides, I don't want to injure the baby's psyche by thinking bad thoughts."

"Is that possible?" Mel asked. That was a level of motherhood she wasn't sure she could handle.

"I don't want to take any chances," Angie said. "You know, some people say I have a temper."

"Really?" Mel asked. She wondered if she managed to feign surprise successfully. "You don't say."

"I know, shocked me, too," Angie said. "But I've read every pregnancy book out there and I just don't want to goof this up, so I've been doing a lot of meditation over the past few weeks and really trying to find my mama Zen."

Mel paused at a red light and turned to look at her friend. Angie had her long dark curls held in a band at the nape of her neck. Her maternity dress was a loosely fitting swing dress in a pretty shade of pink. She looked about as angelic as Mel had ever seen her. She reached across the console and squeezed Angie's hand.

"That is one lucky baby to have you for a mom," she said.

In an instant Angie's eyes filled with tears and she gulped. "You think so? I just want to be the best mom ever."

"You've got this," Mel said. "No doubt."

She handed Angie a tissue from the pack in the glove box and Angie blew her nose. It sounded like someone stepped on a goose. Mel turned her head to hide her smile. At least that hadn't changed.

"All right, enough sentiment," Angie said. She waved her tissue at the window. "Aren't there cupcakes waiting for us? Onward!"

Relieved, Mel put the Mini Cooper in gear and headed for the resort.

˹ ˵ ˶ ˺

The Sun Dial Resort was on the north side of Old Town. A classic resort built in the 1950s, the heyday of the tourist district, when cowboys and the Old West were all the rage, the Sun Dial had a very Frank Lloyd Wright mid-century modern vibe going on, which had appealed to Mel and Joe for the wedding reception even before Oz had taken the job as head pastry chef.

Mel parked in the visitors' lot and she and Angie strolled to the main entrance, passing the valet parking attendants and walking up the cobbled pathway under the giant, circular cement structures that provided shade. Succulent gardens lined both sides of the walkway and a fountain trickled in the center of the garden on the right. The base was done in copper with a teal patina, and perched in the middle was an enormous glass orb of delicious swirls of white and apple green with water pumping up through its center to pour out of the top and spill into the basin below.

Mel paused to study the glass-and-copper piece. She

felt an ache in her chest. Angie stepped beside her and linked her arm with Mel's. "One of Rene's?"

"I think so," Mel said. Her voice came out gruff as her throat was tight. Rene had been a local glass artist who had befriended Mel and Angie when they'd first opened their bakery. She had been murdered several months ago, and Mel still struggled with the loss of their friend. Rene had been such a force of nature in the community. Kind and generous, she'd even created the wedding topper for Mel and Joe's cake.

"She's still with us," Angie said. She put her hand over her heart. "I can feel her here."

Mel nodded. She could, too.

She shook her head and turned towards the large double doors. "Let's go find Oz and drown our sorrows in some decadent buttercream."

"Okay, but I get double portions," Angie said. She patted her belly. "I'm eating for two."

Mel laughed. "You've been using that for months. What are you going to do when the baby is born?"

"Well, I'll have to keep my strength up, won't I, to keep up with the rigorous nursing schedule of a newborn?"

"Fair point," Mel conceded.

They strode down the hallway, past the reception desk, through the large dining room. It was a sight to behold, with retro aqua-upholstered square-edged furniture, low kidney-shaped tables, and chrome starbursts decorating the walls. Mel felt as if she were walking back in time with the stonework walls and curved wood completing the mid-century vibe.

The swinging doors that led into the kitchens loomed

ahead and there, in his chef whites, with his chef toque perched on his head, was Oz. Mel felt a smile curve her mouth when she saw him. It was ridiculous to feel as if she hadn't seen him in months. He lived above their bakery in her old apartment and popped down to visit a couple of times each week. Still, he wasn't in their day-to-day lives anymore, and she missed him. Partly, because he was the best at wrestling Marty, their octogenarian wildcard, into line, but also because he just had that Oz essence of calm competence that she enjoyed so much.

At six foot four, he was tall with wide shoulders and muscled forearms. He looked as if he'd be more at home on a football field or wearing a tool belt than an apron, but no. Not Oz. His enormous hands could craft the most delicate flower petals out of fondant, and his intuitive taste for mixing new combinations of flavors like Earl Grey and lemon or rose and pistachio was unparalleled.

"Oz!" Angie let go of Mel's arm and darted forward. She held her arms wide, and when she was within range she launched herself, hugging him hard around the middle. Oz let out an *oof* but didn't stumble, and bent over and hugged her back. The affection between them was tangible and Mel knew Angie missed Oz as much as she did.

"Good to see you, Ange," he said.

"Yeah, yeah." She tipped her head back to look at his face. "'Can I use the facilities? 'Cause being pregnant makes me pee like Seabiscuit.'"

Oz barked out a laugh and then, because it was a long-running game between them, he identified the movie she had just quoted. "Juno."

"Nailed it." Angie held up her hand for a high five. Oz slapped her palm and then pointed across the dining room to an alcove that had the word *Restrooms* on a sign above it.

"Be right back," Angie called to Mel. "Don't start taste testing without me!"

"We have to wait for Joe," Mel reminded her.

Angie sent her a thumbs-up as she disappeared around the corner. Mel turned back to Oz and stepped in for a hug.

"This is not the Oz I'm used to seeing, in his Metallica T-shirts and ripped jeans," she said. After a quick squeeze, she let him go and stepped back, taking in the professional Oz in front of her.

"Since working here, I've gotten more into the Grateful Dead," he said.

"'Sugar Magnolia'?" she asked.

"'Ripple,'" he said. "This place can harsh a dude's mellow, if you know what I mean."

"Oh, yeah. During my first high-end kitchen gig, I used to bake at work and then go home and stress-bake and eat," Mel said, "Productive but also rather sad."

Oz laughed, "I'll stick with tunes, thanks."

"Smart choice."

She glanced around the dining room. It was massive and overlooked the golf course. In contrast, the room she and Joe were going to hold their reception in was a smaller venue set aside specifically for events. Their wedding was a small gathering of about fifty people, give or take a plus-one, because that's the way they wanted it.

A clattering noise came from the kitchen behind them and Oz visibly started. Mel frowned.

"Are you happy here, Oz?"

She had never asked him during the past six months if he was happy. Partly, she didn't want to know if he was. It was childish, she knew, to want him to regret leaving their bakery family, but it was what it was. She missed him and she wanted him to feel the same. If he said he was ecstatic and only regretted not leaving sooner, she'd be crushed flatter than rolled-out fondant.

"*Happy* is such a nebulous term," Oz said. He shrugged. "I mean, what is happiness anyway?"

"Being mindful and living your life with intention," Mel said. She'd thought long and hard about all of these things when she was just starting out. It was why she'd given up her misguided stint in the corporate world to open her bakery. If this was a pop quiz, she'd get an A. "You know, like going to work every day, doing something you enjoy with people you like."

"I'd say I'm running at about sixty percent," Oz said.

Mel latched on to the number. "So, you're not happy."

He smiled at her with a knowing look. "I'm not *not* happy."

"I'm confused," she said. "That percentage is not awesome."

"Sorry." He gestured to the kitchen behind him. "This is just a bit more complicated than the cupcake bakery. Lots of personalities, lots of hidden agendas, and power plays. I just want to bake."

"You're a purist," Mel said. "I get it. You might be better served having your own bakery, you know, like a franchise of a successful place but one you could call your own."

Oz looked at her. "I can't afford to buy into the Fairy Tale Cupcakes franchise," he said.

"But—"

"No *buts*." Oz held up his hand in a stop gesture. "I have to be able to stand on my own in the industry. I don't want to be your charity case."

"Oz, you're a brilliant chef," she said. "You don't have to have a franchise. We could make you an executive chef in charge of new flavors."

"I thought that was your job," he said.

"I could share," Mel said. "I'm getting married and Joe and I are considering having kids. I might have to make some changes and there's no one I would trust more in the research and development of Fairy Tale Cupcakes than you."

Oz bowed his head. A tinge of pink colored his cheeks. For years he'd worn a long fringe of hair that covered his eyes, but he'd recently cut the bangs off and it still disconcerted Mel to see his pretty long-lashed eyes, which were a soft brown, looking at her with shy embarrassment.

"Thanks," he said. "That means a lot."

"I mean every word."

"Is she trying to talk you into coming back to Fairy Tale Cupcakes?" Angie asked as she joined them.

Oz grinned and said, "She's—"

A horrific crash sounded from behind him, and he jumped and spun around. Before Mel could blink, he was pushing through the swinging doors to the kitchen.

Mel and Angie exchanged a look and hurried after him.

The yelling started almost immediately.

"Of all the worthless, stupid, idiotic sauciers I've ever had, you are the absolute worst." An older male chef was yelling at a young female, who stood trembling under his wrath. "It's a good thing you're easy on the eyes or I'd fire you right here, right now!"

Two

"Hey, Chef." Oz strode forward. His voice was cheerful, as if he could put out the other man's fiery temper with his own positive attitude. "Can I assist?"

The man turned to face them. Up close, his face was loose-jowled and puffy-eyed, with the bone structure of a man who'd formerly been good-looking. It was clear that he wasn't being treated kindly by the years. He had the red-nosed look of a man who drank too much and there was a mean twist to his lips. He did not look pleased to see Oz.

"Did I ask for your assistance, Ruiz?" The chef's tone was scathing.

"No, Chef," Oz answered. He didn't sound fazed in the least.

The rest of the kitchen staff stood frozen, as if they

didn't move then the chef wouldn't notice them and yell at them, too.

"Well, he seems like a peach to work with," Angie whispered to Mel. Except she didn't whisper.

Oz glanced back and shot her a wide-eyed look, clearly indicating she should hush.

"Sorry." Angie mouthed her apology. Oz nodded and turned back to the head chef.

He raised his hands in a placating gesture. "We're all on the same team, Chef." He glanced at the young woman, who stood with her head bowed and asked, "You all right, Sarah? You didn't get hurt, did you?"

The young woman blinked back the tears that filled her eyes. She shook her head. Her blond braid swung across her back and she sucked in a breath and said, "I'm fine. I just—"

"Well, I'm glad *you're* fine," Chef interrupted, his tone scathing. He balled his fingers into a fist and slammed it on the steel worktable, causing everyone in the kitchen to start. Very dramatic. "My dinner is ruined and it'll take my reputation with it. Do you have any idea what an honor it is to work for me, Miles Gallway, in *my* kitchen?"

Sarah flinched and cowered, but Oz drew himself up taller. Mel knew how he felt about bullies. She wondered if Chef Miles knew. She was betting no. She glanced at Angie, who was not known for letting acts of aggression go unchallenged, and noticed that the mother-to-be had put her hands over her belly, as if she would protect her wee one from the hostility pouring off the indignant chef.

"Chef, come on," Oz cajoled. "Accidents happen all the time. Kitchens are crazy, you know that. We have time to make it right and dinner will be fine."

The executive chef, or chef de cuisine, glared at Oz. He was not going to be talked out of his anger.

"You work for me, Ruiz," Chef said. "You exist in this kitchen at my pleasure and there are a million pâtissiers who would jump at the chance to take your job, and don't you forget it."

"Yes, Chef," Oz said. His mouth was a thin line and Mel suspected he was forcibly holding in his temper. The two men stared at each other for a long moment.

"Don't you have some buttercream to mix?" Chef Miles snapped. He managed to slight the position of pastry chef, and Mel felt her own temper heat.

"Nah, *my* kitchen is perfectly in order," Oz said. He made a careless shrug as if he hadn't just delivered a barely veiled insult.

Mel was in awe. Her mild-mannered former sous chef was not the least bit intimidated by the head chef. Had she been in Oz's shoes at his age, she would have hidden in the walk-in freezer until she either froze to death or the chef calmed down. The hierarchy in the kitchen was sacrosanct. One simply did not butt heads with the chef de cuisine even when he was wrong. It was always "Yes, Chef" or "*Oui*, Chef." Period.

"If this imbecile hadn't dropped tonight's tomato sauce then my kitchen would be just fine," Miles snapped. "But no, I've been saddled with a saucier who is too stupid to live."

A single tear slipped down the young woman's cheek.

"That's enough, Chef!" Oz snapped. He looked like he wanted to punch Miles in the mouth and Mel wouldn't have blamed him a bit. "Sarah, go grab two of the busboys to help clean up the mess."

The young woman nodded and dashed away, clearly relieved to be out of the room.

"How dare you undermine me in my own kitchen," Miles hissed. If Oz didn't tower over him by at least eight inches, Mel was certain he'd take a swing at him. "You think you're such hot stuff, Ruiz, then take over tonight's dinner."

He yanked off his coat, which was almost comical when he didn't pause to unfasten it and tried to tug it over his head. He staggered around a bit and then ripped the coat free and tossed it on top of the crushed tomatoes that had been spilled on the floor.

Mel, Angie, and Oz watched as he tipped his chin up and stormed from the kitchen. Oz glanced at Mel and rolled his eyes.

"Any chance you two are free to help me prep dinner?" he asked.

"My savory skills are a bit rusty, but I'm in," Mel said. "Angie, are you up for it?"

"Of course," she said. She glanced between them. "It'll be fun."

᛭

It was not fun. It was chaotic and messy and Mel wondered if she and Angie were more of a help or a hindrance in the prepping of the resort's dinner. The restaurant wouldn't open for a few hours but there was much work to be done beforehand.

The resort kitchen operated in the brigade style, meaning the chefs were assigned stations and specific tasks, such as Sarah the saucier, who was in charge of sauces, hot appetizers, and finishing touches on the meat. The concept had been popularized by the famed French chef Auguste Escoffier.

Angie and Mel stepped in to help by preparing stations. Angie fetched and carried from the larder as directed, while Mel stocked stations with olive oil, bottles of water, and clean kitchen cloths. She had a flashback to her cooking school days and remembered why she'd been drawn to the sweet side. Aside from her love of baked goods, she hated the stress of the timing required for meals. Plating everything, presenting it all, getting multiple meals to customers on time and hot. It completely stressed her out.

Oz hunkered down at the saucier station with Sarah. Together they re-created the ruined sauce, and even from where Mel was standing on the other side of the kitchen, it smelled divine. Oz had savory skills—who knew?

Utilizing her former teaching skills, Angie started to banter with the chefs. In no time, she had the mood of the kitchen elevated. Mel had never appreciated Angie's people skills more. She had a magical way of rallying the troops when it was needed.

Oz worked the kitchen like a champ. He had everyone moving with the rhythm of those accustomed to working as a unit in a high-pressure situation. He consulted with the butcher and the larder chef, and they both nodded as he directed them around the evening's menu, which he already knew even though he was in charge of the bread and desserts. Mel was sweating, literally, over the rub she was applying to a rack of ribs, when another chef entered the kitchen.

She was very tall, slender but curvy, had enormous

blue eyes, and dark brown hair in a bun at the nape of her neck. She surveyed the kitchen and a frown line appeared between her eyes. She zeroed in on Mel.

"Who are you? Where is Miles?" she demanded.

Mel glanced at Oz. He was inspecting the prep work being done on the fish station and didn't notice her.

"Excuse me, I asked where is Chef Miles?" The female chef's voice went up to shrill and Mel winced.

Oz glanced over at the woman and said, "He stepped out for a sec, Ashley."

Ashley crossed her arms over her chest and stared Oz down. "And you just thought you'd step in and take over?"

"Not exactly," Oz said. He seemed completely unperturbed by the woman's ire. "There was a spill, so when Miles . . . had to get some air, I thought I'd make sure dinner stayed on schedule."

He gave her a pointed look and Mel suspected that Ashley was Miles's sous chef and should have been here to step into the breach, but she hadn't been.

So much drama in the kitchen. Mel wondered how Oz could stand it.

Mel noticed that none of the other chefs looked particularly happy to see Ashley. Kitchens were pretty high-stress environments. It really mattered who was in charge and so far it looked as if this kitchen had two of the most miserable chefs Mel had ever seen running things.

"*I'm* here now," Ashley said. "You can go back to your pastries and cupcakes."

Oz glanced around the kitchen. He made eye contact with the staff as if to be certain they were okay with his leaving. His gaze lingered on Sarah. She gave him a tremulous nod and Oz turned back to Ashley.

"All right, here's the rundown," he said. He proceeded to tell her the progress of the dinner prep, at which Ashley looked completely uninterested, even going so far as to inspect her manicure. Mel frowned. Ashley's highly polished red talons were not those of a real chef. Kitchen work was hard on the hands and didn't allow for that sort of thing. She wondered if Ashley had ever had an acrylic tip break off in someone's food. Oh, horror.

Mel handed the bowl of rub over to the chef closest to her. She and Angie tossed their borrowed aprons into the laundry bin and headed for the door. Before they reached it, Miles slammed back through the doors with so much force Angie jumped and let out a curse word.

Mel steadied her on her feet and they both watched as the chef de cuisine glanced around the kitchen with a sour look on his face. He strode forward and demanded, "What is going on in my kitchen?"

At this, Ashley snapped to attention and repeated everything Oz had just told her, but rather than give Oz any credit, she spun it so it sounded as if she'd been there running the show. Oz rolled his eyes as he walked towards Angie and Mel.

"And you, Ruiz!" Miles yelled after him. "Stay in your own kitchen!"

"With pleasure," Oz said. He strode past Mel and Angie, pushed open the door, which he held for them, and led the way to the pâtissier's kitchen, which was its own contained room at the end of the narrow hallway.

"Is it normal for resorts to have separate kitchens for savory and sweet?" Angie asked.

Oz shrugged. "We do so many weddings and special events here that there needed to be a separate kitchen for baking. Can you imagine trying to bake a cake in that chaos? We also have a separate kitchen for banquets as well. The banquet chef is super chill, which is amazing because we do get some high-maintenance brides coming through."

Mel shuddered. She couldn't imagine trying to bake cupcakes in the insanity of Chef Miles's kitchen. "The drama."

"Exactly," Oz said. He pushed through another set of double doors and the scent of all good things engulfed Mel like a hug. Chocolate, cinnamon, lemon, vanilla, butter, all the smells that comforted her and made life worth living, as far as she was concerned, filled the air.

Standing by a large steel worktable was a tall man with broad shoulders, wavy dark brown hair, and a smile that still made Mel weak in the knees. Joe. The man who in a matter of weeks was going to be her husband.

"Hey, cupcake, where've you been?" he asked. He stepped forward to kiss Mel, before turning to hug his sister, Angie. He maneuvered around her big belly and grinned when she wobbled on her feet. He steadied her, helping her onto a nearby stool. Then he turned and shook Oz's hand.

"Hey, Joe."

"Good to see you, Oz."

"Chef, I've started working on the lemon curd." A young man in a black chef beret and white coat approached, juggling an armful of ingredients.

Oz stepped forward to help him out and consulted with him by the stove, where the curd was cooking. Mel watched as he moved over to speak to the other two chefs in the large, well-lit space. One was kneading dough for the evening's dinner rolls while another dipped fat red strawberries into a pot of liquid chocolate. Yum.

It hit Mel again how much of a grown-up Oz had become. Running a kitchen, ordering people around in that upbeat, confident way he had. She felt a burst of pride rocket through her as she remembered the awkward teen who had arrived at the bakery's front door a few years before.

No, she didn't take credit for how well he had turned out. Okay, maybe just a little. But she had to admit that his decision to leave the bakery and go out on his own had been a good one. He was clearly ready to be his own man—in fact, he was thriving. When he rejoined them he met Mel's stare.

"What?" he asked.

"What what?" Mel countered.

"You're staring at me with that *proud mom* look you get," he said.

"Am I?" she asked. She grinned. "'Don't ever let anybody tell you they're better than you.'"

"Mrs. Gump," Angie said, identifying the character who said the movie quote.

"*Forrest Gump*," Oz clarified.

"Just so," Angie said. They exchanged a knuckle bump.

"All right, let's get down to business," Oz said. "I'm going to get the samples I made for your wedding reception. I went for romantic but with plenty of subtle flare. I'll be right back."

Mel and Joe exchanged a look. "I'm the romance," he said. "You're the flare."

Mel laughed. "I'm quite certain I'm the romance, given that I'm the one in the poofy dress and all."

"What about me and baby?" Angie asked. "I'm quite certain we're the flare." She gestured around her large belly and Mel nodded.

"I'm going to have to give you that one."

Oz returned bearing a fully loaded tray. Mel gasped at the sight of the cupcakes. They were decorated with incredibly elaborate flowers, all done in shades of pale pink and sunset orange, and at the end of the tray sat a bride cupcake in a lacy paper cutout wrapper, sporting a veil on the elaborate swirl of vanilla frosting, and beside it was a cupcake in a tuxedo paper liner with a tiny top hat perched on top of its chocolate frosting.

"Bride and groom cupcakes," Mel sighed. She clasped her hands over her heart. "They're perfect."

"I know you have that glass cake topper from Rene," Oz said. "And I plan to make a small cake in the same sunset colors as the cupcakes that you can take home and save for your first anniversary, or some random night at midnight when the mood strikes, but the bride and groom cupcakes can be eaten at the reception while Rene's piece will stay on display for the whole event."

"Genius," Angie chimed in.

"Agreed," Joe said.

Mel nodded. She had wanted her friend Rene's glass sculpture to be featured. "That's perfect. Thanks, Oz."

He grinned. "All right, now let's discuss flavors. We've got a lot happening here."

Joe rubbed his hands together. His sweet tooth was legendary. "Hit me."

"All right, this one is the classic flavor of chocolate cake with vanilla icing but with a twist." Oz picked up one of the cupcakes that had very pretty sweet pea blossoms piped on top of it. He plated it and then handed it to Mel and Joe with two forks.

"Ahem," Angie said. Oz grinned and gave her a cupcake all to herself. "You get your own, because you're eating for two."

"See?" Angie asked Mel with a grin, then she laughed.

Angie beamed and helped herself to a forkful. Mel studied the cupcake in front of her. Given that Joe, local district attorney, was marrying her, a cupcake baker, she felt that the cupcakes had to have a wow factor of epic proportions. Their guests were mostly family and friends, but she still felt appearances mattered, and there was no one she trusted more than Oz.

Her fork slid through the delicate petals of pale pink icing and into the decadently moist cake. She tried to have a fifty-fifty ratio of cake to frosting on her fork. She glanced at Joe and noted that he had done the same, instead of stuffing the entire cupcake into his mouth, which she had seen him do before on occasions of high stress. She didn't judge. She'd had a few days in her life where if she could have mainlined frosting, she would have.

"Count of three," Joe said. She nodded. "One, two, three."

Mel bit down on her fork. The first taste was one of the pleasantly comforting commingling of cake and frosting. Yum. Was there any greater source of food in the world? No, there was not. Then a sneaky explosion of flavor crept up on her and she straightened up and glanced at Oz. A small smile played on his lips. She chewed slowly, processing the flavor of melted chocolate within the chocolate cake. She gasped.

"I know, right?" Oz asked.

"Ermagawd." Joe swallowed and went in for another forkful. "It's like you made a chocolate lava cake in the cupcake."

Oz rocked back on his heels, clearly pleased. "Just wait until you get to the daisy-shaped one."

"What'd you do to the daisy?" Mel asked. Oz plated one for her and pushed it in front of her. The palest pink icing had streaks of a deeper rose color, but the flower's shape was that of a daisy with a burst of colorful sprinkles filling the center of the flower. Mel used the side of her fork to slice through the vanilla cupcake, cutting out a wedge as if it were a mini cake and she was serving tiny pieces. She stabbed the slice with her fork and when she lifted the morsel, the center of the cupcake spilled out in a river of sprinkles.

"Ha!" Joe laughed. "The kids at the reception will love that."

"That was the plan," Oz said. "I figured the kids would lock on the cupcakes with the sprinkle centers."

"Oz, that's genius," Mel said. She turned to look at Angie. "Why did we let him go?"

"Shortsighted," she said through a mouthful. "Clearly, we should have kept him locked up in the pantry for our own good."

"What's this? Is someone trying to steal my pastry chef?" A man entered the kitchen. He had a deep tan and was wearing golf attire, a bright green polo shirt over equally bright green and blue plaid shorts. He had on a visor and a right-handed glove. He'd obviously just gotten off the course.

"Afternoon, Mr. Perry," Oz said. He turned to them and said in a low voice, "That's Mr. Perry, he owns the

Sun Dial Resort." As the man joined them, Oz said, "This is Joe DeLaura and Melanie Cooper. Their wedding reception is going to be here in a couple of weeks. And this is Angie Harper."

"Matron of honor, at your service." Angie nodded at the man, while Mel felt herself get a little dizzy at Oz's announcement. Sure, she knew their wedding was just a few weeks away, but hearing someone else say it made it so much more real. It was hard to believe. After all this time, she and Joe were finally getting married. It felt like a small miracle.

"Joe DeLaura, as in Assistant District Attorney Joe DeLaura?" Mr. Perry asked.

"That's right," Joe said. He wiped his fingers on a napkin and shook the man's hand. "Nice to meet you, Mr. Perry. You have a beautiful resort."

"Thank you. Call me Clay," he said. He turned to Mel and shook her hand as well. He extended his hand to Angie but turned it into a wave as she had moved on with trying the flavors and was now double-fisting with a cupcake in each hand.

"This one is loaded with caramel," she said. "Soooo good."

Clay laughed. He turned to Oz and said, "Hiring you was one of my best decisions to date."

"Was it, was it really?" a voice asked from behind them. "Do you have any idea of what he's done?"

They all glanced at the door to see Miles Gallway standing there. He had his arms crossed over his chest, a dripping ladle in his hand, and his chef's toque perched low on his brow. He used the ladle to point at Oz. "He ruined tonight's main course!"

Three

Clay looked from Miles to Oz and back. He frowned. "Explain."

"I leave my kitchen for one minute and this puppy steps in and takes over, as if a pastry chef"—Chef Miles paused to sneer—"could even attempt to manage the demands of the main kitchen. I studied for years in the kitchens of the finest restaurants around the world."

Mel glanced at Oz. He crossed his arms over his chest, looking unimpressed with Miles's tantrum.

Clay opened his mouth to speak, but Miles wasn't done. "And where did *he* train? Some silly little cupcake bakeshop in the tourist trap portion of the city under the tutelage of some woman who likely wouldn't know a spatula from a garlic press—"

"Oh, now he's done it," Joe muttered. He maneuvered

himself in between Angie and Miles, as if he could body-block her when she pounced. Mel prepared to dive into the fray as well. She didn't even want to think about what Tate would have to say if his firecracker of a wife got into a brawl during her advanced months of pregnancy.

Angie, who was working her way through what looked like a lemon-filled cupcake, glanced up at them and asked, "What?"

"Nothing." Joe shrugged. "Just, you know, making sure you're not upset."

"Why would I be upset?" Angie asked.

"Because we just got insulted," Mel said. "Like *really* insulted."

Angie blinked. Mel braced herself for her fiery friend to launch her attack. She didn't. Instead, she looked past them at Chef Miles, tipped her head to the side, and said, "Meh."

Mel glanced over her shoulder and saw Oz blinking in confusion. Loyal to the end, Angie never took insults to her friends well. In fact, if she even perceived a deroga-tory statement about someone she cared about, she deliv-ered a stinging rebuke, sometimes accompanied by a physical takedown.

"You're not even going to insult him back?" Oz asked in surprise.

Angie looked Chef Miles over again and shrugged. "He's one of those types. You know, the ones who have an overinflated sense of their own worth. He's not worth the time or effort."

Gallway looked like he was about to pitch a fit, but Angie continued unperturbed.

"If every amazing woman had the confidence of a mediocre man"—she paused to give Chef Miles a dismissive look—"then whatever the silly man said to diminish the woman really wouldn't matter, now, would it?"

Chef Miles sputtered and choked. "Who are you calling mediocre?"

Angie studied her cupcakes, not even bothering to look at him. "You," she said.

"How dare you." The chef drew himself up to his full height. "Do you know who I am?"

"The guy who had better not get spittle on my cupcakes or we're going to have a problem," Angie snapped.

Chef Miles must have seen something in her hard stare, because he toned it down immediately. It was the wise choice.

"Now, Miles, settle yourself," Clay said. "Oz is still new here. Whatever he did, I'm sure it was an innocent mistake."

"No, it wasn't," Oz said. He, too, drew himself up to his full height, which allowed him to loom over Miles. "You screamed and insulted your saucier and then stormed out of your kitchen right in the middle of prep. So, I stepped in and made tonight's sauce using my own recipe because I didn't have access to yours."

"Oz, it is not okay to alter the chef de cuisine's recipes," Clay said. His tone was a gentle rebuke.

Oz shrugged. "Well, when the chef leaves the kitchen in a snit, you do what you can to help."

Chef Miles held up the ladle under Clay's nose. "Taste this. Tell me if you think this is fit to serve under the name Miles Gallway."

Clay shrugged and dabbed his finger into the ladle. He popped his finger in his mouth and let the flavor of the sauce Oz had created with Sarah settle for a moment. Then he smiled and turned to Oz. "What did you put in there? It's an excellent tomato sauce but there's something different about it. I can't put my finger on it."

Ignoring Chef Miles, he dabbed the ladle for another taste. "It's exotic and yet familiar." He narrowed his eyes at Oz. "What is it? You have to tell me."

"Cinnamon, allspice, and nutmeg," Oz said. "A little bit of Greek influence."

"Fantastic!"

"This is not my signature sauce," Chef Miles snapped. "And the last time I checked this was *my* kitchen."

Clay's smile vanished and he nodded vigorously. "Quite right. Sorry, that flavor combination was just so intriguing. I could taste it on a nice linguine."

"You can't be serious!" Chef Miles blustered. "How can you even think of encouraging this *thug* in my kitchen?"

He emphasized the word *thug* and Mel was certain she could hear a soufflé collapse in the ensuing silence. Then Chef Miles decided to double down on the insults.

"You—" With his pointer finger Chef Miles jabbed Oz in the chest. The wall of muscle that was Oz did not budge. "You're a child. Untried. Untested. Try doing more than slam out cakes and pastries in the safety of the pâtissier's kitchen and then you can talk to me about how I manage mine."

He sounded so superior. It chafed and Mel found herself rising to Oz's defense even when she had promised herself she would stay out of it.

"I don't know." Mel shrugged. "As a Cordon Bleu graduate myself, I'd say he handled your kitchen just fine."

Oz grinned at her and Angie nodded in approval. Joe

put his hand around Mel's waist in an obvious show of support that also signaled to Chef Miles not to come after her. Mel appreciated the gesture but she didn't need backup. She'd dealt with a slew of Miles Gallways in the culinary industry. He could take his best shot and he still wouldn't be able to rile her.

"I ought to quit," Chef Miles declared. "That would show you! You don't deserve the brilliance, the artistry, of Miles Gallway."

Joe gagged. They all turned to look at him and he said, "Sorry, choked on some frosting."

Given that he wasn't eating at the moment; it was a flagrant fib. Miles, clearly not wanting to lose the momentum of his histrionics, ignored him.

"That would show you!" he declared. He scowled at Clay. "I'll leave and then what will you do? You need me. You need my name recognition to make your tired old resort the hip and happening spot it is. You need me!"

Clay rocked back on his heels. He pushed his visor back on his head. He studied Miles for a beat or two and then he nodded slowly, as if coming to terms with what Miles said. "You're right. You're probably too big of a name for the Sun Dial. You likely have offers to be the executive chef in high-end restaurants all over the world. We can't keep you here."

Chef Miles looked uncertain for a moment. Clearly he'd been hoping he'd bring Clay to his knees by threatening to leave. Having Clay agree with him put him in an awkward spot, but he was in too far to back out now.

"It's a shame, really," Clay said. "I've got Simon Marconi coming into town from the Foodie Channel. He's looking for the next big star. Of course, I told him you were here, and he thought maybe it was time for you to make your comeback, but if you're out, you're out." He turned his back on Miles and looked at Oz. "Ever think of cooking on television, young man? You've got the skills."

Oz's eyes went wide with horror. "No. Never."

Mel smiled. He was still her shy Urban Tech High School student at heart.

"Pity," Clay said.

"Well, I can see you're in a bind," Miles said. His bluster vanished and with his free hand he smoothed the front of his chef's coat—not the one he'd thrown on the floor, judging by its lack of stains—as if he were preparing to go into battle. "I suppose I'll stay just to help you out. It wouldn't do for me to leave and have the food be subpar in my absence."

They all looked at him without speaking. How he had twisted the conversation to make it sound like he could save the day, Mel had no idea. And who did he think he was fooling with his abrupt one-eighty the minute the Foodie Channel was mentioned? It certainly wasn't anyone in their group. Mercy, what an ego this guy had.

Miles looked at them expectantly and when no one said anything, he said, "You're welcome." Then he turned on his heel and stormed for the door. Once he reached it, he spun back around, pointed his ladle at Oz, and while tomato sauce dripped onto the floor, shouted, "And, you, stay out of my kitchen!"

The door swung shut behind him and Clay sighed. "What a horse's ass he is."

No one argued.

"I'm sorry he came after you, Oz," Clay said. "Just try

to steer clear of him. He's a prima donna but he's harmless and, sadly, I do need his name recognition to get butts into the restaurant chairs."

"No worries," Oz said. "We're going to be slammed with events over the next few weeks, so Miles and I will be too busy to cross paths."

"Excellent," Clay said. He leaned back and studied Oz. He scratched his chin and said, "Are you sure you're not interested in doing a spot on television? You'd be a smashing success."

"No, thank you, but no," Oz said. "That is not my scene, at all."

"If you ever change your mind . . ." Clay let his words hang in the air. He clapped Oz on the back and left the kitchen.

"Who knew there was so much drama in the world of professional kitchens?" Angie asked. "I always thought that Foodie Channel stuff was made up to draw in the viewers."

Oz shrugged. "There's a lot of ego involved in the culinary arts."

"Which is why I like running my own shop," Mel said. "And our franchised bakeries can manage their own shops their own ways. No drama."

She glanced at Oz to see if he had any reaction to her words. He did not. So frustrating.

"What *is* in this?" Joe asked. He had gotten back to the work at hand and was eating a chocolate cupcake with a peony frosting flower on top. His face had gone slack and he looked like was sliding into some sort of sublime sugar coma.

Oz smiled knowingly. "It's my chocolate orange cupcake. Chocolate cake with orange buttercream with a handmade chocolate orange truffle tucked in the middle. It's not bad."

"Not bad?" Joe asked. "It's the best thing I've ever—" He stopped speaking and glanced at Mel. He swallowed. "What I meant to say was—"

"Uh-huh, try and save yourself, big brother," Angie said. She grinned and propped her chin on her hand, enjoying watching him squirm.

"It's the best I've ever tasted that wasn't Mel's," Joe said. He looked quite proud of himself.

Mel gave him a dubious look, then gently elbowed him aside and tucked her fork into the decadent flower-shaped frosting. It was so smooth, it looked sinful. She dug deep into the spongy chocolate cake, making sure she got a bit of the truffle as well. As the first bite touched her tongue, she thought her eyes might roll back into her head.

"Oz, that is the most amazing thing I've ever tasted," she said. Sort of. It came out more like *Owz, dat's de mos amzing ding I'b eber dasded*. The whole manners thing of not talking with your mouth full going right into the garbage bin as the truffle melted on her tongue, followed by the luscious cake and silky-smooth icing.

Mel dropped her fork. She grabbed Oz by the shirt-front. "What wizardry is this?"

Oz laughed. It was his first hearty laugh of the day and it made Mel feel better that he could laugh, given the hostile environment in which he was working. Not that it was any of her business, but still.

"All right, give it here," Angie said. She pulled the plate in front of her and tucked her fork in. She took a bite and blinked. "Oh, wow, oh, my, that is . . . something."

"See?" Joe asked.

He went to take the plate back but Angie held on to it. They started a sibling tug-of-war, which Oz ended by plating another two peony cupcakes and putting them in front of them. "I made plenty. Don't make yourselves sick."

Angie's eyes lit up as she reached for the plate closest to her.

"So, what do you think?" Oz asked Mel. Joe had an opinion, of course, but they both knew Mel would be the deciding vote.

She glanced at the array of cupcakes. Oz had outdone himself.

"Let's take a walk," she said.

Joe and Angie both paused in their eating to look at her. She gave them a tiny nod to let them know it was all right. Relieved, they went back to eating.

"Okay," Oz said.

He frowned in confusion but led the way out of the kitchen through a side door that opened up onto a patio that contained a small kitchen garden. Mel paused to take in the pots of herbs and small citrus trees. She glanced at Oz and he shrugged. "Fresh ingredients are best."

She grinned. She always hit the Old Town farmers' market, but having a kitchen garden was genius. Oz really was flourishing here.

He led the way onto a path that circled the resort. They walked side by side in silence until Oz finally asked, "If you didn't like the cupcakes, you could have told me in front of Angie and Joe. I'm not that sensitive."

"This isn't about the cupcakes," Mel said. Now that they were out of the kitchen, she wasn't sure how to broach the subject. She was Oz's former boss, his current landlord, and his friend. His life wasn't any of her business, except that she cared about him.

"Oh, god, it isn't Marty, is it?" he asked. He sounded panicked. "What's wrong with him?"

"No." Mel rushed to reassure him. "Marty's fine. Everyone is fine."

"Oh." Oz gave her a side eye and she could see the confusion on his face.

"Are you happy here, Oz?" she asked. They paused beside the golf course. The sweep of green lawn rippled all the way to the edge of the rough-and-tumble desert beyond.

"I don't know if *happy* is the word I would use," he said.

"It should be," Mel said.

"Should it?" he asked. He turned and squinted out across the meticulously groomed fairway. "Isn't there a certain amount of paying your dues that you have to do when you start out? You know, time in, punishment served, and all of that?"

Mel considered the question. She had so despised her postcollege career path in marketing that she'd saved a chunk of money and dumped it all into attending cooking school, which had included a semester in Paris. When she'd returned, she'd worked a few jobs in professional kitchens and hated it. When her friend Tate had offered to stake her in her own bakery, she'd jumped at the chance.

"I suppose it doesn't hurt to know what not to do," she said. "It seems like Miles Gallway has given you an exemplary hands-on lesson in that."

Oz snorted but he didn't confirm or deny. Mel wanted to ask a million questions. She wanted to butt right into his business, but she held herself back. Oz was a grown-up and if he wanted her advice, he'd ask for it.

"He's not so bad," Oz said. He didn't sound very convincing.

Mel snapped her head in his direction. She pressed her lips together to keep from saying anything when what she wanted to do was blast him with a *What?!*

Oz met her gaze and said, "All right, let it out before you hurt yourself."

"He's awful!" Mel said. "I know his type. He's a bully and he enjoys running his kitchen by making everyone afraid. He wields his authority like a weapon and it sucks, sucks, sucks."

"Don't hold back," Oz said. "Say what you think."

"He's puffy and I noticed his hands shake," Mel said. "Closet drinker, there. And why do you think he screamed at Sarah? Youngest and female, easy pickin's. Oh, I know his type, all right. You should steer clear of him. You've made an enemy and I'm betting he'll do something to exact revenge. His sort always does."

"He's like half my size," Oz protested. "What exactly could he do?"

"Ruin your kitchen," Mel said. "You want rats in your pantry?"

Oz's eyes went huge and he shuddered.

"He'll do it," she insisted. "Trust me, I've seen that kind of behavior before. Petty and mean."

Oz glanced back at the resort. He looked mildly panicked.

"He's not going to do it now," she said. "But seriously, watch your back."

"Noted." He studied the features of the mid-century modern resort with its molded cement work and natural stone. "You know, I just wanted to have my own kitchen. I wanted to be the boss, prove myself, and start experimenting with my own desserts."

"That chocolate orange truffle cupcake was a heck of a start," she said.

Oz smiled. "But this"—he paused and gestured at the building with his hands—"this drama festival was way more than I bargained on."

"You were right before. There is tremendous ego in the culinary arts," Mel said. "It's changing as abusers get called out, but chefs like Miles Gallway will always think that they are lord and master over their kitchen staff, and because you're kitchen adjacent and technically under his executive management, he thinks you're his whipping boy, too. That's why he was so furious when you stepped up in his kitchen."

"What was I supposed to do? Let Mr. Perry down by letting dinner get ruined?" Oz seemed genuinely perplexed.

"I don't think that would have happened," Mel said. "The thing about chefs and their egos? They can't have their reputation tarnished by serving a bad meal. Miles stormed off, like a kid who gets tagged out and then quits the game, but he fully expected everyone to come and beg him to come back to the kitchen because they couldn't function without him. You proved that they could, and he'll never forgive you for that."

"Snap," Oz said. "Do you really think he'll put rats in my pantry?"

"Or weevils in your flour," Mel said. "It might not be rats in the pantry, could be pantry moths. Or he'll ruin you in other ways, like arranging a power outage during a big bake."

"Why?" Oz asked. He was genuinely puzzled. "Aren't we all trying to represent the resort kitchen in its best possible light?"

"Ego," Mel said. "Never underestimate the ego of some chefs."

Oz shook his head. "Let's go. I keep the pantry locked with the key on the doorframe above, but I think I need to hit the store and buy some heavy-duty plastic storage containers. I can't have critters in my pantry."

They walked back towards the resort. "Oz, you don't think Miles would go off the deep end and try to hurt you, do you?"

Oz blew out a breath as if he'd been considering it but was holding it in until Mel said something first, allowing him to let it out. "I honestly don't know."

Four

"Shut the front door!" A shout sounded from the front of the bakery, and Mel snapped her head at the swinging doors, expecting to see her octogenarian counter help, Marty Zelaznik, appear. He did not.

Angie was seated on a stool across the steel worktable from her. They were decorating a batch of specialty gender-reveal cupcakes so the frosting was half-pink and half-blue. Inside the cupcakes was a pink center of raspberry cream, because the baby was going to be a girl. They had not done the same thing for Angie because, much to everyone's chagrin, she and Tate had decided not to find out if Baby Harper was a boy or a girl.

"What do you suppose that was about?" Angie asked.

The swinging doors slammed open and Marty appeared. His bald head was pink and shiny and his navy blue Fairy Tale Cupcakes apron was askew and had a smear of buttercream on the bib.

"Turn on the TV, Channel Nine," he cried.

"What?" Mel asked.

"Why? Is there a fire?" Angie asked.

She was already in motion and pushed off her stool and crossed the kitchen as swiftly as her pregnant belly would allow. She grabbed the remote and switched on the television they kept in the kitchen. It was mounted on the wall, as Mel liked to watch old movies when she pulled an all-nighter on a special order.

Angie flicked through the channels, pausing on Channel 9. In seconds, the beaming smile of Oscar Ruiz, former employee of Fairy Tale Cupcakes, was smiling out at them as he demonstrated the proper technique when piping icing out of a pastry bag.

Mel felt her mouth drop open. "Oz? That's our Oz!"

"I know! Look at him!" Marty clapped a hand onto his bald head. "He looks like a movie star."

"But he said . . ." Angie paused and bit her lip. She looked at Mel and asked, "He did say he wasn't interested, right? My pregnant brain didn't make me hallucinate that, did it?"

"No, that's what he said," Mel agreed.

"Hush, he's talking," Marty said.

"Then you want to hold the bag at an angle and pipe the frosting in a thick swirl, working from the outside to the center," Oz instructed.

"My, you do have a wonderful technique," Stella, the morning-show host, purred as she leaned up against Oz.

Angie made a low rumble in her throat. "I didn't know Stella was so handsy."

They watched as Oz handed Stella a pastry bag and helped her decorate a cupcake. He was handsome and charming and the camera loved him. When he flashed a smile, two dimples appeared in his cheeks, which clearly charmed the socks off Stella.

"Hoo boy, look at him," Marty said. "He's like the Henry Cavill of cupcake baking."

The segment ended with Stella biting into one of Oz's cupcakes and fake-swooning. Oz deftly caught her in his arms and then smiled at the camera. Marty was right. He was 100 percent movie-star Foodie Channel material.

"How?" Mel turned to Angie.

Angie shrugged and switched off the television as it segued to the weather. "Search me. He sounded like he'd rather be dipped in honey and tied to the top of a hill of fire ants when the owner of the resort suggested it."

"So, he must have changed his mind," Mel said. "But why and when?"

Marty pulled out his phone and rapid-fired a text. "I don't know, but we're going to find out."

"Hey, is anyone working here?" A man in black leather pants topped with a blue silk shirt unbuttoned down to his chest hair, allowing the thick gold chain around his neck to be seen, poked his head around the door.

"Yeah, yeah, keep your shirt on," Marty said. Then he squinted at Ray, one of Angie's brothers, and added, "In your case, please, keep your shirt on. No one needs to see that much hair when trying to eat a cupcake."

"What? Chest hair is a sign of manliness." He extended his arms wide as if shocked by any insinuation otherwise.

"Right," Marty said. "Very *GQ* that shag carpeting you're sporting."

He strode towards the door, glancing back at Mel as he went. "If you hear from Oz first, you tell me what he says."

"Same," Mel said.

"Yo, Ange, how's my little namesake doing today?" Ray asked. He crossed the room and leaned down to kiss Angie's cheek.

"I am not naming the baby after you, Ray," Angie said. "We've been over this."

"You'll change your mind," he said. He seemed very confident. "After all, how else can you show your affection for your favorite brother?"

"I don't have a favorite," Angie said. "I hate you all equally most of the time."

Ray laughed. He looked at Mel and said, "Just a couple of weeks until the big day, eh, Sis?"

His eyes twinkled at her, and while Ray might not be Angie's favorite brother, he was Mel's. Mostly because they had a bit of a checkered history of escaping from gunmen together. In-laws that run from bad guys together bond, plus, Ray made her laugh.

"Yeah, it feels like it came up really fast," she said.

"You're not getting cold feet, are you?" he asked. One hairy eyebrow shot up higher than the other.

"Nope," she said. "I've never been more sure of anything in my life."

"Excellent," he said. "Melanie DeLaura, it's got a nice ring to it."

Mel and Angie exchanged a look but neither of them said anything. No need to make Ray fret over Mel's indecision about her surname.

"Did you want cupcakes or what?" Marty poked his head back through the door to yell at Ray.

"Keep your apron on, I'll be right there," Ray said. Then he swiped one of the gender-reveal cupcakes on his way out.

"Ray!" Mel and Angie protested together.

"What?" he asked. "They're pretty." He chewed and a look of sublime happiness made his features relax into a dopey puppy look. "And tasty."

"Those are for a baby shower," Angie said. "Not for public consumption."

"Sorry," he said. He glanced at Mel. "They're really good though. I like that pink goo in the middle."

"It's raspberry cream not goo, but thank you," Mel said. "And don't worry, I made extra." She always made extra.

"Cool." Ray slipped out the doors and they could just hear the murmur of Marty and Ray harassing each other. Mel shook her head. So much testosterone in her little pink bakeshop.

She turned back to the gender-reveal cupcakes. They had piped ruffles of half-blue and half-pink icing on top of the chocolate and vanilla cupcakes, and now they just needed to be topped off with white fondant question marks.

She began placing one on each top while Angie watched. She hugged her belly and asked, "Do you think we should have found out if it's a boy or a girl?"

Oh, dear, what was the best answer here? Mel wasn't sure. Angie'd had a pretty unremarkable pregnancy so far, but she didn't want to say anything that set her friend off into some existential crisis of pregnancy. She did not have enough extra cupcakes on hand for that sort of comfort eating.

"Do *you* think you should have found out the gender?" Mel asked. When all else failed she'd always found it best to turn the question back on the questioner.

"I don't know," Angie said. She looked exasperated. "That's why I'm asking."

"How does Tate feel about it?" Mel asked. Deflect, deflect, deflect!

"He wanted to wait," she said. "He said there aren't any surprises in life anymore and wouldn't this be a great one?"

"He has a point," Mel said.

"He also has a waistline," Angie said. "Which makes me think he really shouldn't get a say."

"Also a worthy opinion," Mel said.

She could feel a fine sweat beading up on her forehead. Angie had been nothing but sunshine, daisies, and buttercups since she got pregnant. It was alarming mostly because it was so out of character. Was now the moment she cracked and the feisty Angie of their youth came back?

Having carried the baby for months, with her feet beginning to swell, her back aching, and her bladder shrinking, was Angie done being nice and about to let loose the wrath that had been bottled up for so many weeks?

"Nah, he's the dad," Angie said. "Of course he has a say; just, you know, less of one."

Mel glanced at her friend and there was a small smile on her lips and a twinkle in her eye.

"So, you're okay with not knowing the gender?" Mel asked.

"Yes, I mean, I wanted to wait, too," she said. "It's just that we're so close. I mean, the nursery is painted a brain-engaging green with blue sky and clouds along the upper walls and ceiling. Perfectly neutral, just like all of the clothes. Lots of yellow and green in there. I hope the baby doesn't look jaundiced."

Mel grinned. "It won't, because the minute you know whether it's a he or a she, the mothers are going to go into a frenzy of shopping. You know this."

Angie laughed. "Yeah, I do." She hugged her belly. "We're cutting it awfully close to your wedding day. Are you sure you don't want to prepare a backup matron of honor?"

"Nope," Mel said. "You're it. You and Tate are our only attendants, and you're not due for at least four weeks after the wedding. We've got this."

"If the baby makes a break for it, I'll just cross my legs and tighten it all up down there," Angie teased.

Mel laughed, relieved that Angie seemed to be maintaining her momma Zen.

"There is one other thing we need to talk about," Angie said.

Mel glanced up at her. "What?"

"We have a meeting in fifteen minutes. Actually we have three meetings," she said. "But it'll take less than an hour, I promise."

"Three?" Mel gaped. She hated meetings to begin with, so to have three of them starting in less than fifteen minutes, she was not a happy camper. "Why? What's going on?"

"We have to hire Oz's replacement," Angie said. Mel opened her mouth to protest but Angie put up her hand in a stop gesture. "I'm going to be out on maternity leave for months, and it's already been a struggle to get the baking done and cover the front counter without Oz. Without both of us, you and Marty are doomed. Plus, you're getting married and going on a honeymoon. Who exactly is going to take care of things?"

"I . . . maybe we could close?" Mel asked. She really hated the idea of replacing Oz. Angie would be back; she and Tate had already decided that she could work a few hours per day so that she could get out and he would watch the baby so that he could bond as a primary caretaker as well, but that was months away. Closing wasn't practical, but Mel found she was very protective of the dynamic they had in the kitchen.

"We're not closing," Angie said. "What would Marty do with his time?" She gasped. "He might go work for Olivia!"

They exchanged an alarmed look. Olivia, Marty's girlfriend, owned a rival bakery and would be happy to steal away her man to go work at Confections.

"All right, you win," Mel said. "When are these interviews starting again?"

Angie glanced at the clock. "Ten minutes."

Mel heaved a sigh. She did not want to do this.

The first candidate was late. Mel was already scratching a line through their name when the front door to the bakery flew open and a woman came in on a cloud of patchouli and wearing a tie-dye maxi dress in the colors of the rainbow. She had long, light brown hair that almost reached her waist, and she was slender but had a prominent nose and chin, which weren't flattered by the middle part she was rocking. She also carried a bakery box. The sight of it made Mel nervous.

"She brought food?" she whispered to Angie.

"I asked them to bring samples of their cooking, given that it is a baking position."

"Ah." This did not reassure Mel in the least.

The woman approached the counter and Marty looked her over and pointed to the booth where Mel and Angie sat waiting.

"Hi, sorry I'm late," the woman said. She slid into the booth across from them. "Ruby Gillespie, pleased to meet you."

"Hi, I'm Angie and this is Mel," Angie introduced them.

Ruby smiled and nodded. "I'll clarify and say I'm not really late."

"No?" Mel asked. It was five minutes after the scheduled interview time.

"No, you see, I'm in my time of flow, and as such I can't be held accountable to the chronological constructs of the patriarchy," she said.

Mel blinked. She had no idea what this woman was talking about.

"Time of flow?" Angie asked. Then her eyes went wide and her mouth formed an O. "Never mind."

"When you say you can't be held accountable to the chronological constructs of the patriarchy," Mel said, "how do you see that impacting your work schedule?"

Ruby shrugged. "I am woman. I am synced to the moon. The imaginary fetters of man can't constrain me."

47

"So, that's a no on having a set schedule?" Angie asked.

"It is set by the tides," Ruby said.

"We're in the desert," Mel pointed out.

Ruby shrugged as if this was of little consequence. She then pushed the box towards them. They sat there with the plain white box in the center of the table. Finally, Angie reached across the table and pulled it close. She blew out a breath and popped the lid.

They both leaned over and glanced inside. Mel gasped. Inside were four perfect cupcakes that looked so delicate and artistic it was as if they'd been conjured by magic. One was a lavender-colored cupcake with a glittery ball of spun sugar sitting on top of it. Another was a dark ganache with a delicate bird's nest complete with three little eggs nestled on top. The other two were equally inventive, one with a detailed fondant flower and the other a traditional vanilla but piped with a thick swirl. It was clear Ruby had tried to showcase her abilities. Despite her unusual ways, Ruby clearly had skills.

"These look amazing," Angie said. "We'll be tasting them and evaluating them later."

"Excellent," Ruby said. She gave them a small smile. "I'm sorry I have to go. I'll let you know what I decide about the job later."

Mel's mouth dropped open. She wondered if she should correct her or just let it lie.

"I really like the aesthetic here, you know," Ruby said. Her gaze swept the bakery. "Very good energy."

"Cool," Mel said. She flashed Ruby a peace sign. The woman bobbed her head in response and headed out the door.

"I don't even know what to say," Mel said.

"The cupcakes look amazing," Angie countered.

"True."

Angie closed the lid and pushed the box aside. Marty was approaching their booth with a middle-aged man wearing glasses and standard-issue accountant attire. His hair was styled in a militarily precise cut and he had a slight overbite, making him appear younger than the stray gray hairs threading through the brown would indicate. He wore creased pants and a plaid dress shirt with short sleeves. The shirt was tucked in and his brown belt matched his loafers. Mel wondered how he'd feel about getting messy in the kitchen.

"This is Kevin Morgan," Marty said. He didn't look impressed.

Kevin thrust a plastic container at Mel. It was a standard-issue grocery store cupcake container and inside were six identical vanilla cupcakes with vanilla icing and sprinkles.

"Hi, Kevin," she said. She gestured for him to take a seat. He did, looking wary, as if he were there for an interrogation instead of a job interview. "I'm Mel and this is Angie."

He nodded but didn't speak. He didn't make eye contact, either. With his slumped shoulders and overall downtrodden appearance, he wasn't really selling a happy cupcake vibe.

"Did you bake these?" Angie asked.

He glanced up and away. His gaze fixed on a spot in the corner and he said, "Sort of."

Mel and Angie exchanged a look. What did "sort of" mean?

"Well," Angie said. She fingered the label of the grocery store on the plastic container. "Are you a grocery store baker then?"

He shrugged.

Mel could feel her patience wearing thin. She wondered when Angie would send Kevin packing because, truly, this was beyond awkward. There was no way they could hire a guy who didn't speak when they weren't even sure if he could bake.

"What would you say your greatest strength in the kitchen is?" Angie asked. Mel was shocked. Angie was showing a fortitude that she herself seriously lacked at the moment.

Kevin stared down at his hands and mumbled something that Mel couldn't hear. She was done. If Ange had gone soft and Mel had to be the bad guy, so be it.

"All right, thanks for stopping by," Mel said. "We'll call you if you're chosen for the position."

Kevin gave them a curt nod and slid out of the booth with a decided air of relief. At the door, a woman who wore the same wire-rimmed glasses and had a matching slight overbite stood waiting. Her hair was white, her face finely wrinkled, and she looked to be an older version of Kevin. Mel assumed it was his mother. As soon as he joined her, she smoothed his shirt at his shoulders and then gave him a nudge with her elbow to straighten up. Yup, definitely his mom.

The woman glanced past Kevin and sent a little finger wave to Mel and Angie, which they returned.

"Okay, I'm really not feeling this process," Mel said to Angie. "Where did you get these people from?"

"I put up an ad online," Angie said. She sounded defensive. "You think these are bad? You should have seen the applicants I rejected."

"You sure you didn't mix them up?" Mel asked. She tapped the store-bought cupcakes with her index finger.

Angie rolled her eyes. "I can't help it if his mom filled out his application for him."

"Hi! Oh, wow, is it really you?" a voice interrupted. "I'm going to die, just die."

Mel and Angie turned to see a petite young woman standing at the edge of the booth. She was cute with big brown eyes and honey-blond hair that she wore all one length at her chin. Her smile was wide and warm and she clutched a large box in her hands, which were trembling.

Marty was beside her but when he went to speak she ran right over him. "Hi, I'm Madison Jacobson and I'm so excited. You're them, aren't you? Mel and Angie, the owners of the bakery? I've been such a fan of yours for so long. I follow all of your social media accounts and, oh, I just love you guys."

Angie perked up. She had been running their Instagram account for years. She loved it. Taking photos, looping in cupcake influencers and fans from all over the world. Mel still had no idea what that even meant or why it helped their business in any way, but it made Angie happy so whatever. Judging by Madison's overwrought fangirl moment, it was more important than Mel had previously realized.

"I would just love, love, love to work with you." The girl burst into tears.

Angie clucked and pushed out of the booth. She immediately put her arm around the sobbing young woman. "There, there, honey, it's okay."

Mel and Marty exchanged a look of horror. "I'm going to be over there," he said. "Way way over there."

Mel envied him. She had no idea what to say to the sobbing young woman. Angie helped the girl into the booth and said, "Just take a minute to catch your breath and we'll look at your cupcakes, okay?"

Madison nodded. She snatched a napkin out of the silver holder and sobbed into it. Angie slid back into the booth and smiled at Mel in a way that said she was charmed by their young fan. Mel could see the appeal. Who didn't like worship? But this was about finding an assistant baker, not a groupie.

Angie popped the top on the box and they looked inside. "Oh, wow," Mel said.

Five

Staring back up at them from inside the box were cupcakes made to look like Mel and Angie. Cartoonish depictions with exaggerated features, but definitely them, as one had short spiked blond hair—Mel—and the other boasted Angie's long dark curls. There were several of each of them with different degrees of finesse but on the whole they were . . . terrible.

Mel had no idea what to say. While she could see the effort that had gone into them, they were in a word, hideous, and most likely would scare people off their food. But there was no way in heck she was going to tell the overly excitable and emotional Madison that.

In that moment, Mel found she had great sympathy for the judges of baking shows like *The Great British Bake Off*. How did you tell someone who had obviously worked very hard that their creation was a bust? Maybe they wouldn't taste that bad. She tried to imagine biting into her own head. Nope, just nope. Too weird.

"These are incredible," Angie said. "I can see how much effort you put into them, Madison. Truly, a lot of effort."

Mel said nothing. She was speechless, plus she felt like the cupcake in the middle was staring at her and she was afraid to look away as it might jump out of the box and try to kill her. Yes, it was that creepy.

"You don't like them?" Madison asked. She was looking at Mel. "I can see it on your face."

Mel swiftly shut the lid, breaking the staring contest with the cupcake. She forced a smile and said, "Are you kidding? In all my years as a baker, I have never seen anything like these."

"Really?" Madison asked. "That's so nice of you to say . . ." Her words got drowned out on a sob.

With a helpless look Mel turned to Angie. She had no idea how to help a crying stranger. She felt like she should hug the girl or something, but her introverted tendencies held her back. Angie was not shy about it at all. She abandoned their side of the booth and slid in next to Madison.

"Sorry, I'm not usually so emotional, but . . ." Madison's words trailed off, and Mel was half-afraid she would say it was her time of flow and then Mel would have to lock herself in her office and never come out because the world was officially too crazy for her.

"I'm just so nervous," Madison said. "I cry when I'm nervous."

"Really?" Mel asked. "I giggle. It's so embarrassing."

Madison stared at her for a second and then gestured to her face with an expression of chagrin. "Worse than this?"

"Well, no." Mel laughed and she was relieved when Madison did, too. Okay, so the kid could laugh at herself, that was definitely a point in her favor.

"Why don't you take a minute to get yourself together," Angie said. She pointed to the public restroom in the corner. "And we can discuss the job here when you get back."

They watched Madison leave and as soon as the door shut, Mel said, "You want to hire her."

"I like her enthusiasm," Angie said. Mel stared at her. "And it wouldn't hurt to have someone who could take over the social media account while I'm away. She's young. She's probably super on top of all the trends, like a real hashtag expert."

"But I need her to bake in the kitchen," Mel said. She gestured to the box. "I don't think this is going to cut it."

"Maybe they taste better than they look," Angie said.

She opened the box, reached in, and grabbed one of her own heads. So weird. She broke it in half and handed a chunk to Mel. It was an eyeball, the mouth, and a gob of the hair.

"Bottoms up," Angie said.

Mel bit into the cupcake. Buttery rich chocolate cake with a nice texture, topped with a frosting that was all vanilla but not too sweet, and it complemented the chocolate cake perfectly. She was pleasantly surprised. She turned to Angie, who was looking equally pleased.

"We can teach her what she needs to know about decorating," Angie said. "These are a solid start."

Mel nodded while she chewed. "But the crying?"

"She'll calm down," Angie said. "You'll see."

"Let's not do anything too hasty," Mel said. "We should at least taste Ruby's before we make a final decision."

"Of course," Angie said.

They wiped their fingers on napkins and closed the box. When Madison reappeared, she looked serenely composed, as if she'd finally conquered her nerves.

"So, Madison, when can you start?" Angie asked.

WHAT?! Mel was grateful she didn't shout it out loud.

Unsurprisingly, another Madison weepfest ensued, and Mel made an excuse to go and hide in the kitchen. Apparently, Madison would be starting at the bakery next week, and Mel figured they were going to need to up their supply of tissues. She honestly had no idea what Angie was thinking to offer the young woman the job without even calling her references.

She was going to give in to Angie's intuition on this one, but she was also going to prepare Madison for the reality of a baker's life. People could be persnickety about their baked goods and not shy about expressing their persnicketiness. She was going to have Madison train on the front counter with Marty for a week. If she survived that then she could come and work back in the kitchen.

It was depressing to remember how easy it had been to hire Oz. He'd just walked in the door and made the job his. Mel hadn't thought finding a decent replacement was going to be such a challenge, but now it looked like they might be in a time of high turnover for a while. She really didn't think Madison had what it took to work with demanding customers.

Angie strode through the swinging doors, carrying

the samples the interviewees had brought. "What should I do with these?"

"Since you've already offered the job to Madison, I'd say you can pitch them," Mel said.

"Don't be mad," Angie said. She dropped the boxes in the large bin they kept in the kitchen. "My intuition dinged and I just knew she was the one."

"We should have discuss—"

The back door opened with a bang, interrupting what Mel had been about to say, which was just as well as the damage was already done, and lecturing Angie at this point wasn't going to change the outcome.

"Marty! Stop texting me!" Oz yelled at the swinging bakery doors as he stepped into the kitchen.

Mel and Angie turned to look at him. He was still in the chef's coat he'd been wearing on television earlier, the one with the Sun Dial Resort logo embroidered on the left breast. His hair was disheveled and he looked sweaty, as if he'd run to the bakery.

"Marty's out front," Mel said. The television was still on, although it had rolled to the next program and was muted.

"You all saw?" Oz asked, glancing at the screen.

Mel nodded and Angie said, "You're a natural. Plus, Stella was clearly warm for your form."

Oz blanched. "She's old enough to be my mom."

His phone chimed again from his pocket. He pulled out his phone and glanced at the screen and then at the door to the front of the bakery.

He fired off a text and had barely hit send when the swinging door to the kitchen blasted open and Marty strode in.

"Well, look who decided to grace us with his presence— the movie star," Marty said. He sidled up to Oz and clasped his hand under his chin, then he batted his eyelashes at him and simpered, "Can I have your autograph?"

Oz lifted one eyebrow and glanced over Marty's head at Mel. "He's loving this, isn't he?"

Mel laughed. "Yeah, you just made his week, possibly his year."

Oz cracked and laughed. He nudged Marty with an elbow and said, "Get a celebrity a cup of coffee, would you? I had to be at the studio so early I didn't get any, and I think I'm getting a caffeine headache."

Marty dropped his hands and strode over to the coffeepot that was kept in use all morning at the bakery. "So, I'm a gofer now? Can I shine your shoes, pick up your dry cleaning, go get your lunch?"

"Well, if you're offering . . ." With a grin Oz took the mug Marty handed him.

"Come on, come on." Marty rolled his hand in a circular motion. "We want the deets."

"We really do," Angie chimed in. She sat and scooted her stool over to make room for Oz at the steel worktable.

He slumped onto the round metal seat and sipped his coffee. "There's not much to tell. Miles was supposed to be on the morning program but he didn't show. Clay called me in a panic because he didn't want to lose the free publicity for the resort, so I stepped in and did some cupcake-decorating demos. Really, not a big deal."

"That's it?" Marty asked. He looked disappointed. "I thought you'd been hired to be their new foodie guy."

"Sorry, no," Oz said. "Just a stand-in."

"Well, you were really good," Angie said. "Although I might have let the fainter hit the floor."

"Yeah, what was up with that?" Oz asked. He shrugged as if to say *Women* without actually saying it.

"Isn't Miles going to be furious with you for usurping what I'm sure he thinks was his spot?" Mel asked.

Oz shrugged. "Maybe. But Clay said that Simon, the producer, had set up the shoot and he would freak out if someone didn't show. I was just trying to help."

"I doubt that Miles is going to see it that way," Mel said. She got a sick feeling in her stomach. This was the same thing she always felt when she was nervous about something or about someone being disappointed or upset with her, but she was transferring her angst to Oz's situation. Things had been so tense at the resort the other day, she really didn't want him to get into trouble with the executive chef, who could clearly be petty and mean.

"When will you have to deal with Miles?" she asked.

"Technically we don't cross paths much, but if he's going to be nasty about the show this morning, it'll probably happen while we're prepping for dinner this afternoon," Oz said.

"Huh, it turns out Joe and I are meeting with Courtney, the reception coordinator, to go over the room and any extras we might want," Mel said. "She's pushing the ice sculpture hard, but I'm holding the line on that."

"Really?" Angie asked. She sounded disappointed. "I bet you could have a supercool swan the size of a small car, with its wings spread out." She gestured and Marty shook his head.

"Nah, you want a mermaid," he said. "Life-size with a huge tail and big—"

"We get the picture," Mel interrupted.

"Eyes," Marty said. He quirked an eyebrow. "What did you think I was going to say?"

"Eyes," Mel lied.

Oz snorted and Angie giggled. Mel grinned. It felt good to have the team back together.

"As I was saying," Mel continued. "Joe and I will be there this afternoon, so if you get into a jam, we can help out."

"I really don't see him coming after me," Oz said. "His beef would be with Mr. Perry or Simon, don't you think? They're the ones who sent me to the station."

"Is this Miles a coward?" Marty asked. He poured himself a cup of coffee, pausing to hold the carafe up to Mel. She shook her head. She didn't need any more go juice today.

"I don't know if he's a coward," Oz said. "He's definitely a bully."

"Then he's a coward." Marty sipped from his mug as the bell chimed from out front. He walked towards the swinging doors and then paused to turn around and say, "Be careful and watch your back."

Oz exchanged a look with Mel. This confirmed what she had already told him. She nodded. "He's right but don't worry," she said. "I'll have Joe be at his most lawyerly this afternoon."

"Thanks," Oz said. He took a sip of his coffee and said, "But I'm sure it'll be fine. Really."

Mel wasn't sure whom he was trying to convince, them or himself.

⌁⌁⌁

"Are you sure you don't want an ice sculpture?" Courtney asked for the fifth time. It was clear she was definitely supposed to push the ice artistry.

Mel glanced around the moderate-sized room where they planned to have their reception. It was enough to accommodate fifty people, who were their families and a handful of friends. Mel was introverted enough that the thought of a big wedding was enough to give her hives, and Joe had made it very clear that he didn't care what they did so long as they managed to get down the aisle this time and were a Mr. and Mrs. at the end of it.

There was a small dance floor, space for a band, and the room had floor-to-ceiling French doors that opened onto to a private veranda that overlooked the resort's gardens. It was perfect.

Despite the badgering about the ice sculpture, Courtney was adorable. Twenty-three years old with a sleek mane of long blond hair, and wearing the requisite purple Sun Dial Resort polo shirt with the same logo that Oz wore on his chef's coat, only she'd paired her top with a black pencil skirt and stiletto sandals. Mel glanced down at her Keds and wondered how Courtney managed an entire day in those arch crampers.

Courtney had the bubble and sparkle of an event coordinator—she was clearly born to this, and Mel liked her even though the young woman made her feel about a thousand years old, which was why she'd refused the ice sculpture. It felt like a young-person thing, and Mel and

Joe were not in the bloom of youth anymore. Mel attempted to refuse in the nicest way possible.

"Sorry, but no ice sculpture for us," she said. She pointed to Joe. "He's allergic."

Joe didn't even bat an eyelash at this flagrant fib. Instead, he nodded and said, "They make my throat close up. Very dangerous."

A tiny vee formed between her carefully sculpted eyebrows and Courtney said, "Wow, I had no idea that was a thing."

"Oh, yeah, it's a thing," Joe said. "But very rare."

Mel felt a twinge of conscience as Courtney looked so reassured that this wasn't something she was going to have to worry about with future clients. Mel decided that escaping was their best option.

She held out her hand and said, "I think everything we've discussed will be perfect. We're trying to keep the day simple and not too fussy."

"Of course." Courtney grinned. She shook Mel's hand and then Joe's. "You leave it to me and I will make sure your day is picture-perfect."

"Thank you," Mel said. When Courtney went to walk them out, Mel added, "We're going to stop by the kitchen and say hi to our friend Oz, the pastry chef."

"Oh, right." Courtney's face turned pink. "He's so ho—such an amazing chef."

Mel and Joe exchanged a small smile. "He is really talented."

"If you have any changes or concerns, let me know," Courtney said.

"I will," Mel promised.

Courtney walked them out of the small banquet room

and with a wave, she turned to go down the hall that led back to her office. She had her phone out and was texting while walking. Mel was surprised she didn't run into a wall since she never looked up, but maybe it was a new sense that was evolving in humankind. The ability to perceive obstacles without looking up from their phones. Handy.

"You don't suppose Oz has any more cupcake samples, do you?" Joe asked as they went down the opposite hallway, through the lobby, and turned down another passageway that led to the resort's public dining rooms and on to the kitchens.

"I can ask," Mel said. She took out her phone to text Oz that they were here. She assumed he was in his kitchen, but he might be out in his little garden or on a break. She waited but no dots appeared to indicate that he was writing back. She put her phone back in her purse. "He's not answering. Should we wait or just go on back there?"

"Let's go back," Joe said. "Worst case scenario, if we get busted by security, we'll say we got lost."

"So devious," Mel teased, shaking her head.

"Obviously I've been spending too much time with my brother Ray."

Mel laughed. They crossed the mid-century modern dining room, which was empty at this hour of postlunch, predinner purgatory, and pushed through the doors that led to the kitchens. She led Joe past the main kitchen, which she noticed was awfully quiet. The last time she'd been here at this time, they'd been busily prepping for dinner. She shrugged and continued down the short hallway that led to Oz's kitchen.

She checked her phone again just to see if he'd texted back. He hadn't. Mel pushed open the set of doors that led to the smaller pastry kitchen and stopped short. Joe plowed into her, catching her before she went sailing forward.

"Mel, are you all—?" Joe glanced over her shoulder and sucked in a breath.

Oz was crouched on the floor, leaning over the inert body of Miles Gallway.

Six

"Oz!" Mel yelled, and she ran towards him.

Joe grabbed her by the elbow, slowing her up. "You help Oz, and I'll check the chef."

Mel nodded. She ran around the body to get to Oz. His hands were covered in blood and he was shaking.

The door on the opposite side of the kitchen crashed open and the sous chef, Ashley, stood there. She took in the scene at a glance and shrieked the rafters down. "Chef! Chef! What's happening? Chef!"

"Quiet!" Joe snapped at her as he crouched beside Miles, placing his fingers at the base of his throat. He dropped his hand, looking grim.

In the silence, Ashley pointed a well-manicured finger at Oz and screeched, "You! You killed him!"

Oz blanched, his face going pale. He turned to Mel

and hissed, "I just came into the kitchen, I swear, and I found him like this. I think he slipped and fell."

Mel glanced past Oz at Miles. He was lying on his right side. His face, what she could see of it, was covered in blood and it had pooled beneath his head. Mel felt her stomach churn as the distinctive coppery smell hit her nose.

Joe put his hand on Miles's chest. Joe's face was grim. "Call 9-1-1."

Mel fumbled for her phone. She stared at it, trying to remember how to make a call. Nine-one-one was not computing.

Joe rolled Miles fully onto his back. Something was lodged under him and Joe lifted his shoulder and pulled out a wooden mallet, the kind used to tenderize meat. He began trying to revive him, using CPR, counting out the chest compressions as he went. He glanced at Mel and said, "It's okay, cupcake. You can do this."

Mel blinked, shook her head to focus, and opened the phone icon on her cell and dialed 9-1-1. It was difficult to talk with Oz beside her, trembling, and Ashley, still shrieking a constant, "Oh my god. He's dead. Oh my god!"

More staff appeared in the kitchen and stood, watching in horror as Joe tried to get Miles's heart started. The dispatcher answered and Mel went into fact mode.

A man had been found unconscious, with an apparent head injury, he was nonresponsive. She gave the address and waited while the dispatcher sent an ambulance to the resort. Joe was muttering to Miles while he worked on him. Sweat was beading up on Joe's forehead and he was looking tired.

One of the line cooks, a robust Black man, stepped forward and crouched down beside Joe. "I know CPR, brother, let me give it a try."

His voice was deep with a thick, rich drawl that sounded like Georgia or maybe North Carolina. Joe moved aside and the muscular man stepped in. He was direct, putting one hand over the other and pushing down on Miles's rib cage, hard enough to crack it. Mel winced even as she knew it was likely Miles's only shot.

Everyone stood still, watching the big man work, hoping he could bring the chef back. There was no response. Miles didn't cringe or wince or give any indication that he was feeling anything that was happening to him. That's when Mel knew. There was no saving him. Miles Gallway was dead.

✌︎ ︎ ✌︎

"How is it that you two just happened to be here when a chef was found dead?" Stan Cooper, Scottsdale homicide detective and Mel's uncle, was pacing back and forth across the dining room. He had taken a roll of antacid tablets and was popping them like they were Pez. "And, you, what were you doing with the body?"

This last bit was directed at Oz. He was seated at a small table with Mel and Joe and staring at his shoes as if he could find the answers to the universe in the scuffed toes and frayed laces.

"Uncle Stan, go easy on him," Mel said. "He found Miles in his kitchen. He's a little freaked out."

Uncle Stan stopped pacing and stared at Oz. "Sorry. You okay, kid?"

At this, Oz glanced up. He met Uncle Stan's gaze and gave a quick nod. It was a brave showing, because Mel could see that he was still trembling a bit and his eyes were wide, his face pale, and he hadn't said a word since Joe had started giving Miles chest compressions. Both he and Henry, the name of the man who had helped Joe, had moved aside for the EMTs when they arrived. The medics had jumped in but there was nothing to be done. As Mel had suspected, Miles Gallway was dead and judging by the dent in his skull and the pool of blood he'd been lying in, he'd been murdered.

The thought made Mel shiver. She couldn't pretend to have liked Miles Gallway. He was a bully and everything she loathed in a chef, driven by ego and unchecked power in his kitchen. Still, no one deserved such a horrible and grisly death. Not even an egomaniacal gasbag like Gallway.

"As for why we were here, we were just here to consult about the reception," Mel said. "We finished meeting with Courtney, she can verify, and then came to the kitchen to say hi to Oz."

She didn't mention that they were there to run interference in case Gallway came after Oz for taking his television spot. It wasn't relevant, or so she told herself, because there was no way Oz had harmed Gallway and she wasn't going to give Uncle Stan any reason to suspect Oz, beyond his finding the body, which had to be just sheer bad luck.

At the mention of their wedding, Uncle Stan looked momentarily misty-eyed. Mel had asked him to give her away with her mother, Joyce, and to her surprise he had gotten weepy and been unable to speak. Joe had assured her it was a good thing and that Uncle Stan was honored as opposed to horrified.

Things were complicated in the Cooper family. Mel's father, Charlie, had passed away when she was in her early twenties, leaving Mel, her mother, Joyce, and her brother, Charlie Junior, devastated.

Her dad, Charlie Cooper, had been larger than life. He loved his family, red meat, stinky cigars, and a couple fingers of single-malt scotch, in that order. He was always quick with a joke and gave the best hugs, real two-arm bear hugs, that let the huggee know that he loved them all the way down to his squishy center. There was not a day of her life that passed that Mel didn't miss her father, especially his big booming laugh, the sort that made you laugh with him whether you thought the joke was funny or not.

It had been over ten years since Charlie's departure to the big distillery in the sky, and Uncle Stan, who had never married or had kids, had stepped in as a father figure to Mel and Charlie and had looked after Joyce. Recently, Joyce and Stan's relationship had changed into a romantic one. Mel was still wrapping her head around it, even as it seemed appropriate. Uncle Stan gave the same bear hugs as her dad, which had been the greatest comfort to her after her father passed. And he always had her back—no matter what happened, Uncle Stan was there for her.

"Your reception, right," Uncle Stan said. His eyes were still watery and he blinked a few times. He looked like that every time the wedding was mentioned, and Mel wondered how he was going to get through the day without breaking down completely. It was equal parts endearing and alarming.

His voice was gruff when he continued, "Okay, that makes sense." He turned to Oz. "What were you doing in the kitchen with him?"

Oz's eyes were huge. Mel reached over and patted his arm. "Just tell Uncle Stan exactly what happened. It's okay."

"Your attorney is with you," Joe said. He gave Oz and then Stan a meaningful look.

"You're a prosecutor," Uncle Stan said. He made a low rumbling noise in his chest, at which Joe shrugged.

"At the moment, I am Oz's representation," Joe said.

"Do you think he needs that?" Uncle Stan countered.

"No, but still, I have the skills so . . ." Joe shrugged.

Oz glanced between them as if watching a Ping-Pong match. He seemed unclear as to who the winner was. Mel shook her head.

"Just tell Uncle Stan what happened," she said. "Joe will step in if you need him."

Oz nodded. He swallowed hard and then said, "I was in the walk-in cooler, preparing to feed the Beast."

Stan held up a hand, "Stop. Beast? Who or what is the Beast, and what's it doing in a restaurant's cooler?"

"Sorry. That's our sourdough," Oz explained. "You use a starter to get it going and then you have to feed it water and flour every day until it's ready. It's like a living thing, so we call it 'the Beast.'"

"Did anyone see you feeding it?" Stan asked.

"No, everyone else was out on the loading dock, helping with a delivery, but my bread guy, Tomas, can verify that I add to the Beast every day. He and I are the only two who touch it and he'd be able to look at it and know

I fed it, as it doubles after a feeding when it's ready to bake, and ours should double today," Oz said. He looked thoughtful. "Except he's on vacation right now."

Uncle Stan nodded. "We'll worry about that later. Continue."

"I got finished with the Beast and came into the kitchen and washed my hands. I was just drying them when I saw Miles on the floor. Well, technically, I saw his shoes. I came around the corner and there he was. I thought he'd fallen and cracked his head. I grabbed a towel to sop up the blood and tried to rouse him without moving him, because it was clearly a head injury, but he didn't wake up. I was just going to call for help when Joe and Mel appeared."

"So, how long would you say you were with him?" Uncle Stan asked.

"I don't know," Oz said. "Time was moving really weird at that point. Maybe a minute, possibly two, but I was in the kitchen washing my hands for a few minutes before."

"What was your relationship with Miles?" Uncle Stan asked.

"And now we're done," Joe said. "That has no relevance to Oz finding Miles on the kitchen floor."

Joe had witnessed Miles's abusive behavior towards Oz previously and Mel had enlightened him about Oz taking Miles's place on the television show this morning. She wanted to ask Oz if he knew why Miles hadn't shown up, but she didn't want to mention it in front of Uncle Stan and give him the idea that there was bad blood between Oz and Miles. Just because they'd had a kitchen squabble didn't mean they were enemies. Chefs fought all the time, but she knew people outside the industry didn't understand it.

"Doesn't it?" Uncle Stan asked. "As I understand it, the baking kitchen is Oz's domain. Why was Miles Gallway in there?" He looked at Oz, who wisely said nothing. "Miles has his own kitchen, doesn't he?"

"Yes, but he's the chef de cuisine," Mel said. "So, he's technically in charge of all kitchen operations, including Oz's."

"So, he's your boss?" Uncle Stan persisted.

"I prefer *supervisor*," Oz said.

Uncle Stan stared at him with one fuzzy gray eyebrow raised higher than the other. If he was getting the inkling that there was no love lost between Oz and Gallway, which Mel was quite certain the sous chef, Ashley, would be sure to confirm, he didn't say so.

"Detective," a uniformed officer called to Stan from the kitchen door. "The crime scene investigators would like a word."

"Be right there," Uncle Stan said. He gave the officer a brisk nod and the uniform disappeared. He glanced back at Oz and asked, "Between you and me, do you know of anyone who would want to harm Miles Gallway?"

Oz froze. He looked like Uncle Stan had just kicked his knees out from under him. Mel wanted to jump in before he could say anything that might incriminate himself but she also didn't want to look like she was afraid of his answer.

"Professional kitchens are volatile on their mellowest days," Joe said. His voice was even as if he weren't trying to preemptively poke holes in Uncle Stan's question. "I'm sure things are said by the heat of the grill that don't mean anything at the end of the day. Would you say that's correct, Oz?"

Oz nodded. "Sure. It can get pretty intense."

"So, there's really no way Oz can accurately answer that question," Joe said. "Right, Oz?"

"It would be hearsay," Oz said. He glanced at Joe. "That's the right word, isn't it?"

"Yes," Joe said.

Stan gave them a look of chagrin. "Fine. Wait here. I need to check in with my team, but I may have more questions."

He strode towards the kitchen and Mel watched him go, feeling terrible that they were on the opposite side of things at the moment. Because there was no doubt that Oz would be considered a suspect, and Mel would do whatever it took to prove her friend's innocence. She knew it didn't look good for Oz to have Miles dead in his kitchen, especially given Miles's animosity towards Oz, which had probably escalated since Oz took his spot on television that morning. She had no doubt that someone was going to tell all, making Oz look like a prime suspect.

As soon as Stan was out of range, she asked Joe, "What do we do?"

"We let the police do their job," he said. "We help them in any way we can, but we don't offer up Oz as a sacrifice to the wheels of justice."

"I really don't like my name and the word *sacrifice* in the same sentence," Oz said.

"Understandable," Joe said. "But that scene with Miles storming into the kitchen the other day was witnessed by enough people that someone is going to tell Stan and then you're going to have questions to answer."

Mel glanced at Oz, who looked like he might be ill.

"But I would never . . ." he said.

"We know, Oz," Mel assured him. She made her voice firm. She didn't want him to have any doubts. "Don't worry. Joe is going to make sure you're not a suspect. Right, Joe?"

Joe glanced at Oz and said, "Absolutely. You really don't need to be concerned. Stan knows you and he knows you didn't have anything to do with what happened to Miles. It's going to be okay."

He put enough lawyerly oomph on the words that Oz's shoulders dropped and he took a deep breath. "Okay."

Mel glanced around the dining room. Uncle Stan's partner, Tara Martinez, was deep in conversation with Clay Perry. Clay looked distraught and Mel wondered if he was more upset that he'd lost a renowned chef or that Miles was dead. Then she immediately felt bad for the uncharitable thought. Clay had seemed like an affable guy. Although, Miles had certainly put him through it. She wondered if Clay'd had enough and lost his temper with the chef. He was a golfer, maybe he had a righteous swing.

"What are you thinking?" Joe asked.

"That Clay Perry, the owner, might have had a motive," she said.

"Like what?" Joe asked.

"Annoyance is the first thing that comes to mind," she conceded. "Probably not enough to commit murder on that alone."

Mel glanced back at the owner and noted the woman

standing behind him, scrolling through the phone she held in one hand while holding a martini in the other. Everyone else in the room was either dressed in chef clothes, golf attire, or business casual. Not this woman. She was wearing a red string bikini and stiletto sandals with a sheer flowing beach cover-up that looked more like something to wear over a negligee. Her hair was pulled back in a messy bun and her sunglasses were perched on top of her head. Her skin was a very deep shade of sun-enhanced bronze and Mel suspected her life was spent poolside, as this was the sort of tan in which hours were invested.

"The woman beside him?" Mel asked, although she already suspected.

"That would be Mrs. Perry," Oz said.

Mel nodded. Just as she figured.

Mrs. Perry looked up from her phone at her husband. She tipped her head in the direction of the resort and the pool beyond and he shook his head no in refusal. She heaved a very dramatic sigh, made a bored face, and went back to her phone. Clearly the pesky death of the resort's executive chef was of no interest to her.

"What about the guy over there? Who's he?" Joe pointed to a man in the corner of the room. He was prowling around his area with the restless energy of a caged big cat. He was bald with round glasses and a dress shirt and skinny jeans that oozed into a pair of combat boots.

"That's Simon Marconi," Oz said. "He's the producer who is scouting talent for the Foodie Channel. Supposedly, he was hoping to resurrect Miles Gallway's television career."

"Didn't Gallway get fired for being inappropriate with some of the staff on his show?" Mel asked. She had done some research on the chef after their altercation last week.

"Marconi felt like he was due for a comeback," Oz said. He shrugged as if he had no idea how the producer had come to that conclusion.

They sat silently, watching the television producer pace. He was stopped by people occasionally, and he acknowledged them with a terse nod but he didn't pause to chat.

"Well, someone didn't think it was time," Joe said.

Mel couldn't argue with that. From what she knew of the very brief time she'd spent with Gallway, she didn't think he warranted the time of day, never mind a television career. That being said, she didn't believe he, or anyone, deserved to be murdered. Let him live his life out in shame with no glory, sure, but not murder. Of course this was assuming he had been murdered. She supposed that was what Uncle Stan and the crime scene unit would determine.

"Did either of you notice a weapon of any kind?" Mel asked. She kept her voice low so that no one around them could hear.

Oz shook his head. "I only saw him and a whole lot of blood."

"Maybe," Joe said. "When I went to move him, there was a wooden mallet under his shoulder."

Mel snapped her fingers. "That's right, the meat tenderizer."

Oz's eyes went wide. "Why would that be in the baking kitchen? We don't use those."

"Exactly," Joe said. "The only reason that would have been under his body was because someone used it on him or maybe he was using it to defend himself."

"A crime of passion, then," Mel said. "I can't imagine anyone put much thought into killing him if they just grabbed a meat tenderizer and walloped him with it."

"So much blood," Oz said. He sounded queasy.

Both he and Joe looked down at their hands. They'd cleaned up after the EMTs had arrived but Mel knew they could feel it still there on their skin. The same thing had happened to her once when she found a dead man in a ball pit, and sometimes she still dreamed about it. There was no recovering from finding someone murdered. It stayed with you as you pondered their last moments, what they were thinking, feeling, or doing. Were they frightened, angry, or taken by surprise? The endless loop of questions never stopped. She shivered.

Joe immediately put his hand on Mel's back in a comforting gesture. She leaned into it. It was one of those silent moments of communication that they had come to share. It was this bond, this simple understanding of each other, that made her more certain than ever that marrying Joe was the best decision of her life.

She had crushed on him since she was twelve and he was sixteen, but he hadn't noticed her until she was a grown-up. Oh, he said he'd recognized that she was going to be a knockout when she was a teenager, but by then he was already in college, living a different life as he pursued a career in the law. It hadn't been until Mel opened up the bakery that Joe had reappeared in her life as he stopped in to visit his sister, Angie, and mooch a cupcake or two.

The bakery had given Mel many things. The achievement of her dream of being a chef, financial independence, and the ability to work with her best friends, but the most significant thing it had brought into her life was the return of Joe. For that, she would be ever grateful.

"Why are you asking me all these questions?" a voice snapped.

Mel glanced across the room to see Ashley standing with Clay Perry, Uncle Stan, and Detective Martinez. The young woman had her hands on her hips in a belligerent stance.

"We're just trying to establish what happened," Uncle Stan said. He was using his calmest talk-the-angry-person-down voice.

Ashely didn't respond well. In a shrill voice that had a bit of a slur in it, she continued, "Questions, questions, questions! Everyone knows who killed Miles Gallway. It's the same person he had a fight with last week, and he's sitting right over there."

She turned and pointed right at Oz.

Seven

Every eyeball in the dining area turned towards Oz. He shifted in his seat, uncomfortable with the scrutiny. Marconi stopped pacing and snapped his head in their direction and then strode towards them. The overhead lights shone off his bald dome, and his glasses and overly large nose gave him the look of a bird of prey.

He stopped at their table and studied Oz. "It's a damn shame," he said.

Mel didn't know if he was referring to Chef Miles or something else. It was as if he'd started the conversation in the middle and expected everyone to know what he was talking about.

"Yeah," Oz agreed. The confused expression on his face made it obvious he wasn't clear on what Marconi was talking about, either, but he was playing along.

"You would have been great. You have the looks, the

skill, the camera loves you. I'm telling you, you're the whole package, but now . . ." Marconi raised his hands in the air and let his voice trail off.

"I'm sorry," Oz said. "What are you talking about?"

"Your television career," Simon said. He looked exasperated, as if Oz wasn't getting the big picture.

"I thought you were talking about Miles being dead," Oz said. His voice was tight.

"That, too, sure," Marconi said. He nodded. "Real tragedy."

Mel glanced at Joe to see if he was getting this. Anything resembling a human emotion like empathy or compassion was seriously lacking in Marconi's voice. It was, in fact, chilling. Joe was frowning, a deep groove appearing and holding in between his eyes.

The television producer, oblivious to their scrutiny, put a hand on the back of his neck. "Not for nothing, but this really puts me in a bind."

"How so?" Joe asked. His voice was hard.

Marconi turned and acknowledged Mel and Joe for the first time. He looked them over. "You aren't professional chefs, are you?" He didn't wait for an answer. "Because a team would be amazing for ratings. Husband and wife? That'd be great. We could do some real tense moments over a hot stove, you know, build up the drama between the two of you."

"She's a baker," Joe said. Marconi's eye lit up. "But I'm a county district attorney."

"Oh." Marconi's face fell. He looked wary and disappointed. "That really won't resonate with viewers of the Foodie Channel."

"Didn't think it would," Joe said.

"Well, this whole thing was a wasted trip," Marconi said. "I'm going to bounce."

He turned on his heel and aimed for the door when Clay Perry intercepted him just a few feet from their table. Per usual, Clay was dressed in golf attire, as if he'd just come off the links.

"Where are you going, Simon?" Clay asked.

Simon held his arms wide. "You're kidding, right? I'm getting out of here and heading back to LA."

"No, you're not," Clay said. "We had a deal. You were going to pick one of my chefs to base a show around. That hasn't changed."

Mel, Joe, and Oz exchanged a considering look. This seemed like significant information.

"Hasn't it?" Marconi asked. "Miles is dead and the only other contender for a television career found his body and is probably a suspect in his murder. I can't make the magic happen without the talent, Clay."

Mel glanced at Oz and saw him blanch at offhandedly being accused of being a murderer. She patted his arm in reassurance and he expelled a breath, releasing some tension.

"What about me?" Ashley strode up behind Marconi. She dragged her hand across the top of his shoulders as she inserted herself in between the two men. "I could be your star." She batted her false eyelashes at him and Marconi rolled his eyes.

"I'm going to save you some time, sweetheart," he said. "You don't have the cooking chops and there's nothing interesting about you. You're like whipped cream.

Pretty and fluffy but you only accent the more substantial tastes, like peach pie or Irish coffee. No one wants a bowl of plain whipped cream."

Ashley's lip curled. She looked like she wanted to slap him. Instead, she tossed her dark hair over her shoulder and said, "I'll show you." She stared at him. "I was more than Miles's sous chef, and I know things."

There was a pause and Marconi studied her as if assessing the threat level she posed. Then he shook his head, unimpressed, and said, "Not about cooking, you don't."

Oz snorted and Ashley snapped her head in his direction and glared at him. Oz quickly feigned interest in the tablecloth. Satisfied, Ashley stalked off, looking like she was going to make someone pay for the slight.

"Thanks for nothing," Clay said. "I need her to step into Miles's spot until I hire a real chef."

Marconi shrugged, not looking repentant in the least.

"We'll talk later," Clay said. "I'm holding you to our deal. You need to find a talent among my staff for your cooking program. This is not negotiable. Remember you owe me."

Marconi watched Clay leave, and then he glanced back at Oz one more time before he walked away, shaking his head in disappointment.

"Is it just me?" Joe asked. "Or does it seem like no one is particularly broken up about Miles Gallway being found dead?"

"Not just you," Oz confirmed.

"And I think it's safe to say that Miles Gallway wasn't just found dead," Mel said. "I think he was murdered."

"Then what happened?" Joyce asked. "Did dear Joe save the day?"

Despite the trauma of the day, Mel almost laughed. Her mother had been calling Joe that from the moment he and Mel had gotten together. Joyce simply adored Joe, which was going to make married life interesting as Mel was quite certain if ever there was an issue, Joyce was going to take Joe's side. She consoled herself that she always had Angie, who would back her to the end.

She resisted laughing, however, because Alma Rodriguez, the fashion designer who had cut down Mel's mother's voluminous white satin dress from the '80s and created something brand-new, with about a hundred yards to spare, was doing her final fitting and Mel didn't want to mess it up and have Alma stab her with a pin. It had happened before.

"He tried to," Mel said. "But after Marconi left, the whole thing got pretty ugly with most of the line cooks rushing to Oz's defense while Ashley and a few of the chefs and floor staff higher up than Oz sold him out to Detective Martinez."

Joyce's lip curled just the tiniest bit. Since she and Uncle Stan had become a thing, she had gotten to know his partner, the feisty detective Martinez, and she struggled with the woman's inexplicable animosity towards Mel.

"Stand still," Alma ordered. "Or I won't be responsible for sticking you."

"I was!" Mel protested. She glanced down at Alma Rodriguez, who despite her success as a fashion designer was still the sourest person Mel had ever met. Alma was glaring at her and also holding a very sharp pin. "Sorry, it won't happen again."

Mel sent her mother a mock-alarmed look and Joyce smiled.

"Well, I'm sure the tragedy will get sorted," Joyce said. With a burst of pride, she added, "Stan is a brilliant detective."

"He is," Mel agreed. She was just beginning to get used to the new relationship between her mother and her uncle. Now that she was getting married, she was glad that her mom had someone special in her life. It hit her then that this scene could easily be reversed. Her mother could be standing on the dais while Mel looked on.

"Um, Mom," she said. "Can I ask you something?"

"Yes, sweetie." Joyce was fussing with her old veil, which Alma had modernized and minimized as well, again, by taking off about a thousand yards of organza and silk roses. Joyce had clearly been enamored with the whole Princess Di vibe back in the day.

"Do you think you and Uncle Stan are going to get married?" Mel asked. She hoped her voice came across as neutral and not as if she was freaking out, because she wasn't, she told herself. She was completely okay with however Joyce answered. Really.

She glanced at her mother, who had gone completely still. "I . . . we . . ." Joyce stammered. "I don't know. It's never come up. Would it bother you if we did?"

"No!" Mel said. Maybe with a bit too much force as Alma rocked back on her heels and gave her a look.

"Overselling," Alma said, barely under her breath.

"I mean, I don't care either way," Mel said. She shrugged. "You do you."

"Underselling and a total buzzkill," Alma said. She shook her head in disgust.

Mel tried again while resisting the urge to kick Alma. "What I'm trying to say is, whatever you crazy kids decide is A-okay with me. One hundred percent. I'll even be your matron of honor."

"Now you're upselling," Alma said. "Try shutting your piehole and just listen to your mom."

Mel glared at her but Alma was oblivious as she went back to pinning the hem on the underskirt. If the dress wasn't the most glorious thing Mel had ever seen, she'd have flounced off the dais by now. But it really was spectacular.

Joyce's wedding gown had been made out of a sea of white satin with a ton of matching silk rosettes sewn onto the ten-foot train, the top of the puffy sleeves, and across the bodice. When Mel was young, she had thought her mother looked like a fairy princess with her long blond hair swept up in a French twist and under a heavy organza veil that was embroidered on the edges and weighted down with even more silk roses. And her father, young and buff, wearing a black tuxedo and with a full head of hair, looked like the hero on a Harlequin romance novel. Mel had gone through their wedding album so many times, she'd worn out a few of the pages.

Alma, with Joyce's approval, had reimagined the dress. The rosettes had been plucked off, the train trimmed, the bodice simplified, and the puffy sleeves removed. Now the gown was a form-fitting white satin sheath with a delicate organza overlay that had been embroidered with tiny seed pearls along the hem and the bodice. The rosettes had been redistributed on the headpiece for Mel's veil, which hung all the way down her back to the floor. The dress made her look long and lithe but also curvy, which was some feat of fashion wizardry that Mel could only guess at. When she looked in the mirror, Mel didn't even recognize herself.

Mel met her mother's amused glance and said, "What I'm really trying to say is that I just want you to be happy."

Alma grunted. It sounded like approval.

Joyce grinned. Mel knew her mother had always been a looker but when she smiled like that, it was easy to see why not just one but two Cooper men had fallen for her.

"I can tell you this," Joyce said. "Whatever happens, you and your brother will be the first to know."

This was not as reassuring as Mel would have supposed.

"So, you've been fired?" Marty said. He sounded outraged.

"Not exactly," Oz said. "Just put on a leave of absence since Mr. Perry is concerned about resort guests being put off their food by a possible murderer in their kitchen."

"That's ridiculous!" Marty exclaimed. His bald head went a shade of crimson that would have alarmed Mel if she hadn't seen it before. Marty took aspersions to the characters of his people very personally. "Just because you found the body doesn't make you a suspect. I'm going to have a word with that Perry guy, and I'm going to ask some questions and find out just what is going on at that place."

"Please don't," Oz said.

"But we need to know what—" Marty began but Oz interrupted him.

"'You're a very nosy fellow, kitty cat,'" Oz said.

"*Chinatown*," Angie identified the movie quote.

"Well done," Mel said. They exchanged a high five.

"It's unfortunate we don't have someone on the inside at the Sun Dial Resort. You know, someone who could give us the inside scoop," Angie said.

"What about one of the brothers?" Mel asked. "Do any of them know someone who works there? Collectively, they've dated about every woman in the Valley of the Sun."

"It's possible. I can check," Angie said. "Sal has the worst reputation and he does love his hostess girlfriends. There was one at the Ritz who pursued him for years. So long as he hasn't broken any hearts at the Sun Dial, we might have an in. Given that all the brothers have that distinctive DeLaura look, I don't think we'll be able to slip a brother by anyone who might have dated one of them."

Oz frowned. "I can't help. I wasn't there long enough to make any real allies except the ones in my kitchen, but they're all afraid of losing their jobs so there's not much they can do for me."

"Well, it's a good thing you have me," Marty said.

Mel glanced at him. "You can't bully the staff of the resort into telling you things."

"I would never," he said.

"Then what's your plan?" Oz asked.

"I'm going to be a guest," he said. "I'll cozy up to Clay Perry and his wife and find out what's going on."

"This seems like a bad idea," Angie said. "What if they connect you to the bakery?"

"They won't," he said. "I've got a sweet set of custom-made Callaway golf clubs that are just aching to be broken in. Believe me, one look at those clubs and they'll be begging me to stay and then they'll tell me everything."

"What's so great about a set of golf clubs?" Oz asked. He was not a golfer, having grown up in Phoenix and spent his youth on his skateboard.

"You can't play without the right equipment," Marty said. "It's a status thing."

"And how's your golf game?" Angie asked.

"That doesn't signify," Marty said. "I don't keep score."

"'Then how do you measure yourself with other golfers?'" Mel asked.

She glanced at Angie, who picked up on the movie quote and responded with the answer, "'By height.'"

"*Caddyshack*!" Oz identified the movie quote, raising his hands in the air, like a referee calling a touchdown.

"Har har har," Marty said. "You laugh but when I'm out on the links with Perry, getting all the inside dirt, you'll be singing a different tune."

Oz, Angie, and Mel simultaneously broke into "I'm Alright," the movie's theme song, while imitating the furry fake gopher who danced in the movie credits.

Marty lifted his apron over his head and tossed it at Oz. "Since you're available, you can train the new girl on the counter. She should be here in a few minutes."

With that he left the kitchen through the back door, shutting it none too gently behind him.

"New girl?" Oz asked. He looked surprised and, Mel thought, a little hurt.

"We needed someone to cover my maternity leave," Angie said. Her expression was blank when she said it, giving no indication that the new girl was also filling Oz's vacant spot.

"So, she's temporary?" he asked.

Mel shrugged. "Depends upon whether Angie comes back or not."

Angie said nothing even though they both knew she had every intention of coming back. By silent agreement, they didn't want Oz to feel as if he was being replaced.

"Since you're on leave, Oz," Mel said. "Do you mind helping out around here?"

"Not at all," he said. He pulled the apron over his head. "It'll be a relief to have something to do to keep me from thinking too much."

Mel nodded. She got that. Whether Oz had liked Miles or not, the fact that he was murdered in Oz's kitchen had to leave him wondering how, who, and why. And being considered a suspect made it personal, very personal.

Eight

"So, Oz, is that really your name?" Madison gushed. "It's so cool. Like rock star cool."

Oz looked over the petite blonde's head at Mel. He looked pained, like a dog being forced to listen to a siren's wail without howling.

"Yeah, it's my name," he said. "Try not to wear it out."

Madison tipped her head to the side. "M'kay. So, tell me about cooking school. I was in college, but the math did me in, like totally, it's not my gift, you know? So, now I'm trying to figure out who I am. I think I'd be a really good influencer because my friends say I have an amazing aesthetic."

Oz stuck his finger in his ear and wiggled it around then he looked at the tip.

"What's wrong?" Madison asked.

"Just checking to see if my ears are bleeding," he said. "Because you haven't stopped talking for over an hour now."

Mel had to turn her snort into a cough. Madison must have loaded up on an energy drink before she got here, because Oz was right, she had not stopped talking from the moment she crossed the threshold. Had Mel been here alone, she would have started banging her head on the steel table. Oz had her sympathies, but not enough to relieve him of the chatterbox.

Mel finished loading the display case with a batch of butter rum cupcakes, a buttery cake topped with a brown-butter-and-rum-flavored icing, and was about to head back to the quiet of the kitchen when the front door to the bakery opened and in strode Marty and Ray DeLaura.

Marty was dressed in standard golf attire, beige shorts and a teal polo shirt, but Ray was, well, Mel had no idea what Ray was wearing. Argyle knee socks with a matching vest and a hat with a pom-pom, over a pair of short pants in a shade of red that made her eyes water. Good grief.

"What is that?" Oz asked. He circled his finger at Ray.

"My golf outfit," he said. He puffed out his chest and put his hands on his hips. "Like it?"

"No." Oz shook his head. "You look like a clown without the face paint."

"I'll have you know this ensemble is the height of fashion in the golf world," Ray said.

"Did you go on the Internet unsupervised?" Mel asked.

"He did," Marty said. He sent Ray an annoyed look. "Everyone knows if you want the right information about something, you ask a librarian. Sheesh."

"You didn't give me enough time, old man," Ray defended himself. "Besides, it's perfect as it will distract from your subpar game."

"My subpar game?" Marty sputtered. He was turning an alarming shade of red.

"When are you playing?" Mel asked. She hoped to distract them from an argument.

"We're meeting up with Clay Perry and Simon Marconi for a ten o'clock tee time," Marty said. He glanced at his watch. "In fact, we need to go. Are you all right here? Golf takes a long time to play."

"Sure," Mel said. "I have Oz and Madison. We'll be fine."

Madison stepped forward. "Hi, Mr. Zelaznik, great to see you again. I hope you have a terrific game."

Marty smiled. "Thanks, kid. It should be—"

"Don't you worry about a thing here," Madison interrupted. "I will make sure everything is done to your specifications. I run a tight ship, you'll see." She turned to Oz and clapped her hands. "Chop chop, there is cleaning to be done. Let's get on these countertops, Oz. Move it. Move it."

Marty sidled over to Mel, and said, "I like her. She's got spirit."

Mel gave him a side eye. "You just love that she's giving Oz a hard time."

"That, too." Marty nodded. He turned around and led the way to the door, "Come on, Fancy Man, we've got balls to hit."

"Roger that," Ray said. He grabbed a peanut butter and chocolate cupcake out of the display case and followed Marty out the door.

Mel watched them go, trying not to worry. Ray wasn't the subtlest person on the planet, and if Clay Perry put him together with Joe, then their quest for information would be short-lived. Maybe his crazy outfit was a good call. She tried not to worry and went back to the kitchen, leaving Oz to fend for himself with Madison. When he cast her a pleading glance, she said, "Survival of the fittest, dude."

\'-\ \ \

The day passed quickly as there were several big orders picked up and the beautiful weather outside had the locals and tourists roaming Old Town, making the most of the moderate temperatures before the Arizona summer hit full force.

Mel had been tracking the weather every day, not wanting to be caught in a ninety-plus-degree day on her wedding. She wasn't worried about herself so much as she was about Angie. Being close to term, the heat could make or break the matron of honor. So far, it looked like it was going to linger in the low eighties. Phew!

Madison punched out in the early afternoon and Oz did not look sorry to see her go. He glanced at Mel when the front door closed behind her, "That one doesn't have an off switch, does she?"

Mel laughed. "Nope. Maybe she'll be good for Marty in your absence, unless you're thinking of coming back as more than temporary?"

She tried to keep her voice even, not wanting to sway him either way.

"I don't know what's going to happen," he said. He looked nervous and Mel rushed to reassure him.

"It's going to be all right," she said. She picked up a fresh cleaning rag and a bottle of disinfectant and began to wipe down a small café table in the center of the shop that one of her favorite families of four had left sticky. "I'm sure of it."

"Are you?" Oz asked. "Because I'm not. The fight I had with Miles was in front of everyone. It makes perfect sense that whoever killed him is going to make it look like I did it."

"If he was struck by the mallet found on the floor beside him that suggests it was done on impulse. Maybe he was fighting with someone else, perhaps someone who had a grudge with him came back, or it could have been something more personal and not work related at all," Mel said. "The police will figure it out and it'll be resolved. I'm sure of it."

She was sure of no such thing, but she wanted Oz to feel as if it was possible for this nightmare to have a reasonable outcome that would absolve him of the murder and give him his old job back if that was what he wanted.

As if to make a mockery of her words of reassurance, the door to the bakery opened and in walked Uncle Stan. He was alone, which was unusual as his partner, Detective Martinez, usually came with him if for no other reason than to give Mel a hard time.

"Mel, Oz," he said. "I'm glad you're both here."

The bakery was mercifully empty. Mel wondered if

she should lock the door. She glanced at Oz and noted that he looked mildly alarmed as well.

"What's going on?" Mel asked.

"There's been an accusation leveled against Oz." Uncle Stan stared at Oz from under his bushy eyebrows.

They both gasped.

"What kind?" Mel asked.

"The murder kind," Uncle Stan said. He turned fully to Oz and asked, "Can you tell me about your relationship with Kasey Perry?"

"Mrs. Perry?" he asked. "The resort owner's wife?"

"That's the one."

"That's it, that's the relationship," Oz said. "She's my employer's wife."

"She's much younger than Mr. Perry," Uncle Stan said. He was staring at Oz in that way he had that made guilty people squirm. Oz was as still as the counter he leaned against.

"What's that signify?" Mel asked. "And she's not that young. I saw her across the room after the murder and even I could tell she's almost fifty and has had a lot of work as she tries to hang on to thirty-five."

Uncle Stan ignored her and kept his penetrating gaze on Oz.

"Can you tell me where you were on April twelfth at one in the afternoon?"

Oz put his hand on his neck as he tried to remember the date. "I'd have to check my calendar. I'd assume I was at work."

"According to Mrs. Perry, you were with her in a vacant room on the resort," Uncle Stan said.

"What would I be doing with her in a vacant room?" Oz asked. Both Mel and Uncle Stan stared at him while he put it together. It took a second. *"What?! NO!"*

He looked horrified and shook his head. Mel got the feeling he was trying to hide behind the bangs he used to wear over his eyes to protect himself from the world. A spurt of anger blasted through her as she thought of Kasey Perry accusing him of such a thing.

"Surely, you don't believe her," Mel said.

Uncle Stan shrugged, never taking his eyes off Oz.

"But that's so . . . ugh." Oz shuddered.

Mel turned to Uncle Stan. "I believe him. She's lying."

"I think so, too," he said. "But an accusation is an accusation and I can't pretend she didn't say what she said about Oz."

"What exactly did she say?" Mel asked. "Did she say he was having an affair with her? And even if he was—" Oz opened his mouth to protest but Mel held her hand up in a stop gesture. "Even if he was, which he wasn't, why would that have anything to do with Gallway's murder?"

Oz looked from Mel to Uncle Stan and said, "Yeah, what she said."

"Mrs. Perry said you wanted to be promoted to executive chef so that you could provide for her in the way she was accustomed to being cared for," Uncle Stan said. "Basically, she said you murdered Gallway for her."

"What?!" Mel cried, echoing Oz's earlier outrage. "That's insane. Chefs simply don't make that much money, even executive chefs."

"Um, not really the point," Oz interrupted. "Let's start with I wasn't having an affair with her and end with I wasn't having an affair with her, adding for the record that I'd never hook up with a married woman. Ever."

"Well . . . duh," Mel said.

She was about to elaborate when the kitchen door slammed open and in came Marty with Ray right behind him. They were still wearing their golf outfits and Ray's caused Mel's vision to blur, interrupting her thoughts.

"Oz, man, you have to get out of here before the Five-O come— Oh, hi, Stan," Marty said. He looped his arm through Oz's and tried to haul him away from the counter. Given that Oz had at least seventy-five pounds on the older man, this was no easy feat. He leaned close and whispered in Oz's ear, "You really need to come with me now."

"Get him out of here," Ray said out of the corner of his mouth. "I'll cover you."

"Cover us?" Marty whirled around. "How? By blinding everyone with your vibrant tartan?"

"Hey!" Ray straightened up and put a hand on his hip. It was hard to take him seriously when the pom-pom on his hat bobbed.

"Is this about my affair with Mrs. Perry?" Oz asked.

"Ah!" Marty yelped and dropped his arm. "It's true?"

"Well, well, well," Ray said. He looked Oz up and down. "The kid's got layers."

"I do not," Oz protested. "I'm not a kid and there are no layers here. I didn't, I wouldn't . . . ugh, I think I'm going to throw up."

"Everyone, settle down," Uncle Stan said. "Listen, I knew Mrs. Perry was lying, because she didn't even get your name right. She thought your first name was Oliver."

Oz quirked an eyebrow up at that. Marty looked at him, made a face, and said, "Oliver?"

Oz shrugged.

Uncle Stan said, "I figured if she was really having the long-running affair with you that she claimed, she'd at least get your first name right."

"You'd think," Oz agreed.

Uncle Stan turned to Ray and Oz and asked, "How'd you two find out about what she said?"

"We were golfing with Clay Perry and Simon Marconi," Marty said. "Men talk, especially when the beer cart keeps coming around."

"Clay Perry told you?" Mel asked.

"No, Simon told us when Clay was trying to punch out his ball from the desert. That guy is lousy down the fairway but is amazing with the punch-outs."

"Focus, Marty," Mel said.

"Sorry," he said.

"Marconi said that Kasey told him that she and Oz had a wild affair and that she was going to have to go to the police because Oz told her that he would kill for her."

"Seriously, going to be ill," Oz said. "Like, get me a bucket."

Ray's eyes went wide and he ducked behind the counter to grab a trash can. He thrust it at Oz, who hugged it to his chest.

"Did Marconi believe her?" Mel asked.

Ray shrugged. "He seemed to. He said it was a damn shame since Oz could be an overnight sensation in the cooking world if he wanted to be."

"I don't want to be," Oz said.

"Here's the thing that's bothering me," Uncle Stan said. "Why would she lie about that? She had to know you'd call her out." He looked at Oz. "Why you?"

"No idea," he said. He frowned. "I have a hard time picturing Mrs. Perry coming after Miles with a wooden mallet. That seems like a depth of feeling she's not capable of."

"Maybe she had someone else whack him?" Mel asked.

"Literally," Ray said. They all ignored him.

"Maybe she and Gallway were having an affair and it went wrong," Uncle Stan said. "Or perhaps he knew she was having an affair with someone else and was blackmailing her. Truly, who knows? I've heard it all a million times. The key is to get her to admit she lied. I've had no luck, she is standing firm on her story, but I think you might be able to break her, Oz. Are you willing?"

"Break her?" Oz sounded horrified. "What exactly does that mean?"

"More importantly, can I help?" Ray asked.

Stan glowered at him. "Aren't you dating my partner?"

"Just trying to be of assistance," Ray said. He raised his hands in the air in a gesture of innocence.

"Don't bother," Uncle Stan said. Ray looked like he was going to protest but Marty shook his head at him.

Everyone knew that Ray was the black sheep of the DeLaura family. He considered the rule of law as more of a suggestion. He and the local Scottsdale Police Department had a complicated relationship made even more so by his recent relationship with Detective Tara Martinez.

"What I'm suggesting"—Uncle Stan paused and glanced at them all—"is that you have a conversation with Mrs. Perry and while doing so wear a wire."

"A wire?" Oz looked alarmed. "I can't wear a wire. First off, how am I supposed to approach her and second, a wire? Don't you need to have some sort of training for that?"

"Nah," Uncle Stan said. "It's easy. Mel's worn one."

"It's true," she said. "But I see your point about approaching her out of the blue when you're on a leave of absence. I don't see how you can finesse that."

"No problem," Ray said. "Have Mel go with you."

Mel looked at him as if he was mental. Not out of the realm of possibility with Ray. "I'm getting married in a week. I don't have time to play detective."

"I understand," Oz said. "It's cool."

His eyes looked so sad. Mel felt her insides twist.

She had a full schedule; she was supposed to be meeting with their wedding coordinator, Judi Franko, and making sure the flowers were ordered for the church; the small jazz band they hired for the reception was confirmed; that her brother and his family were all settled in at her mother's; and so on. There were details, picky pesky details, even for their small wedding. She was not supposed to go and interrogate the wife of a wealthy resort owner about the murder of their executive chef.

She tipped up her chin, planning to hold the line. Oz met her gaze and gave her a closed-lipped smile of understanding. Damn it!

"Fine, I'll go, but only as your backup," Mel said. "You have to be the one to approach her."

Oz perked up and Mel felt a surge of happiness, the sort that came from helping a friend in need. Surely, questioning Mrs. Perry wouldn't be that bad. Oz would wear the wire, they'd get her to admit she lied, and Oz would be cleared. Nothing could be easier. Right?

Nine

They drove Mel's Mini Cooper to the resort and Mel parked in her usual spot. She watched Oz closely to see if he showed any signs of distress. She didn't want him to suffer some horrible posttraumatic episode, which was way out of her wheelhouse when it came to employee wellness. Although Oz wasn't an employee anymore, he was still family.

"I think I'm allergic to the adhesive on the tape they used to attach the mic to my chest," he said. He pulled the front of his Hawaiian shirt away from his body and stared down at his chest while they walked towards the resort. "Yup, hives."

"Maybe you're allergic to the shirt," Mel said.

Oz had borrowed it from Ray. Since they were trying to fit in with the guests at the resort, they'd decided it was best to be wearing resort attire. Oz was in navy blue drip-dry shorts, the sort that could be shorts or a bathing suit, with his loaner Hawaiian shirt, which featured enormous leaves in eye-searing shades of orange, blue, and green. While Mel was in a conservative one-piece bathing suit, with a white crocheted beach cover-up that reached down to her knees. They were both wearing large hats and sunglasses, completing their disguises.

"It's not the shirt," Oz said. He scratched his chest, trying not to disturb the mic.

"Have you been allergic to adhesive before?" Mel asked. "Do you break out from bandages and such?"

"Not that I remember," he said.

"Then it's probably nerves," Mel said. "Try some deep-breathing exercises."

Oz paused and took a deep breath. "I can't do this." He turned and started walking back to the car.

"Yes, you can!" Mel protested. She ran around him so that she was in front of him, blocking his path. "Oz, stop. Listen, I know this is lousy but Uncle Stan is right. This is your best chance at proving your innocence by calling Mrs. Perry out on her lies. Otherwise, she's going to make it sound like you did it, and then the police will have to treat you like suspect number one."

"But I'm not," Oz protested. "I would never, especially in a kitchen, that's my sacred space."

Mel smiled. She understood that completely. "I know, but it doesn't look good. Let's review what's stacking up against you."

"Can we not?"

"Gallway was found in your kitchen, potentially murdered; and willingly or not, you were in competition for a television career against him. You have no alibi other than feeding your sourdough. You had a very public spat with Miles a few days before he was killed, and now the resort owner's wife is claiming that you plotted the whole thing to try and earn her love. It's reads like a really bad true crime story."

"This is a nightmare," Oz said. "I can't believe this is my life. I feel as if it's falling apart."

"I know it seems that way," Mel said. "But concentrate on the good things. The murderer will get caught. You'll get your job back. You have all of us, your family, your girlfriend, Lupe. It's going to be all right."

He looked pained. He opened his mouth to speak and then closed it.

"What is it, Oz?" Mel asked. "What are you thinking?"

"What if it's not all right?" he asked. He clapped a hand over his chest as if he could block sound to the supersensitive microphone taped to his chest. "What if I'm arrested for a murder I didn't commit, get found guilty and sent to prison, and my entire life is ruined? What then?"

"Well, we're getting married in the DeLaura family church," Mel said. "We'll be sure to offer up a prayer for you in the middle of the ceremony."

"That's it?" Oz's eyes went wide with horror, and Mel realized this was no time to be joking around with him.

"Sorry, I'm kidding," she said. She looped her arm through his and tried to pull him along. It was like trying to move a vehicle in park. "Come on, Lupe coming to town should be more motivation for you to get this cleared up."

"Yeah, well," Oz said. If anything, his expression became even more grim. Mel wondered what that was about.

"Listen," Mel cajoled him. "If nothing else, this awful woman has besmirched the character of one of my former employees, who is also a fine pastry chef, and I can't let that stand. Besides, we're not looking for a confrontation but rather we are going for information."

"It sounds so much better when you put it like that," Oz said. He began to move and Mel was relieved. She'd started to build up a sweat.

"Any idea where we can find Mrs. Perry at this hour of the day?"

"Oh, yeah, she's always in the same place. Poolside with her flag up and beverages coming in a steady parade."

"Oh, goody."

She remembered the woman she'd seen standing beside her husband in the resort dining area after Miles Gallway's body had been found. Mel suspected that she was the sort of woman who evaluated people on their looks, rating them as worthy or not at a glance. Mel had met her type before and the encounters always made her feel less than. This was not something she needed to be dealing with right before her wedding.

Mel didn't want to revisit her own body insecurity but there was no way that woman's manufactured dips and curves weren't going to give Mel a twinge or four.

The parking valet nodded to Oz when they walked by, so it was clear Oz hadn't been banned from the premises. Mel was relieved that even though Simon had blabbed the gossip to Marty and Ray, he hadn't said anything to Mr. Perry, apparently.

Still, Mel didn't want to have any unpleasant scenes during their visit, so they needed to avoid Clay like a pandemic. They walked through the lobby and Mel scanned the area, looking for potential threats. She saw an officer whom she recognized from the Scottsdale police department, a detective named John Gonzalez, who worked with Uncle Stan. He was standing at the bar and his eyes met Mel's for just the briefest moment, letting her know that he was there to make certain nothing bad happened to her or Oz. Good old Uncle Stan always had her back.

"This way," Oz said. He went in the opposite direction of the kitchens. He led Mel past the main entrance to the pool and around to a side gate. He used his staff badge to unlock it. The lock clicked open and they slipped inside, walking as if they belonged. Oz paused to visually sweep the area.

"Is she here?" Mel asked. She looked but with the array of sunscreened bodies lounging around the pool she couldn't pick out the one that might belong to Mrs. Perry.

"There she is. In the blue lounge chair to the right," Oz said.

Mel took in the sight of a well-oiled woman, covered by the barest scraps of orange fabric that could still be called a bathing suit. Much like the last time Mel had seen her, Kasey Perry wore her hair in a tight ball on the top of her head, sported overly large dark sunglasses, and her wrists, throat, and ankles dripped gold, diamond-encrusted jewelry. Wow, just wow.

Sure enough, as they watched, a male waiter in shorts and a polo shirt approached with a frosty margarita on his tray. Mrs. Perry handed him her empty glass and took the new one. When he held out the bill for her to sign, she waved him off.

"I can't," she said. "I'm all oily." She gestured to her

body, which was deeply tanned and covered in body oil. The waiter nodded and she gave him a flirtatious finger wave, checking out his backside as he departed. Ew.

Kasey up close in the flesh was a bit more than Mel had been expecting. She was clearly the queen bee of the poolside as she waved to other guests and took selfies on her phone, drinking her beverage by puckering her vibrant pink lips around her straw. Mel would bet she had quite the lively online presence, which could prove to be very informative. Still, she was a lot to take in.

"'Surely, you can't be serious,'" Mel said.

"'I am serious . . . and don't call me Shirley,'" Oz retorted.

"Airplane!" Mel identified the movie. They exchanged a look of amusement.

Mel glanced back at Kasey. She squinted, taking in all of the skin and hair and jewelry. It was like watching something in a nature documentary. She listened, half expecting to hear Morgan Freeman narrate how the female of the indigenous poolside species selected a male to mate with but then ripped his head off if he wasn't fast enough with the drinks.

"All right, let's do this," Oz said.

He strode forward, leaving Mel to hurry in his wake. With her yellow flip-flops with big plastic daisies on them, and her overly large pool covering, she felt as sexy as someone's grandma, but that was fine. She wasn't here to compete in a swimsuit competition. This was an information-gathering mission.

Oz stood beside Kasey's chair, effectively blocking the sun. Kasey had put down her drink and was in full recline.

Without opening her eyes, she said, "Do you mind? You're blocking my sun."

Oz said nothing. He just stood there, arms crossed over his chest as if to keep himself from strangling her. Mel stood beside him, wondering if she should say something. She waited.

With a huff, Kasey sat up in her chair and snapped, "I said, could you move out of my sun?"

"Sure." Oz sat sideways on the chair beside hers. "I just have a few questions."

Kasey shielded her eyes against the sun and glanced at Oz. When the recognition hit, she sent him a small smile and in a low voice said, "Hi there, Tiger."

What?! Mel was relieved that she didn't say it out loud.

"Don't call me that," Oz said. He glared.

Kasey pouted. "But I always call you that."

"You've never called me that," he said. "In fact, you've never called me anything but Chef."

"Well, I thought it," she said. She leaned forward, giving him an eyeful of her cleavage. Oz glanced away.

"Spoilsport," she said. Her gazed shifted to Mel, who sat down beside Oz, and Kasey's eyebrows looked like they wanted to shift into a frown but were incapable of moving. "Who's that?" She pointed a very long, bright pink fingernail at Mel and picked up her drink.

"A friend," Oz said. "Mrs. Perry—"

"Call me Kasey," she said.

"No." Oz shifted in his seat. "Mrs. Perry, why did you—"

"Nuh uh uh." Kasey wagged a finger at him. "I'm not talking to you until you call me Kasey."

She shifted so that her posterior was turned in Oz's

direction, and she looked at him over her shoulder in a come-hither pose.

Mel had a sudden memory of being at the Phoenix Zoo as a kid and seeing one of the female baboons present itself to the male. Kindergarten had gotten a whole lot more interesting that day. She could still remember Mrs. Diaz clapping her hand over Mel's eyes and hauling her away from the exhibit. When she got home and told her dad, he'd laughed so hard he popped a button on his shirt. She glanced at Oz and realized he'd probably prefer the baboons right now.

His face had turned a hot shade of red and he was sweating. While it was warm outside, he was a native Arizonan and as such usually didn't break a sweat until the temperature was over one hundred.

Mel leaned close and whispered, "Need backup?"

"Yes, please," he answered. His voice sounded strangled.

Mel nudged him aside and moved so that she was in front of Kasey. "You stay like that and you're going to throw your back out."

"Who are you?" Kasey flopped onto her back and repositioned her seat back to support her as she sat upright. "And why are you here?"

"I'm here because you're a big, fat liar," Mel said. She didn't feel the need to sugarcoat the truth. "And I want to know why."

"What did you say to me?" Kasey snapped. "Do you know who I am?"

"Yes, you're married to the resort owner, Clay Perry, blah blah," Mel said.

"I'll have you thrown out," Kasey said. She lifted her

hand as if she'd make it happen with a snap of her fingers. Mel was not intimidated. She'd had her share of irate customers in the bakery. Like, just try dealing with two customers who arrived at the same time and both wanted the last red velvet. It got ugly.

"I doubt that, given that my husband-to-be is the county district attorney and he'd love to have the police drag you and your husband in for questioning in the murder of Miles Gallway," she said. Of course, Joe had no intention of doing any such thing, but she felt that was on a need-to-know basis. She studied her bare fingernails as if she'd had a fabulous manicure.

Dang it! That was one more thing on her to-do list for the wedding, which she'd forgotten about.

Kasey shook her head. "If you're to be married to an attorney, what are you doing with him?" She waved her hand dismissively at Oz.

"He's my friend," Mel said. She glanced at Oz and smiled. It was true. He'd become one of her best friends and when she thought about the garbage this woman was saying about him, she wanted to slap the drink right out of her hands or, even better, pour it over her head.

"Friend?" Kasey asked. She lowered her sunglasses and studied the two of them. "Right."

"What's that supposed to mean?" Mel asked.

"We're getting off topic here," Oz said. "Mrs. Perry, why did you tell the police that I was . . . that we were . . . when I'd never . . ."

"I don't know what you're talking about." Kasey sipped her drink. Mel couldn't be sure but she thought that Kasey was amused.

"You told the police that I . . . that I . . ." Oz stuttered to a halt. He couldn't even make himself say what Kasey had said. Mel could see the weight of his embarrassment crushing him and she felt another spurt of anger for what this woman was doing to a guy easily half her age, if not younger.

"You told the police that you and Oz shacked up in an empty room at the resort where he told you he was going to kill Gallway so that he could take his spot as executive chef in order to provide for you in the way you're accustomed," Mel said. "Does that lie ring a bell?"

"What makes you so sure it's a lie?" Kasey asked. She looked so shrewd and self-satisfied that Mel was compelled to take her down.

Without thinking it through she said, "Because at the time you said he was with you, he was actually with me."

Oz's head snapped in Mel's direction and his eyes went wide as if she'd just confessed to murdering Gallway herself. She had, of course, meant that Oz was in the bakery with her but that wasn't how it sounded and it wasn't how Kasey took it, because of course she didn't

Kasey reared up in her chair, snatched the sunglasses from her face, and studied Mel like she was trying to figure out what anyone could possibly see in her. It made Mel feel as awkward as an adolescent and she had to force herself to stay still and meet Kasey's contemptuous look head-on.

"What can you possibly see in *her*?" Kasey snapped at Oz.

"Excuse me?" Oz blinked. He was clearly struggling to keep up.

Kasey leaned forward. The tiny triangles covering her privates strained to the breaking point and Mel wondered if she should offer the woman her cover-up, lest there be a wardrobe malfunction that would leave both her and Oz mortified for life.

"You heard me," Kasey hissed. She waved a dismissive hand at Mel. "Look at her with her butch haircut, lack of makeup, and doughy skin. She's about as sexy as vanilla pudding."

"Hey!" Mel protested. She knew she was in the unremarkable range when it came to looks, but it didn't need to be pointed out so bluntly.

"What?" Oz glanced between the two women as if he couldn't understand a word Kasey was saying. "Are you kidding me? There is nothing plain about Melanie Cooper."

Aw. What a nice guy. He was defending her. Mel was touched.

"She's kind—" Oz began but Kasey interrupted with a *pffth*, leaving them in no doubt about how much she valued kindness.

"Which matters," Oz said. "She's also funny, smart, and beautiful."

Kasey rolled her eyes, which made it quite clear what she thought of Mel's looks. Mel would have been offended but given that she felt the same way about Kasey's manufactured looks, it felt like it was a fair assessment. Two polar opposites were never going to see the attractiveness of the other.

"Don't!" Oz said. He sounded angry. "Don't do that. Mel happens to be the sort of woman who is not only beautiful but she is also completely unaware of how lovely she is. It makes her even more breathtaking."

"Breathtaking?" Kasey squawked. She looked at Mel

as if she were a three-headed troll who'd just popped out from under a bridge. "Are you crazy?" She hopped up from her lounger, wobbling a bit as the effects of the margaritas kicked in. "Look at her!" she cried, and held her hands out to Mel. "And look at me!" She gestured to herself.

Oz glanced from Kasey to Mel and back.

"And?" he asked. His tone was dry as if he was bored.

"How can you compare this?" She did a shimmy-shake that wiggled her assets right in his face. "To that!" She pointed again at Mel.

Despite her acceptance of her own limitations in the looks department, Mel was beginning to be offended.

Oz stood up and loomed over Kasey. He gave her a dismissive look. "She is more beautiful than you will ever be on your best day," he said. His voice was firm and assured and Mel felt her battered ego pick itself up and dust itself off.

Kasey staggered back as if Oz had delivered a body blow. Mel stood up, fearing that Kasey might fall over her own chair and need assistance.

"Ah," Kasey gasped. She glanced from Oz to Mel and back. She gaped at him and said, "You're in love with her!"

Oz's face went instantly, vibrantly, explosively red. "What?!"

"You are," Kasey accused. She turned to Mel. "You're having a fling with him, aren't you?"

"I . . ." Mel was caught off guard, unable to speak in the face of Oz's obvious hot embarrassment. She felt as if something was happening between them, some rift or shift in the relationship, mentor to student, boss to employee, friend to friend, that she couldn't quite grasp. She tried to shake it off. "No!"

"Liar," Kasey accused. She turned to Oz. "Don't you know that the first rule of shagging an older woman is not to become attached? She's never going to give up her stability for you, and she's going to break your heart."

"No, that's not—" Mel and Oz said together. Startled, they looked at each other. Oz's expression was dismay, as if he'd been sucker punched, and Mel got an uncomfortable feeling that things were being said that would forever change the relationship between them, and she didn't want that to happen.

"Don't be ridiculous!" Mel snapped. "Oz is like a little brother to me."

"Well, that's just perverted," Kasey said. She sounded disgusted.

Mel closed her eyes, seeking patience. She needed to stay on task here. She needed to get Kasey to admit that she'd lied. If she was going to make that happen, she'd have to embrace the horrifically awkward things Kasey was saying about them.

"Okay, fine," Mel said. She couldn't look at Oz for fear she'd crack. She used her thumb to gesture between them. "He and I are having a fling." She felt him stiffen beside her but he didn't deny it.

"I knew it!" Kasey grabbed her margarita, tucked the straw into the side of her mouth, and sucked down the drink until it made the distinctive gurgle of a glass on empty. Mel marveled that Kasey hadn't gotten a vicious brain freeze.

"Which is why I'm here," Mel said. "Why did you lie about having an affair with him? If he gets arrested and sent to jail, you'll have cost me my boy toy." To her credit, Mel thought, she didn't choke on the words. At this point, she figured the only way they'd get a confession out of Kasey was to speak her own seedy gross language where everyone had a price. It worked.

"First of all, I didn't know he already had a sugar mama," Kasey said. She plopped back into her chair and began to arrange her limbs for optimum sun. "Second, how could I ever have expected him to be with someone like you?" She glanced at Oz and asked, "Is she quite rich?"

Oz looked as if he'd been turned to stone. Mel nudged him with her elbow.

"Yes, quite . . . very . . . superrich," he muttered, obviously catching on that they needed to get Kasey to think that they were as morally bankrupt as she was. He looked at the ground at his feet as if hoping for an escape hatch to appear in the pool decking.

"Well, well, well." Kasey seemed mollified by this. "I can't fault you for going for the money. I mean, that's why I married Clay. My return on investment there really paid out."

Mel felt slightly nauseous at Kasey's callous assessment of her own marriage. Given that her own wedding was just a week away, it made the mere idea of marriage feel tainted. Mel shook it off.

"Whatever," Mel said. She sat back down, pulling Oz with her. "I still want to know why you lied."

"None of your business," Kasey said. She flipped the flag on her chair to up and waved at the waiter, who was circling the loungers.

"Maybe not, but since I'm going to have to come forward and admit that Oz was with me," Mel said, "it's going to come out that you lied." Mel leaned back on one hand and feigned an ease she most definitely did not feel. "Your call, but I thought you might want to get ahead of it."

"What do I care if you admit to your own bad behavior?" Kasey asked.

"Um, because when it comes out that you lied, who do you think they're going to look at for the murder of Miles Gallway?" Mel asked. She waited while Kasey mentally caught up to the implications of lying to the police. Kasey blinked in confusion, so Mel spelled it out for her. "They're going to look at the person who lied, which would be you."

"But I didn't kill Miles," Kasey protested. "I mean, why would I kill him when our affair ended months ago?"

Ten

"Affair?" Oz asked.

Kasey slapped a hand over her mouth.

"Do tell," Mel said. She rested her chin on her fist and stared at Kasey.

Kasey snapped her fingers and pointed at them. Her pointy fingernail looked like a dagger. "That's none of your business."

Mel shrugged. "Maybe, but I'm certain the police will want to know all of the juicy details." She rolled up to her feet. "Come on, Oz, I think we're done here."

"It was over a long time ago, and I prefer my men much younger these days. Besides, Miles was a drunk. That's why he missed the television spot the other day. He was passed out drunk and missed it. Simon was ready to murder him," Kasey said. She gave them a pointed look that Mel ignored.

"Says you," Mel said. She paused, enjoying the moment of getting the last word more than she probably should have as Kasey glared up at them, her well-oiled body vibrating with rage and resentment. "But we've already established that you're a liar."

With that, Mel left Kasey to wave down her cocktail waiter. With the day she was going to have when Mel told Uncle Stan what she'd learned, Kasey was going to need all of the liquid help she could get.

Oz fell in behind Mel and they slipped out the same gate they'd used to access the pool. Feeling as if they were making a getaway, they picked up their pace. It wasn't until they were in Mel's car and driving out of the lot that they spoke.

"About what Kasey said," Mel began but Oz cut her off.

"We're not talking about that."

"We're not?"

"No."

That was it. Mel glanced over at Oz, squished into the passenger seat of her admittedly petite car. His chin was tipped down and she suspected that if he could turn back time, he'd never have cut off his bangs and he'd be shielding his face with them at that very moment.

"Okay," she said. They drove back to the bakery in silence. It was excruciatingly uncomfortable.

She felt as if she were sixteen and taking her driver's license test all over again. She'd had a horrible woman, Margie, take her around the first time. Yes, the first time. Mel had failed her test, quite spectacularly, by going through a red light. It didn't help that the woman had shrieked as if Mel had stalled her car on train tracks with a train bearing down on them, instead of going through a light that regulated the traffic flow of the local National Guard base.

There had been no cars in the area at all. Still, Margie had vowed that Mel would never ever get her license so long as Margie drew breath.

Well, Margie was still alive and kicking in south Scottsdale, and Mel liked to wave at her from the driver's seat of her car whenever their paths happened to cross. It was the little things. Still, Mel was quite certain she had never sat in a car with so much tension since the day she failed her test and had to drive Margie back to the motor vehicle office with Margie huffing into a paper bag and then quite dramatically falling to her knees on the pavement as soon as Mel had parked in her designated spot.

She gave Oz a few minutes to decompress then she casually said, "Because, you know, nothing she said was true. She's just a big fat liar."

Oz turned to look at her. His face was the picture of misery. Mel felt her heart squeeze tight. She hated seeing her friend suffer.

"And look on the bright side, we got her to admit to an affair with Miles," Mel said. "That totally makes her a suspect. Not only her but Clay Perry as well. I mean, his executive chef was carrying on with his trophy wife— that had to hurt. Maybe enough for Clay to murder him."

Oz heaved a sigh and glanced up at the ceiling of the car. He looked like he was being tortured.

"Oz, speak to me," Mel said. "What is wrong?"

They were stopped at an intersection and Mel glanced

at him. He reached under his shirt and ripped the mic off, wincing when the adhesive pulled the fine hairs on his skin. He opened the glove box and tossed it inside.

"Better now?" Mel asked. "No more itch?"

"I didn't do that because of the adhesive," he said. He rubbed his chest where the mic had been.

"No?" Mel wanted to look at him but they were moving with the traffic now and she couldn't take her eyes off the road.

"Kasey was right," Oz said.

"About what?" Mel asked.

"I have feelings for you," he said.

Mel jerked her head in his direction. If he'd told her he'd actually had an affair with Kasey, she couldn't have been more shocked.

"But—" she protested.

"I know," he said. "You're my boss, former boss, landlord, or whatever, you're about to marry Joe, who I consider my friend, and you're a little bit older than me."

"Little bit?" Mel asked. "More than ten years, Oz."

He shrugged as if this was no big deal.

Mel put her signal on and made a quick turn into the public parking garage attached to the Scottsdale Public Library. Mel needed air. Fortunately, there was a nice park, called the Civic Center Mall, full of sculptures and fountains, and a man-made pond.

"Come on," she said. "We're going to talk where I don't have to drive, too."

Oz didn't argue but climbed out of his seat and followed her along the path to the pond, where a pair of swans and some mallards swam, looking for handouts from visitors, even though a sign very clearly said not to feed the ducks.

Mel found an empty bench in the shade and sat down. Oz sat down beside her. She didn't know what to say. She didn't want to hurt his feelings but this announcement of his felt like it was coming out of left field and she knew that no matter how much she didn't want it to change the way things were between them, it probably would.

They watched a mother chase two toddlers on the grass. The belly laughs coming out of the kids were contagious, and Mel felt herself smile. The air was sweet, the day was still cool, the sky was the purest blue, and some birds were having a lively conversation. It all felt completely normal in a world that had suddenly veered sideways—hard.

"I'm not sure what to say," Mel said.

"There's nothing to say," Oz said. He spread his hands in a gesture of resignation. "I never wanted you to know but when Mrs. Perry was so nasty to you, well, I couldn't help but defend you, and it got away from me and she figured it out."

Mel nodded. It was clear he was mortified. She tried to think about what she would want someone to say to her if the situation was reversed. She'd had plenty of crushes over the years. What would happen if one of them had found out how she felt? She remembered her French cooking professor during her time in Paris. He had been handsome and charming and every girl in the class was madly in love with him, including Mel. Unlike the other women who could flirt and laugh with him, however, Mel had been so tongue-tied around him that she was positive he thought she was mute.

How would she have wanted him to handle finding out about her feelings? With kindness and understanding.

"Oz—" she began.

"I can't go back to the bakery," he said. "Everyone who listens to that audio will know when Kasey accuses me of being in love with you that I am."

"Okay, stop saying that," Mel said.

He looked at her. He was the picture of misery. "But it's true."

"No," Mel said gently. "It isn't. What about Lupe?"

Oz stared out across the pond, watching the two swans glide across the surface together. "We broke up."

"Oh, I'm sorry," Mel said. "When?"

He shrugged. "A few months ago."

"Months?" she cried. "And you never said anything?"

"I didn't want to talk about it."

"I'm so sorry, Oz," she said. Before, she would have hugged him but now it felt inappropriate. She settled for patting his forearm. "That's a tough one."

"I'm fine," he said. Which clearly meant he wasn't.

"I think maybe your feelings are all jumbled up," Mel said. "That happens sometimes after a breakup."

"I know how I feel," he protested.

They sat quietly for a while.

"Oz, do you remember when we first met?" she asked.

"Yeah, I came to the shop to be your high school intern," he said.

"You were also dealing with being bullied and we gave you a sanctuary," Mel said.

He nodded. "I remember."

"Feeling safe for the first time can make for some powerful emotions."

"Maybe," Oz sighed. "You were the first person who ever believed I could be a chef."

Mel smiled. "It wasn't hard. You're talented, and I know you're going to have an amazing career."

He shrugged. "If I don't die of embarrassment."

Mel laughed, relieved to see a glimpse of the old Oz.

"I don't think it's a fatal condition," she said. "As for the recording, anyone who hears it is going to hear a predatory woman, trying to use her position of power to manipulate a person in her husband's employ. Your defense of me was just loyalty in action. Her accusation that you're in love with me was just her ego trying to deal with the rejection."

"You think?" he asked.

"Yes," she said. "Oz, don't you think your sudden feelings for me have more to do with your breakup with Lupe? First heartbreaks are a doozy."

Oz put a hand on the back of his neck. He looked even more uncomfortable, if that was possible. "Actually, you were one of the reasons we broke up."

"Oh." Mel had no idea what to say to that.

"Lupe asked me to move to California and get an apartment with her, and I said no. She accused me of being too attached to my life here instead of her. I denied it, but then she said she got tired of our conversations being 'Mel this' and 'Mel that.' I didn't even realize it until she called me out." He looked rueful.

"Here's the thing about those feelings you're having," Mel said. "They're going to pass."

He looked like he'd deny it, but Mel shook her head.

"They will. What you're feeling isn't being 'in love'— that's a feeling that has to be reciprocated fully to survive. But a crush or an infatuation, it feels so much like being in love that people get it confused with the real thing. But it isn't real, because love can't be a one-way street. When you find the real thing with a person who feels the same way about you, then you'll really be in love."

"And that's what you have with Joe?" he asked. Mel nodded. Oz sighed. "You're sure?"

"Positive." She laughed at his beleaguered expression. She put her hand on his arm. "I do love you, you know, but—"

"As a little brother," Oz finished her sentence, looking resigned.

"Yes," she said. She leaned against him, shoulder to shoulder. "You're very special to me and I'd never want to cause you any pain. If it would be easier for you to not bake the cupcakes for the wedding and to skip the day entirely, I'll understand."

He reared back and looked at her as if she'd just cursed a shocking blue streak. "No! Absolutely not. I might be carrying a torch for you, but I am a professional and those cupcakes are going to be the most amazing thing anyone has ever seen. Besides, if I can't get you to consider a younger man—" He paused to grin at her and she was relieved to see his eyes twinkle with humor. Still, she shook her head no. "Then I'm really happy you're marrying Joe. He's a great guy."

"Yeah, he is," Mel agreed. It hit her then that her wedding was coming up fast. While it was an intentionally low-key affair, she felt like it should be occupying more of her brain than it was. She felt a sudden need to go over the details with her wedding planner. She would never hear the end of it from her mother if she forgot something major. Heaven forbid.

"Come on," she said. She rose to her feet. "We need to rendezvous with Uncle Stan at the bakery and turn your mic in."

Oz reluctantly stood. "I have a feeling this is not going to go well for me."

"Better to face it down than to try and duck," Mel said. "Besides, I really don't think anyone is going to think anything of it. I mean, I was there and I didn't catch on."

Oz smiled at her. "That might be because you're thick, no offense."

Mel laughed. "None taken." She couldn't really argue the point. She'd really had no idea how Oz felt about her. She wondered if the others suspected, but she couldn't imagine that Angie and Tate wouldn't have said anything.

Mel and Oz arrived at the bakery to find Uncle Stan standing beside the surveillance van. James, the IT guy who ran the van, collected the mic from Oz and said, "Good work. Given the noise of the pool area around you, you managed to get her loud and clear." He turned back to Uncle Stan. "I'll get started on a transcript. See you back at the station."

"Right behind you." Uncle Stan nodded. He turned to them. "Nice work, Oz."

He clapped Oz on the shoulder when he said it, which Mel suspected was to make Oz feel better about what the recording revealed.

Mercifully, the only people who had heard the conversation were Uncle Stan and James, who had been in the unmarked police van during their confrontation with

Kasey. Mel knew that Uncle Stan wouldn't say anything and that he'd make sure James didn't either, so at least they'd dodged that bullet.

"So, now you can scratch Oz off your suspect list?" Mel asked.

"Not entirely," Uncle Stan said.

"What? Why?" Mel cried.

"Because while you got Kasey to admit that she lied about being with Oz—nice work there—it doesn't change the fact that Miles was found dead in Oz's kitchen with Oz hovering over him after they'd had a fight, and Oz's alibi is shaky at best," he said.

"But the Beast!" Oz protested.

"Not really an eyewitness," Uncle Stan said. Oz sighed and Uncle Stan added, "Sorry."

"But she also confessed to having an affair with Miles," Mel said. "That must count for something. Maybe Kasey murdered him, or possibly Clay. Isn't jealousy one of the main motives for murder?"

"Except we already know about the affair," Uncle Stan said. "Clay clearly wanted to get ahead of it, and told us about Kasey's affair during our first interview. He also let us know he was out on the golf course at the time of Miles's death while Kasey was poolside, and both had loads of witnesses."

"So, that clears Clay, but it doesn't mean Kasey didn't kill Miles," Mel said. "It wouldn't be that hard to leave the pool to go to the kitchen."

Uncle Stan raised his hands in a calm-down gesture. Historically, this never worked for Mel. There was nothing she resented more than being told to "calm down" when she was legitimately upset.

The front door to the bakery opened and Angie and Tate came outside to join them. Angie stood in front of Tate and leaned back against him. Tate gazed down at his pregnant wife with a look of such tenderness that Mel was warmed just from being in their glow.

"Are we having a meeting?" Angie asked. "Because there was nothing on my calendar."

"Not a meeting so much as a protest," Mel said. Uncle Stan sighed.

"What are we protesting?" Tate asked. "Do I need to make signs? You know I love a good cause."

"I'm your cause," Oz said. Both Tate and Angie looked at him and then at Uncle Stan.

"Protesting isn't necessary," he said. "Just give us a few days and I'm sure we'll have Oz free and clear."

"I'm getting married in a few days," Mel said. "And he's baking my cupcakes. You can't arrest my pastry chef right before my wedding for a crime he didn't commit."

"Arrest—" Tate began but Uncle Stan interrupted.

"No one is getting arrested."

"Pity," Tate said.

"Hey!" Oz said.

"Sorry, I was already mentally surveying my protest-sign supplies," Tate said.

"I'm leaving," Uncle Stan said. He glanced at them all and then lingered on Oz. "I know I don't have to say this, but don't leave town."

Oz blinked at him then looked at Mel. "I'm going to hide in my apartment like there's a horde of murder hornets swarming. Call me if you need me in the bakery."

"Madison is here today," Mel said.

"Then don't call me, unless she leaves," Oz said.

"Will do." She watched him lope across the patio and through the front door. Then she turned to Uncle Stan, "He's just a kid."

"He's legally an adult," Uncle Stan argued. "And if this goes badly, he's going to be tried as one, too."

Mel felt her stomach cramp. Uncle Stan gave her a quick hug and said, "Don't worry. I'll be in touch."

With a wave, he left Mel standing with Tate and Angie, feeling as if her entire world was about to implode right before her wedding.

"Hey, does anyone else work here or is it just me and the new kid now?" Marty's head popped out of the front door and he glared at them.

Duly chastened, the three of them hurried into the bakery to help out. Madison was working the front counter with Marty while Tate and Angie boxed up orders and Mel restocked the front case from the supplies in back. The line of customers was long enough to keep them all busy, and Mel didn't get a chance to get the others up to speed until there was a lull.

"See you tomorrow," Madison called from the door as she headed out.

"I told you she would work out," Angie said through her smile as she waved at the young woman.

When the door shut behind Madison, Mel said, "So far. We haven't gotten her in the kitchen yet."

"Speaking of . . ." Angie paused and looked at the clock. "Break time!"

The bakery crew took advantage of the daily lull and met up in the kitchen for their usual late-afternoon break. Mel took the opportunity to tell them about Kasey's affair, and it was agreed that she was definitely a prime suspect. Mel did not mention Oz's confessed feelings for her, because she would never intentionally do anything that would embarrass him. Instead, they debated who at the resort besides Kasey would have wanted to kill Miles.

"Sex or money," Tate said. "Those are the usual motives."

"What about revenge or a secret?" Angie asked.

"Both of those are usually about sex or money," Tate said.

Mel had plated a variety of cupcakes and they noshed while enjoying a cup of coffee, except for Angie, who went with milk. Mel debated her options, finally choosing a caramel cupcake with salted caramel buttercream frosting. When she took her first bite, it was the first time all afternoon that she felt her stress level drop. A decadent cupcake was always the right answer no matter the question.

"It seems to me," Marty said, "given that the chef was bludgeoned, that whoever did it was angry with him."

"Angry or desperate?" Mel asked.

"Both?" Angie suggested.

"What else did you find out from Clay Perry when you were golfing?" Mel asked. "Did he mention anyone at the resort that he was having trouble with?"

"No," Marty said. "Stan already grilled me and Ray about this. Clay got on Simon's case about picking a chef from the resort to host a show on the network, but Simon balked. There was definitely some tension there. Apparently, Miles was fired for being inappropriate, but he really wanted back on the show. Then there's some other chef, Ashley, who is desperate to be on the show but Simon didn't think she was talented enough. He really wanted Oz to be the pick, but with the murder and all . . ."

"I'm not going to be on television." Oz came into the kitchen through the back door. He knew the late-day bakery schedule and, sure enough, helped himself to coffee and a cupcake. "I told them that."

Tate studied him while chewing on his traditional chocolate cupcake with vanilla frosting. "You'd be great, though. You were amazing on the morning show."

Oz shrugged him off. He met Mel's gaze and shook his head and she was relieved that it felt like old times. There was no residual weirdness between them. Thank goodness, she would have hated that.

"What about this Ashley person?" Angie asked Oz. "Do you think they'll pick her?"

"Simon might not have a choice," Oz said. "Sarah Lincoln—the chef you saw Miles yelling at—told me that Simon has a gambling problem and he is in the hole in a big way to Clay. That's why he's at the resort, looking to film a show there. Clay owns him."

"Would he have killed Miles to get out of it?" Marty asked.

"I would think it would make more sense to kill Clay," Angie said.

"Except"—Marty held up a finger—"Clay owns the resort, kind of a high-profile guy. Miles is persona non grata with the public and, from what I could see, a bit of a liability for Clay, plus he slept with his wife. Could Simon have done Clay a favor and killed Miles in exchange for forgiving his gambling debt?"

"Ooh, you went on a deeply twisted turn there," Tate said.

Marty looked quite pleased with himself.

"The only problem with that theory is that Simon is

still here," Oz said. "If he murdered Miles to even things with Clay, wouldn't Clay let him out of the television deal and he'd be gone?"

"Maybe he can't," Mel said. "It could be Uncle Stan told him the same thing he told you—not to leave town."

"How do we find out?" Angie said.

"Poker game!" Marty cried. They all turned to look at him. "What? It's perfect. I've already established myself as a high roller. I'm sure I can get Ray and some of the brothers to help me."

"Definitely," Angie said with growing enthusiasm. "But keep an eye on Tony. We call him Sticky Fingers for a reason."

"Looks like we have a plan," Tate said.

"Only one problem," Angie said. "Who's going to tell Joe?"

They all turned to look at Mel. She sighed. "Me, I'll tell him."

This, she was not looking forward to.

Eleven

Mel arrived home to find Joe already there. He had Peanut, their rescued Boston terrier, and Captain Jack, their likewise rescued kitten, harassing him while he attempted to prep their dinners at the same time. Captain Jack was up on the counter, sneaking nibbles out of Peanut's bowl while Peanut sat on Joe's foot, staring up at him with her tongue hanging out.

It was a normal, everyday event, and yet, taking in the sight of her three somebodies in their kitchen made Mel's heart swell. The love she felt for her little family was without end.

As if sensing her watching him, Joe turned and smiled at her. "Hey, cupcake, how was your day?"

He'd been calling her "cupcake" ever since they first got together and it never failed to make Mel's heart go pitter-pat. She crossed the room and gave him a quick hug from the side. He turned and kissed her quick, at which Captain Jack howled as attention was being taken away from the making of his dinner. Mel stroked his back to soothe him and bent down and scratched Peanut's ears. A lick on the wrist was her response and Mel smiled.

"My day was informative, how about yours?"

"Dull," he said. "Lots of paper pushing so let's talk about yours."

Mel watched as he served the critters and then went to the fridge. "Wine or beer?"

"Beer, definitely beer," Mel said.

Joe raised an eyebrow and poured them two glasses. "All right, what gives?"

Mel led the way to the living room, where they sat on the couch while she told him about her mission with Oz and the stunning information that Kasey Perry had had an affair with Miles.

"Whoa," he said. "That puts her in prime suspect position, yes? Oz must be happy about that."

"Eh." Mel took a big sip of her beer.

Again, one of Joe's eyebrows popped up on his forehead. "That doesn't sound good."

"The thing is, it got rather weird with Kasey," Mel said. "As in she thought Oz was my boy toy and I had to work that angle to get her to talk to us."

"Oh," Joe said. "Awkward."

"Yeah, when Kasey attacked, Oz felt compelled to come to my defense and . . ." She wasn't sure how to finish the story.

"It came out that Oz has feelings for you," Joe said.

Mel's jaw dropped as Peanut, who had finished her

dinner, came trotting into the living room and took a doggy leap right into the middle of them. Both Mel and Joe shifted to accommodate her and Joe rubbed her tummy, much to Peanut's delight.

"How did you know that?" she asked.

"It's been pretty obvious that he's had a soft spot for you ever since the day you hired him," Joe said.

"Did everyone know about this except me?" she asked.

"I doubt it," Joe said. "I wasn't even sure until he cut his hair and I could finally see his eyes. They light up whenever you enter the room, by the way. When he quit the bakery, I suspected he was leaving to get some space."

"Why didn't you ever say anything?" Mel asked. "I had no idea. I felt completely blindsided."

"It wasn't my business," he said. "I figured if Oz wanted to say something to you he would."

"I don't think he wanted to," Mel said. "The situation with Kasey got out of hand and, of course, he was wearing a mic so the crime scene tech and Uncle Stan heard it all."

"Is that why you told me?" he asked. "Because you think I'll hear about it secondhand?"

"Not so much that as I was hoping you'd tell me if I handled it right," she said. She went on to tell him about her talk with Oz.

"If a guy has to be rejected, I think you did it in the kindest possible way," he said. "Why are you still frowning?"

"It changes everything, though, doesn't it?" she asked.

"Maybe, a little, until Oz finds his own 'cupcake,'" he said.

She smiled. Leave it to Joe to make it so simple.

"Now, tell me what's really on your mind," he said.

Drat, the man knew her too well. Mel took a deep breath. Best to get it over with as fast as possible. *"YourbrothersarehavingapokergamewithSimonfromtheFoodieChanneltofindoutifhemurderedMiles."*

Joe blinked at her. "Huh?"

Mel was panting. Joe was smack-dab in the middle of his seven brothers and, as such, was the family mediator. It had surprised no one that he had gone into law as a profession given that he'd spent his formative years settling disputes between the DeLaura siblings.

"Is this about the poker game?"

"You knew?"

"Brother group chat," he said. "Ray forgot to take me off it when he sent out the call to all."

Mel nodded. "Of course he did. Did you tell them not to do it?"

"Nope," Joe said. "I figure it's a good opportunity to find out more about Simon Marconi."

"They didn't notice you were still in the group, did they?" she asked.

Joe grinned. "No."

"Joe, we're a little less than a week away from our big day. What's going to happen if Uncle Stan doesn't figure out who murdered Miles Gallway before we get married?" she asked.

Joe clasped her hand in his. "That's not going to happen because there's no way we could enjoy our honeymoon while worrying that Oz is going to be arrested. Uncle Stan will figure it out and, who knows, maybe Marty and the bros will get a clue from Marconi that will crack the case wide open."

"I hope so," Mel said. "Do you think we should tell Uncle Stan about the poker game?"

"What poker game?" he asked.

"I'll take that as a no," she said. She lifted her glass to his and said, "To cracking the case."

"I'll drink to that."

"My dude, you look like a pimp," Oz said. He was sitting at the steel table in the bakery, taking in Marty's poker outfit.

"Shows what you know," Marty said. He tugged his shirtsleeves so they were just visible beneath the cuffs of his navy blue velvet jacket.

Angie had her head down but her shoulders were shaking and Mel suspected she was doing her best to keep from laughing out loud. The struggle was real. Mel opted to bite her tongue until the pain squashed any urge that she had to laugh.

"You look very dapper," she said. "Very Frank Sinatra Rat Pack."

"Without the hair," Oz added.

Marty scowled at him.

"Who's ready for some action?" Ray asked as he pushed through the bakery doors into the kitchen. Unlike Marty, he was dressed in black leather pants and an open-at-the-throat dress shirt, which again left the thick gold chain he wore around his neck visible. Mel tried not to wonder how he disentangled it from his chest hair without hurting himself. Al and Tony arrived next, looking reassuringly normal in jeans and T-shirts, followed by Paulie, who had kicked it up a notch by wearing a suit. Neither Sal nor Dominick were participating in the game and so far none of them had realized that they'd included Joe on the group text.

"I'm ready for a big hand," Paulie said.

Angie rolled her eyes. "Paulie, you can't even win at Yahtzee. What are you thinking, trying to play in a high-stakes poker game?"

"Yahtzee is for old ladies," he protested. He ran a hand through his curly hair and tipped his chin up. "Texas Hold'em and me are like this." He held up two crossed fingers.

"Really?" Al asked. "Because the last time you played it was more like this." He made an obscene gesture with his hand and Ray slapped his hand down.

"Not in front of the girls," he said.

"Girls?" Angie turned and looked at Mel. Her expression seemed to say *Can you believe this guy?*

Given that it was Ray, not known to be the most forward thinking of the DeLaura brothers, Mel shrugged. There was simply no enlightening Ray—besides, he was his girlfriend's problem now.

"Tony, how is this going to work?" she asked. Tony was the gadget guy of the family. While no one knew exactly what he did (he went by the generic title *technical director*), he had some serious espionage skills, and Mel and Joe had decided between themselves that he was some sort of corporate fraud investigator. There was simply no other explanation for his high income and affinity for spy gear.

"We're all microphoned up," Tony said. He handed Angie a small portable Bluetooth speaker. "I have the conversation recording to a cloud, but you two can listen in during the game. That way if Ray gets into trouble, you can call for backup from Uncle Stan."

Mel looked at Angie. "Oh, he's going to love getting that call."

"The plan is for you to not need to make the call," Tony said. "You're just backup."

"Gotcha," Angie said. She looked doubtful.

"Where is the game being held?" Mel asked. If things did go wrong, it would help to be able to tell Uncle Stan where they were.

"We're playing in the back room at Mick's tattoo parlor," Marty said. "Of course, I had to pay him for use, but I figured it would keep us on neutral ground with Marconi."

"Good thinking," Tony said.

"Tattoo parlor?" Paulie asked. "They put all of the stuff away, right?"

"What stuff?" Marty asked.

"You know, the stuff," Paulie said.

"The needles," Al explained. "He's afraid of needles."

"I am not afraid," Paulie protested. "I just have a healthy respect for not puncturing my epidermis."

"Like I said, he's afraid," Al said.

"We're in the back room," Marty said. "It's not like the needles are going to fly up and stab you of their own volition."

"I'm definitely going to have nightmares," Paulie said. He ran a hand down the front of his suit as if trying to soothe himself.

"All right, that's enough yapping," Ray said. "We've got to go. We can't be seen coming from here together.

Everyone, out the back, and then we split up to make it look like we arrived separately."

No one moved.

"You heard him," Tony said. He clapped his hands. "Let's go."

The brothers and Marty all headed to the door. Ray turned and looked at Mel and Angie. "Did you see that? I speak and no one moves. Tony claps and everyone jumps to it."

"That's because we're all afraid that Tony knows our deep dark secrets," Angie said.

"Besides, they did start moving when you spoke," Mel said. She couldn't stand to see Ray's feelings get hurt. "They were just slow."

He nodded. "Yeah, I knew that."

He was the last to leave and Angie locked the door behind him. She looked at Mel and cradled her belly with one hand while holding the small speaker with the other. "Why am I worried about those knuckleheads? They're going to be fine, right?"

"Totally," Mel said. She took her cell phone out of her pocket and texted Joe. She noticed Angie was doing the same with her free hand. "Tate?"

"He wanted to be kept in the loop and is going to swing by," Angie said. She glanced at Mel's phone. "Joe?"

"Same." They exchanged a grin.

"Come on," Angie said. "Let's go over our remaining wedding details while we wait."

They left the kitchen and sat in one of the booths in front of the large picture window. The shades were drawn, the doors were locked, and the bakery was closed for the night. This was Mel's favorite time of the day.

In the beginning, this was the only time she'd had the bakery to herself. She'd put in many late nights, listening to the radio, dreaming of the success of her shop while baking until the early hours of the morning. The work was grueling and the potential for failure huge. She'd lived in a constant state of high anxiety back then. Now, weirdly, she missed those early days.

She'd been young and single and living above the bakery. Tate had gone all in and invested in making the place a success. Angie had quit her teaching job to work here, clearing out her savings to buy in. It had been the three of them against the world. It was before Tate realized he loved Angie, who had been in love with him since middle school. It was also before Joe had started coming around, giving Mel hope that maybe he finally saw his little sister's best friend as something more than another little sister.

"So much has changed since we opened the bakery," Mel said.

The nostalgia was feeling pretty thick as she realized Angie might not return from her maternity leave. Now that Tate had managed to successfully franchise the bakery all over the country, they really didn't need to work in the day-to-day operations of the original shop, but Mel couldn't give up her specialty orders and she loved experimenting with new recipes to share with the other Fairy Tale Cupcakes bakeries. While each shop was individually owned and operated, Tate had made certain that they upheld the high standards and signature recipes of the original bakery.

Mel glanced at the counter where she and Angie had

toiled until they'd hired Marty. He'd managed to slip right in, becoming family almost immediately. Then Oz had come along, rounding out their crew. He'd gone to culinary school and even then Mel had known he wouldn't be staying, but she missed him just the same. And now although things had gotten complicated, she missed their big shaggy-haired teen, who'd mostly stayed in the kitchen perfecting his craft, because he'd scared the customers.

"Hello? Mel?" Angie waved her hand in front of Mel's face. "I'm going over the checklist for Friday and Saturday here, you know, for your wedding. Any input you want to add?"

Mel blinked and glanced at the sheet in Angie's hand. "Oh . . . um. No, it all sounds good to me."

"Really?" Angie asked. There was a wicked twinkle in her brown eyes when she asked, "So, that's a yes on you and Joe arriving at the church astride camels? My cousin Judi will love that. And then you'll be serenaded at the reception by a celebrity impersonator, did you prefer Lady Gaga or Bruno Mars?"

"You're hilarious," Mel said.

"I know," Angie chortled. "Can you imagine our mothers' faces if we got a Bruce Springsteen impersonator?"

"They'd mob him," Mel said. "The guy would have to do the famous knee slide right on out of there."

Angie tapped her lips with her forefinger. "Almost worth it."

When their chuckles subsided, Angie glanced at Mel. "What are you really thinking about? You look very introspective for a bride who is finally getting this matrimony thing done." She gave Mel a side eye. "You're not getting cold feet, are you?"

"No! Not at all," Mel assured her. "I'm just remembering our beginnings. It's all changed so much in the past few years."

"For the better, right?" Angie asked. She picked up the speaker and switched it on. They could hear the sound of the brothers arriving at the tattoo shop down the street. Angie glanced at Mel, waiting for her answer.

"Of course, I just . . ." Mel paused. What was she trying to say? She was happy. Life was great. They'd achieved their dreams and were about to embark on even bigger ones. Marriage for her and Joe, a baby for Tate and Angie. It was all good and great and she had no complaints. Really.

"I just miss how uncomplicated it all used to be," she said.

Angie studied her. She nodded. "It was pretty simple back when it was just the three of us. Of course, we were also totally broke and working twenty-hour days. It was just the two of us since Tate had to keep his day job for a while. I remember eating a lot of packaged noodles."

Mel laughed. "I do, too. Ah, those were the days."

"They were," Angie agreed. "But I'm really glad we can afford to eat from the other sections of the grocery store now."

"Same—"

"Hey there, how are you, Simon?" Marty's voice boomed out of the speaker and both women jumped.

Angie snatched up the small portable speaker, searching for a volume control. It was a tiny button on the bottom. She gingerly adjusted it. Mel gave her a relieved look. This would have been a very long poker game if the volume stayed that loud.

"Good to see you, Marty." Mel recognized the voice as Simon's. She mouthed his name to Angie, who nodded.

They settled in to listen as Marty introduced the brothers. It sounded pleasant enough and then Marty explained the rules of the table. It was high stakes so they were starting at a hundred dollars to ante. Mel felt her stomach go a bit queasy at that and she wondered who was staking all of the DeLaura brothers. She suspected it was Marty and hoped his two daughters didn't find out or they'd try to have him committed again.

Marty had worked at the bakery for a couple of years before they'd discovered he was quite wealthy and didn't need to work. He just liked to keep busy and loved working the counter at the bakery. His daughters, concerned about their inheritance, had tried to have Marty locked up, especially when he began his tempestuous relationship with rival bakery owner Olivia Puckett. On that score, Mel could see their point but she adored Marty and if Olivia made him happy, who was she to judge?

After the men settled in, the poker game was quiet except for the sound of chips stacking, cards shuffling, and the occasional grunt. Mel wished they'd had a video feed into the game. She wanted to see who was breaking into a sweat and who was playing it cool. Her money was on Paulie for the sweaty one, Ray the impetuous bluffer, Tony maintaining his usual cool, and Al, as the youngest, the watcher.

"Any luck finding someone for your television show?" Marty asked, breaking the quiet. He explained to the others. "Simon, here, is a TV producer."

"Cool," Ray said. Mel could just picture him giving Simon a view of his best side.

"Not yet," Simon answered. He sounded distracted and Mel thought she heard the scratch of cards on the table as he examined his hand.

Angie glanced at Mel. She noticed the tone, too. Simon took his card playing very seriously, it seemed. The game continued as cards were dumped, hands were folded, and two players remained. Ray and Simon. When Ray finally called him, Simon revealed a full house. Ray threw down his pair of kings and made a sound of disgust.

Although she knew the brothers had plotted out how the game should go, it sounded as if Ray's disgust was the real deal. More shuffling commenced. While they were listening, Tate arrived and slid into the booth beside Angie. Shortly after that, Joe appeared and took a spot beside Mel.

"Did I miss anything?" he asked.

"Just Ray losing, repeatedly," Mel said.

Joe made a face as if he knew how poorly that was going to sit with his brother. "On purpose?" he asked hopefully.

"I don't think so," Mel said.

"All right," Tony's voice came out of the speaker. "Five-card stud, one-eyed jacks are wild, ante up."

The sound of chips landing in a pile sounded and then the swish of cards being dealt.

"I'll open for five hundred," Simon said.

Mel exchanged a wide-eyed look with Angie, who whispered, "I think I'm going to throw up."

"I'll call and raise you another two-fifty," Al said.

There was the sound of shifting in chairs and Joe said, "Am I the only one who's feeling uncomfortable?"

"Nope," Tate said. He blew out a breath. "Seven hundred and fifty on a hand of cards."

"Eight-fifty if you count the ante," Angie said.

"Not helping," Tate said with a grin. He kissed Angie's head and tucked her in close as they listened.

Most of the table folded but Al held in there as did Marty. When it was up to two thousand per player to stay in, Marty folded and then Simon did, too. Called out, Al spread out his cards. He had a pair of threes.

"You . . . that . . ." Ray was apoplectic. "I don't know whether to punch you in the face or high-five you. That was the most epic bluff ever. I was positive you had a royal flush or four of a kind."

"It's always the quiet ones you have to look out for," Marty said, but there was respect in his voice.

"Thank you," Al said. They could hear him pulling his winnings in closer.

The game continued for another hour. Marty and Tony were the most persistent about asking Simon questions about what he thought about the murder of Miles Gallway, but he managed to sidestep each one, keeping his focus on the game.

After two more hands, Paulie was out, and Ray followed on the third. Tony and Al were still in play, as were Marty and Simon. On a winning streak, Simon had proposed that the last hand be winner take all. With a pot worth sixty thousand dollars, the stakes were higher than they'd been all night.

This was it, their last chance to get any information out of Simon. Mel thought she might faint, and judging by the way Angie, Tate, and Joe were hovering over the small speaker with her, they felt the same.

The sound of cards being dealt broke the silence, and then Marty's voice, asked, "So, Simon, tell me the truth. Did you murder Miles Gallway?"

Twelve

"What?" Simon asked. He sounded distracted and angry. "Why would you even ask me that?"

"Relax. I'm just making conversation," Marty said. "Don't get all worked up."

"If you're trying to break my concentration on the final hand," Simon said, "it won't work. I'm hot tonight and nothing can break ruin my winning streak."

"We'll see," Marty said.

There was a tense silence that fairly crackled out of the speaker. Mel felt Joe stiffen beside her. Always the protector, she knew he was ready to run to the rescue if need be.

There was the sound of cards being dealt and studied. One hand was tossed down.

"I'm out," Tony said.

"Me, too," Al said.

Silence stretched to the point where Mel feared the speaker might have broken.

"Together?" Marty asked.

"All right," Simon agreed.

The sound of cards being flipped, a random nervous cough, and then . . .

"You son of gun!" Ray shouted. There was the sound of someone getting thumped on the back.

"Ow," Marty said.

"Look at that!" Al cried. "You had him three of a kind, king to queens. Talk about luck of the draw."

"I think I had a heart attack," Ray said.

"That's a helluva pot of gold," Tony agreed.

The noise of chips being gathered sounded. Mel felt herself relax. They hadn't gotten anything out of Simon, but at least Marty hadn't lost his money.

"So, this was great," Simon said. "I'll have my businessman pop a check in the mail to you."

"Beg pardon?" Marty asked.

"You know, for my share," Simon said. He sounded nervous.

"This is a cash game," Marty said. "Acceptable forms of payment include cash, money order, or bank check, unless you can directly transfer the money from your bank to mine while I watch."

"Right," Simon said. "Sure. I'll just— Damn, looks like I left the bank check at home." The sound of a chair scraping against the floor broke the quiet. Mel wondered if Simon really thought he was going to be able to outrun all of the DeLaura brothers.

"That's cool," Marty said. "I take cards, too."

For Batter or Worse

"Well, I . . . you . . . huh, it seems I've forgotten my wallet as well."

"Really?" Tony asked. "Because I think this is it right here."

Mel glanced at Angie who said, "Sticky Fingers."

Mel grinned but noted that Joe was frowning. He did not like it when the brothers played fast and loose with the rules.

"Hey!" Simon protested. "How did you—?"

"Found it on the ground," Tony said. "But that's you, right? I mean, the license says Simon Marconi."

"Give me that!" Simon snapped. There was a scuffle and Mel suspected that Simon had snatched his wallet away from Tony.

"Listen, the truth is I'm a little short," Simon said. "I'm going to have to do some transfers of funds."

"I get it," Marty said. "These things happen."

"I'm glad you understand," Simon said. "I'm good for it, I swear."

"I'm sure you are," Marty said. "Hey, Mick, come here."

The sound of a door opened and then Mick's unmistakably deep voice asked, "What do you need, Marty?"

"My friend needs a little reminder to pay up," Marty said.

"He sounds like a mob boss," Tate hissed. "Who let him watch *Goodfellas* unsupervised?"

Joe was easing out of the booth and Mel knew he was going to intervene before anything bad happened.

"If he tattoos him, I'm going to throw up," Paulie said. His voice sounded strangled.

"Tattoo? Reminder?" Simon squeaked. "No, no, no. I'll remember. I promise. I'm good for it."

"Really?" Al asked. "Because I heard the only reason you were even at the resort looking at Miles for your television show was because you're in debt to Clay Perry and this was the only way you could break even."

"How did you know?" Simon asked. He paused and Mel suspected he was glancing around the room at the wall of DeLaura brothers and Mick who, with his shaved-and-tattooed head and multiple body piercings, was a fearsome sight to behold.

"I have my sources," Ray said.

"Well, it's not a secret," Simon said. "Even the police know I'm in debt up to my—"

"They do?" Marty asked. He failed to hide his disappointment.

"Yeah," Simon said. "It's common knowledge that I like to gamble and sometimes it gets a little away from me. Clay and I have an understanding, so it's all good. I find that a lot of people prefer to use my skills as a trade for monies owed."

"Your skills?" Tony asked dubiously.

"Yeah, like, look at the four of you," Simon said. "Four good-looking brothers such as yourselves should have your own TV show."

Stunned silence met this statement.

"Oh, hell no!" Joe cried, and he bolted for the door.

Mel and Angie were right behind him. Tate was left behind to lock up as they raced down the walkway to Mick's tattoo parlor.

Joe didn't knock. Instead he yanked the door open—thankfully it was unlocked—and barged into the vacant parlor. He strode across the floor and made his way into the back. The room was a total man cave with squashy leather couches, a giant flat-screen television on the wall, and a large refrigerator.

The brothers, Marty, and Simon were seated at a round table off to the side of the room while Mick hovered in the doorway of the back entrance as if he'd been beckoned from the underworld. They all had beers in front of them and, in Marty's case, a pile of chips.

"Joe," Ray said. "What are you doing here?"

"No television show," Joe said.

"Hi, Mick," Mel said. She waved at the tattoo artist and he waved back with a grin.

"How did you know about the show?" Paulie asked. He glanced at Angie. "Did you rat us out about the poker game?"

"Didn't have to," she said.

"We forgot to take you off the group text, didn't we?" Tony asked. He smacked his forehead.

"Yes," Joe confirmed.

Tony looked at Mel and Angie. "You knew he was in on it and you didn't say anything?"

"Duh," Angie said. "Did you really think we'd let you do something like this without bringing Joe into the loop?"

"That's cold," Al said.

Tate arrived right behind them. "What'd I miss?"

"Nothing yet," Joe said. "But if any of them reaches for a pen to sign anything you have my permission to tackle at will."

"As if we'd sign anything," Tony said with an exaggerated eye roll.

"Speak for yourself," Paulie retorted. He turned back to Simon. "I'll sign."

Simon's head bobbed around the room as if he was trying to keep up with the fast and furious conversation. Mel would have told him not to bother, the DeLauras spoke their own language.

Joe jerked his head at Tony, who rose from his chair and snatched up both Paulie and Al by the backs of their shirts. "Come on, you two. We've got to go. I told Ma we'd stop by tonight."

"What? Why?" Al protested.

"She made zeppole," Tony said.

Both brothers straightened up. "Why didn't you say so?" Al asked. "Night, all, nice meeting you, Simon." Al led the way to the door.

"Yeah, it was great," Paulie said. He made a phone with his hand and to Simon, he said, "Call me."

"Bye." Tony followed the other two out the door and to Mel it felt as if the closed-in space swelled with oxygen.

"So, wild guess here, but this whole thing"—Simon paused to gesture to the table and the room—"was just an elaborate way to try and determine if I was Miles's killer."

There was an awkward silence and finally Marty said, "Yeah."

"Well, I'm not," he said. "Why would I kill him? What possible motive could I have?"

"Money," Ray said. "It's always money."

"I didn't owe him any money. Clay, sure, but not Miles. He didn't have any money, either," Simon said.

"Then sex," Marty added. "Sex is always a motive."

"No." Simon shook his head. "We didn't have that sort of relationship."

"Secrets." Angie snapped her fingers. "What secret did Miles know about you?"

"I don't have any secrets," Simon said.

"You have a gambling problem," Joe said. "That seems like a worthy secret."

"It would be, if it was actually a secret," Simon said. He gestured to Marty and Ray, still sitting at the table. "But clearly, it's not. Besides, even if it was, why would I kill Miles?"

"Maybe someone asked you to do it," Angie said. "Someone you owe a favor?"

Simon shook his head. "I'm not the murdering kind. I'd rather just be sued and then shunned."

Mel felt her hopes deflate. It would have been so nice to have the murder solved all nice and neat with Simon killing off Miles as payment to what he owed Clay, who wanted to exact revenge for his wife's affair but no matter how they tried to make the pieces fit, they just didn't.

"Besides," Simon said as he rose from the table, "if you had just asked me, I could have told you, I have an alibi for the time of the murder."

"Oh?" Angie asked.

Simon looked smug as if he didn't plan on saying a word.

"I'm an assistant DA," Joe said. "I'll find out either way."

Simon frowned. "Fine. I was auditioning Ashley for the television spot."

"When you say *auditioning* . . ." Ray let the sentence hang in the air. They all looked at Simon.

"We were doing a screen test to see how well she did

in front of the camera," he said. "Some people just aren't natural on screen."

"And?" Marty asked.

"And what?" Simon snapped.

"How did she do?" Ray asked. "You can't leave us hanging."

"She blinks," Simon said. He made an annoyed face. "A lot. I don't know if it's a nervous thing or what, but unless she can get that under control, there's no career in television for her."

"And you say you were with her when Miles was murdered?" Mel asked. "And she'll corroborate that?"

"She already has with the police," he asked. "Why?"

"Because she came screaming into the kitchen when we found Miles," Mel said. "It just seems odd timing."

"She'd just left filming," he said. He sounded like he was running out of patience. "Your point?"

"None, except everyone knew Miles wanted back on television, so if she wanted it really badly, she might have—"

"Bludgeoned him with a meat tenderizer to take his place?" Simon asked.

Mel shrugged. At least she hadn't said it first.

"I think you credit her with a lot more ambition than she actually has. It wasn't her," he said. "She was with me."

"Which gives her an alibi, too," Angie said. She didn't bother to hide her disappointment.

Simon grinned at her but it was without amusement. "Just so. Now, if you'll excuse me, I'm leaving."

No one stopped him as he strode out of the parlor, closing the front door behind him with a firm *click*.

"Well, that didn't work out as I'd hoped," Marty said.

"What?" Ray asked. "You don't believe that guy, do you?"

"Don't you?" Joe asked.

They all turned to look at Ray. He stared back, unblinking. "Not one word of it. Dude was lying out of his—"

"We get the idea," Mick interrupted. Despite his rough exterior, he didn't like it when people swore.

"Face hole," Ray continued. "Maybe it takes one to know one, but that man is a stone-cold liar. He knows something that he's not saying and I'll bet dollars to donuts, he knows exactly what happened to Miles Gallway."

◦ ◦ ◦

It was only days until the wedding. Mel had a million things to do, one of which was to drop by the resort and deliver to Courtney the seating chart Joyce had drawn up. There were to be only fifty people in attendance but Joyce had been very clear that the tables not be a free-for-all of seating, as she felt it might get awkward with too many people at one table and not enough at another and so on.

To appease Joyce's need for order, Mel agreed to stop by the resort and drop off the table charts even though she had less than no interest in where anyone sat. She was leaving Courtney's office when she decided to swing by the pastry kitchen so she could report back to Oz on what was happening in his workspace during his leave of absence. She knew he'd been particularly worried about the Beast and whether it was being fed, since Tomas was still on vacation.

She walked through the resort, thinking not about her upcoming reception but rather the fact that Miles Gallway, disgraced Foodie Channel chef, had been murdered right here in this very kitchen and no one knew who had done it or why.

She paused by the door of the big kitchen and peered through the round window. The line cooks were beginning prep and Ashley was marching around them, looking very much like a military general giving inspection to the troops. Mel leaned in and heard nothing but criticism and cutting remarks. Why did every chef think that treating their crew badly made them a rock star? It made them a jerk in Mel's opinion, not that anyone was asking.

She must have made a noise because Ashley whipped around in the direction of the doors and Mel jumped back. She slammed into someone behind her and let out a yelp. She spun around to find Sarah Lincoln, the unfortunate saucier, standing there holding a large tub of mayonnaise. She was grimacing in pain and Mel glanced down and noticed that one of her hands was bandaged.

"Oh, no! I'm so sorry," Mel cried. "Are you all right?"

"No, it's my fault," Sarah said. "I thought you were going in and didn't say I was behind you. I know better."

Mel remembered the training of the high-traffic kitchen. One of the rules was to let other cooks know when you were moving behind them. It spared a lot of injuries in the trenches.

"What happened to your hand?" Mel asked.

"Burn," Sarah said. She cradled the tub in one arm and held up her hand to show her individually wrapped fingers. "One of the hazards of the kitchen. I like to think I'm adding to my collection of battle scars."

Mel held up her left hand. She had a knife scar that ran across the middle of her palm. "I got this my first week in cooking school. I was positive I was going to bleed out and then get thrown out."

"Oh, wow," Sarah said. "New knives?"

"Of course," Mel confirmed. They shared a knowing laugh, the sort only cooking school survivors could understand.

"When did it happen?" Mel asked.

"A few days ago," Sarah said. She shrugged. "I'm sure it'll be fine. No permanent damage, at any rate."

"I'm sorry, are we cooking out here now?" Ashley's voice broke into their conversation as she pushed open the door. Sarah paled as if she knew what was coming. "When I send you to the larder, I expect a prompt return."

"My fault," Mel said. Mercy, she hated bullies. "I was asking for directions." She turned to Sarah. "Thank you. I'll be sure to let Mr. Perry know how helpful you were."

Sarah nodded and then scurried past Mel and Ashley and back into the kitchen.

Ashley glared at Mel, who glared back. She was a bride having her wedding to a prominent district attorney at the resort. If this was a power play, Mel knew she was the winner. Ashley made the most of it, however, doing a very slow pivot and pushing back into the kitchen, dripping with attitude and scorn.

Mel wasn't impressed. She waited until the door shut and then strode down the hall to the pastry kitchen. There was a young man sitting at the counter, staring at a tablet he had propped up. When Mel entered, he slammed the tablet facedown and stood.

"Hi! Can I help you?" He appeared to be in his early

twenties. He was medium in height and build, pale as if he didn't get outside much, with a shock of dark blond hair that stuck out from under his black chef's beanie, a much more practical hat while cooking than the over-sized toque.

Mel looked behind her to see if something scary had followed her into the room because his reaction was so over the top. No one and nothing was there.

"Hi, I'm Melanie Cooper and you are?"

"Sorry, I'm Sam Whitaker."

"Nice to meet you," Mel said. She glanced around the empty kitchen. Sam watched her. He was about as contained as a pressure cooker about to blow.

"Are you okay, Sam?" she asked. He was sweating profusely and she started to worry that he might pass out on her.

"Sure, fine, yup," he answered. He looked even more nervous.

"I'm a friend of Oz's," Mel said. "I just came by to see how things were going without him."

"Great!" the young man said. "Things are great. I am on top of it."

Mel pursed her lips. This kid was the worst fibber of all time. She approached his worktable and flipped the tablet back over. Oz's face stared back at her.

"Really, Oz?" she asked.

Thirteen

Oz's eyes went wide and she laughed at his look of surprise.

"Hi, Oz," she said. "Mentoring your replacement?"

He shrugged. "It's my kitchen."

"I get that," she said. "But if he gets caught talking to you, the police might drag him into the investigation."

Oz sighed. "He's making raspberry cream tarts for tonight's signature dessert. The shortbread crust is not his specialty, however. Sorry, Sam."

"No, it's okay." Sam said. "Totally true."

"I can help," Mel said.

"No, we can't ask you—"

"Sure you can," Mel interrupted. "I don't have anything to do other than to report to my mother's for wedding-favor-making duty. We're bagging up those little Jordan almonds, very traditional, since I refuse to have any sort of favor that isn't edible and those almonds won't melt. My mom and Joe's mom can totally start without me, plus, Angie will be there and I'm sure they'll be consumed with her upcoming delivery. They won't even miss me."

"This would be such a huge help—" Sam said.

"Perfect," Mel said. She turned back to the tablet. "Bye, Oz."

She switched it off before he could argue, which it looked like he was about to do.

"Apron," Mel said. She went to the sink and scrubbed in. Sam brought her a well-worn but clean white apron, and Mel fished her own chef's beanie out of her purse. She always carried one with her for those exceptionally bad hair days.

They went to the pastry kitchen's designated supply cupboards and walk-in refrigerator and gathered their ingredients. Mel talked Sam through her shortbread crust for tarts. He was a quick learner with good instincts. She let him take over the cream portion of the tart while she baked the crusts. It reminded her of the first few days of cooking with Oz in her kitchen. This was what she wanted in an assistant. Of course, she couldn't poach Sam as that would be bad form, but she could definitely find someone similar if Madison didn't work out.

When the tarts were done, they worked side by side, covering them with raspberries, round side up. When they were finished, Mel helped him store the desserts in the walk-in cooler.

"Thank you so much," Sam said. "Tonight would have been a disaster if you hadn't wandered by. Ever since Oz has been gone, well, things have been chaos and no one seems to know who is really in charge. I've tried to lead in here, but Ashley has made it very difficult, undercutting my instructions to the staff at every turn."

He sounded frustrated, and Mel couldn't blame him. She'd seen Ashley in action. Not a pleasant woman.

"It was my pleasure," Mel said. And she meant it. She was enjoying a glass of water and glanced over at the other pastry chefs who had arrived to help with the evening's dinner. She lowered her voice and asked, "I don't want to get too personal, Sam, but were you here the afternoon that Chef Gallway was killed?"

"Yeah, I was," he said. "I was assisting with the larder as we'd gotten in a huge shipment and needed to inventory everything before we put it away."

"I'm sure the police have already asked you, and I don't want to make you uncomfortable by bringing it up, but did you see anything or hear anything that day?" Mel asked.

"Oh, yeah, the police have asked," Sam said. "Unfortunately, I was out on the loading dock with the rest of the kitchen staff. We were hustling to get the shipment unloaded before we started dinner prep and we were running late. I didn't see or hear anything until Ashley started screaming."

Mel nodded. She remembered that scene well.

"We all ran in, thinking the kitchen was on fire or something, but no."

"Instead, Chef Miles was dead," Mel said.

"Yeah, and Oz was covered in blood . . . it looked bad. Well, you know, you were there." Sam shook his head as if he still couldn't make sense of it all. He wasn't alone.

"Did anything else happen that was noteworthy?" Mel asked. "Even in the days before the murder, did anyone freak out or have a fit or anything like that? Was there any kitchen drama that seemed especially over the top?"

"No, not that I can remember," Sam said. "I mean, there are always factions vying for power in a kitchen, aren't there? Both Miles and Ashley wanted to be Simon's next television star, but he was pushing hard for it to be Oz. I was wishing for it to be Oz, too."

"Really?" Mel asked. She was surprised that Sam would be okay with losing a boss he clearly enjoyed working for.

"Sure, bragging rights, you know?"

Mel nodded. That made sense.

"But on that day, everything was weird and wrong. We all just stood around in shock. Then Sarah needed to see a doctor for her hand, but—"

"You mean the burn?" Mel asked.

"Yeah, in all the commotion, she burned her hand on the range—" he began but Mel interrupted.

"Wait—are you saying she was burned the same time that Gallway was murdered?"

"I don't know if it was the same exact time," Sam said. He paused to think about it and took a sip of his water. "We all ran in here when we heard Ashley screaming, and Sarah came in shortly after, cradling her hand."

"Because she'd been burned," Mel said. She wanted to be sure that this was accurate. She found it odd that Sarah hadn't mentioned that it happened the same day that Gallway was murdered.

"Yeah, it was crazy. We all know basic first aid, but

this was a bad burn," he said. "She refused to go to the hospital, though. She said she didn't want to interrupt what was happening with the investigation into Gallway's death, so we did a quick clean and bandage but honestly, I think there was some deep tissue injury. She's still on pain meds."

Mel thought back to the day she and Joe had popped into the kitchen and found Oz over Chef's body. They had paused by the main kitchen first. No one had been in there. No one. So how had Sarah burned herself at the same time the murder took place if she hadn't been in the kitchen at all?

Mel got a sick feeling in her stomach. While she didn't know Sarah very well, Oz's defense of the saucier when Gallway had reprimanded her had made Mel think sympathetically of the girl. No one worked in a high-stress kitchen without working for a Gallway or two in their time, but how well did Oz know her? Could she have been out to get revenge on Gallway for humiliating her? Could she have been the one to bludgeon him with the wooden mallet? Then how did she get burned? And how did he end up dead in the pastry kitchen?

Having lost Simon and Ashley as suspects, although Ashley's screen test still needed to be confirmed, it seemed they could add Sarah to the list, since Mel still considered Clay and Kasey as possibilities. Sure, they had alibis, but they weren't solid. Clay could have come in from the golf course and Kasey could have left the pool. Mel refused to consider Oz. She debated going to the main kitchen to talk to Sarah, but dinner hour was approaching and they would be ramping up with no time to talk. Plus, she wanted to get her alone and not have to deal with Ashley watching. No, it was better to go to her mother's— Ack!

Mel snatched the beret off her head, took off her apron, and threw it at Sam. "I'm late, so late. This was fun. Gotta go. Nice meeting you, Sam."

"Bye!" Sam called after her, but Mel was now in a dead run and barely heard him. She hit the doors and dashed to her car. She wasn't going to speed to her mom's, of course she wasn't, but she certainly wasn't going to lollygag, either.

Mel stopped her Mini Cooper on a squeal of brakes right in front of her mother's house. She hurried out of the car and dashed up the walkway, finger combing her short blond hair as she went. Angie met her at the door.

"You owe me, you owe me so huge," Angie said. Then she glanced at Mel and gasped. "Are you all right? What happened?"

Mel blinked. Was this Angie's way of getting her out of trouble? She'd rather just own her tardiness.

"You're bleeding!" Angie cried.

"What?" Mel glanced down. Sure enough, there were red splatters all over her pale blue sleeveless blouse.

"Oh, holy mother in heaven, she's been stabbed!" Maria DeLaura cried, looking like she might faint.

"What?" Joyce pushed to the front. She grabbed Mel by the hand and dragged her into the well-lit dining room.

"What did you do to yourself?" Joyce clucked as she examined Mel's shirt, looking for a hole where the blood must be coming from.

"Nothing, I swear I'm fine," Mel said. "Those are

raspberry stains. I must have brushed my shirt with my apron when I took it off."

A huge bowl of Jordan almonds sat in the center with stacks of pearl white organza drawstring bags surrounding it. A basket of already-filled bags sat at the end of the table.

"Mom, we've only invited fifty people," Mel said. "How many of these are you making?"

"Enough so that we're not embarrassed if more people show up," Joyce said.

"Always better to have leftovers," Maria agreed. "Then you know no one went hungry."

"Especially for those who always arrive late," Joyce said with a pointed look at Mel.

Mel looked at Angie. "I do owe you big-time."

"Free babysitting whenever I want," Angie said. "I'm just sayin'."

"Done."

"Now, about that shirt," Joyce said. She left the room, coming back with an old T-shirt of Mel's father's. "Put this on."

"Mom, I can take—"

"The stain will set before you go home and ruin your blouse," Joyce said. "Go ahead and change."

Mel rolled her eyes at Angie. She disappeared into the kitchen and came back wearing her father's old ASU shirt. She smelled the shoulder, hoping to get a whiff of cigar smoke and bourbon, two smells she always associated with her dad. The only scent she could register was laundry detergent. She sighed.

"Rubbing alcohol will take that out," Maria said.

"Do you think so?" Joyce asked. She sounded skeptical. "I was going to try vinegar."

Without asking, the two women took the shirt from Mel and headed into the kitchen. Angie watched them go, looking thoughtful.

"Is that going to be us in thirty years?"

"Maybe," Mel said. She grinned at her friend. "There's certainly no one I'd rather debate laundering techniques with than you."

Angie returned the smile. "Ditto." She grimaced and sat down, rubbing her knuckles over her chest. "I'm having wicked heartburn."

"Can I get you something?"

"Nah, I think I just ate too many almonds," she said. "Why are these things so good?"

"I don't know," Mel said. She scooped up a few and popped them into her mouth. She chewed thoughtfully. "We should make a cupcake that reflects our love of the Jordan almond."

"Totally," Angie agreed. "So, why were you really late?"

"I stopped by the resort to give Courtney the seating chart," Mel said. "And then I went to the kitchen to see how they were doing in Oz's absence."

"I bet they miss him," Angie said.

"Terribly. I ended up helping Oz's assistant, Sam Whitaker, make raspberry tarts for tonight's featured dessert."

"Ah, now it comes full circle," Angie said.

"Yes, but Sam also told me some interesting tidbits about the line cook, Sarah."

"The one we watched get dressed down by Gallway?"

"Yes," Mel said. "Apparently, at the time of Gallway's murder, she burned her hand quite badly on the stove."

"Oh, that's awful," Angie said. "Will she be all right?"

"I think so," Mel said. "But the interesting part of this is that Joe and I were in the kitchen where she was supposedly burned right before we stumbled upon Gallway and Oz and there was no one in the kitchen. It was empty."

"She lied?" Angie asked.

Mel shrugged. "Looks like it."

"But why?"

"Maybe she needed an alibi and gave herself one," Mel said.

"Ah!" Angie gasped. "You mean she murdered Gallway and then burned herself? That's pretty twisted. And she seemed so nice."

Mel nodded. It was rather horrifying to think that Sarah had murdered Gallway and then burned herself to cover her crime. How could they prove it? Mel thought about the wooden meat tenderizer. She wondered if there was any evidence that it had been near a flame or a burner. If it was scorched, they could tie it to Sarah. The thought made Mel feel awful for even thinking it, but then again Oz was in the hot seat for murder and Mel would do anything necessary to prove his innocence.

Joyce and Maria came back in a few moments. They looked very pleased with themselves.

"Got the stain out," Joyce said.

"Rubbing alcohol," Maria added.

Joyce looked comically aggrieved but they sat down and started bagging almonds. Mel lost count but she suspected they made over one hundred bags of almonds, all tied with the custom white ribbons Joyce had ordered that read *Melanie and Joseph* in dark blue on one end and the date on the other.

Mel studied the bag in her hands and marveled that if twelve-year-old her had known that one day she would actually be Mrs. Joe DeLaura, she would likely have had a heart attack and keeled over dead right then and there. Good thing she hadn't known.

She glanced up to see her mother, Mrs. DeLaura, and Angie all watching her. She smiled as she glanced from one face to the next. "What?"

"Your dream is coming true," Mrs. DeLaura said. Then she watered up and sobbed. Joyce took one look at her face and began to cry as well.

"Oh, no, here they go. Save it for the church, Moms," Mel said. She smiled and patted their hands. Then she looked at Angie to share her amusement. To her dismay, Angie was crying as well. She handed her a paper napkin from the holder on the table. "Oh, no, not you, too."

"I can't help it," Angie said. "You've loved Joe for sooooo long. It's like something out of a movie for you to finally become his wife and live happily ever after."

This observation set the moms off again, naturally, and as they all wailed into their paper napkins, Mel helped herself to another handful of almonds. She savored their bittersweet flavor. She studied a big fat pink one in the palm of her hand and thought about how it was a perfect metaphor for life. So much nuttiness surrounded by a sugary candy shell. She smiled.

"I can't believe you're not crying," Angie said. She looked at Mel with annoyance. "It's like the end of the romantic comedy when everything works out all right. You're supposed to be choked up."

"Well, the credits haven't rolled yet," Mel said. "We still have to get down the aisle, don't we? And I don't want to jinx anything by counting my wedding vows before they're spoken."

That dried the moms right up.

"Melanie, you're not trying to tell me something, are you?" Joyce asked. She blew her nose with an impressive honk. "I mean, you and Joe haven't had a spat or anything, have you?"

"Which would be perfectly normal just before the wedding," Maria added. She bobbed her head reassuringly and Joyce did, too. "Dom and I had a terrible fight right before our wedding."

"You did?" Angie looked surprised.

"Oh, yes," Maria said. "I almost called off the wedding." Angie's jaw dropped.

"Charlie and I had an argument, too," Joyce said.

"What?" Mel cried. She had never heard of this before.

"It's true," Joyce said. "Your father wasn't helping with any of the wedding plans. It was all on me, and I was convinced that his lack of interest in planning meant he wasn't really interested in marrying me. It was silly but when I threw his ring at him and told him it was off if he didn't step up and start helping, then he got the message."

Maria laughed. "For me, it was Dom's wish to have his ex-girlfriend at our wedding. Can you even believe it? His ex at our wedding?"

The flash in Maria's eyes was one Mel had seen in Angie's many times and it suddenly became very clear to Mel whom Angie had inherited her temper from.

"How have I never heard about this?" Angie asked. "And what did you do? You didn't let him invite her, did you?"

"No, certainly not," Maria said. Then she laughed. "I actually did call off the wedding and then I went to his mother and told her why. She took my side and told Dom he was being an idiot. He finally admitted that he wanted his ex at our wedding to rub it in her face that he was marrying the most beautiful girl in the world." She sighed. "Naturally, I forgave him, but she still wasn't invited."

They all laughed and then they each looked at Mel inquiringly.

"No," Mel said. "Nothing like that has happened."

"You haven't changed your mind, have you?" Maria asked. She gave Mel a look of gentle reproach.

"No!" Mel shook her head. "But Joe and I have tried to get down the aisle a couple of times now, and something has always stopped us, so I'll just save my happy tears for after the service."

"You're right," Angie said. She dabbed her face with a tissue. "I don't even know why I was crying. Oh, wait, yes, I do." She patted her belly. "Sorry, the little one has just made me so sentimental."

"Understandable," Mel said. "Are you hungry? Maybe something besides almonds would level you out."

"I do feel a bit peckish," Angie said.

Both Joyce and Maria hopped up from their seats, declaring, "We'll fix you something."

They disappeared into the kitchen and Mel grinned at Angie.

"That was devious," Angie said.

"I prefer to think of it as giving them something useful to occupy themselves with," Mel said. "Besides, I'm starving."

"Me, too," Angie laughed. They exchanged a grin and then Angie sobered and asked, "Straight talk, though, are you at all nervous about the wedding?"

"Not at all," Mel said. "I mean, we're keeping it simple precisely so that the potential for disaster is averted, so what could possibly go wrong?"

Fourteen

Mel couldn't sleep that night. She supposed it could be wedding anxiety kicking in, not that she was worried about anything, she told herself. But she suspected that it was more that she was concerned for Oz. No other suspects had proven out as yet and Oz'd had an altercation, witnessed by many, with Gallway over Sarah.

And then there was Sarah. Mel couldn't get the woman's burnt hand out of her mind. It just didn't jive with what she knew, that there had been no one in the kitchen right before Oz found Miles, so when had the young woman been burned? And why had she refused to get treatment?

When she talked to Joe about what she'd discovered, he agreed that it was odd. He remembered the main kitchen being empty when they'd walked by, and Mel told him what Sam had told her about the staff being out on the loading dock.

Feeling restless and worried about Oz, Mel decided she would take the wedding favors over to Courtney at the resort and just have a walk through the Sun Dial to see what was what.

She didn't mention her errand to Joe because she was quite certain he would not approve. Besides, she assured herself, she wasn't going to be that long. Just a pop-in on a legit errand. No big deal.

Again, she parked in what was beginning to feel like her usual spot. She said hello to the parking attendants, the front desk personnel, and the security guard. With her basket of almonds, it was obvious why she was here and no one questioned her.

Courtney was happy to keep the basket in her office until it was time to set up the room for the reception. She went over a few details with Mel and then her phone rang. Mel waved bye to her from the door, feeling impatient to be on her way. Courtney, in her usual bubbly way, blew Mel a kiss and gave her a little finger wave. There was a sincere cuteness to Courtney that Mel would never be able to replicate. Not in a million years.

She walked towards the kitchens, hoping she'd run into Sam. He'd been a fountain of information and she had more questions. She checked both kitchens but there was no sign of anyone she recognized. The breakfast crew was a completely different set of chefs. Very disappointing.

Mel meandered through the resort. When she passed the lounge, she saw Kasey Perry sitting with Simon Marconi. Hmm. It seemed an odd pairing. Marconi was much older than the young men Kasey admitted to preferring, and why would Marconi get involved with the wife of the man he owed money to? Seemed like a dicey situation, but then again they were out in public, so maybe they were friends. No, neither one of them seemed to be the type to have friends.

Mel tried to read their facial expressions to see if it was a pleasant meeting or not. Given the tightness of Kasey's face, it appeared not. Hmm.

She tried to stay out of their line of sight while maneuvering closer. Since their heads were pressed together and they were staring at each other quite intently, it wasn't that hard. She slid into the booth behind them and opened a menu, pretending to peruse the offerings.

It took her a moment to realize she had picked up the individual dessert menu. Huh. She recognized a few of Oz's specialties as he had tried out many of his signature desserts on the bakery staff when he was in cooking school. Her attention was caught by a pistachio crème brûlée.

Yes, please! While her mother would likely consider it a bad breakfast choice, Mel couldn't disagree more. It contained eggs and cream. Why, it was practically an omelet.

A waitress came by and Mel quietly ordered the dessert with a cup of coffee. If the waitress thought the request odd, she didn't show it.

Mel continued to look at the menu, while listening to the snippets of conversation she could hear behind her.

"There's something not right about her," Simon said.

Mel wondered who they were talking about.

"Obviously," Kasey said. "No one in their right mind would willingly be Miles's assistant."

Ah, Mel thought, it had to be Ashley. She had to agree with their assessment, there was something wrong with Ashley. A lack of empathy was the first thing that came to mind.

"She's desperate to be your next Foodie Channel star," Kasey said. "She's the only chef who wanted it as badly as Miles."

"Too bad for her, she's going to lose out," Simon said. "She's as interesting as a boiled potato and she has a nervous tic or something. She's constantly blinking. There's no way she's television material, and also, she's a terrible chef."

"Then why did Miles make her his sous chef?" Kasey asked. "Do you think he was sleeping with her?"

"Probably," Simon said. "He got booted off his original show for being handsy with the female chefs, but I don't think he learned a thing. He was your typical narcissist: nothing was his fault, and he wanted what he wanted when he wanted it."

"Well, I can't really fault him for that," Kasey said. She gave a throaty laugh that Simon didn't return. "You know Clay is expecting you to pick someone from the kitchen."

"Yeah, but the only one who could carry it off has been put on leave," Simon said.

"Oz?" Kasey asked. She practically purred his name. It made Mel's hair stand on end in alarm.

"He's got it all: the looks, talent, and charm," he said.

"I'd let that one go if I were you," Kasey said. "He killed Miles. It's just a matter of time before they prove it."

Mel sucked in a breath and then hunkered down in her booth in case they heard her.

"What? How do you know that?" Simon asked.

"I just do," Kasey said. "Now, I don't mean to tell you your business, but I think you're overlooking some real potential in the kitchen."

"Who?" Simon asked. He sounded dubious.

"Sam Whitaker," Kasey said.

"Who?"

"Sam Whitaker," Kasey said. She sounded offended that Simon didn't know whom she was talking about. "He's got the looks and the talent."

"He's Oz's assistant, right?" Simon asked. "Skinny guy, doesn't look old enough to drive?"

"He's twenty-two," Kasey said.

"A baby," Simon said. "You want me to make a show around a baby chef?"

"He's not," Kasey snapped.

"He's no Oz," Simon countered.

"Who is a murderer."

"Yeah, damn it. Oz seemed like such a nice guy," he said.

"They always do." There was a pause and then in a hesitant voice, Kasey said, "So, what about Sam?"

"You mean 'Tiger'?" Simon asked.

Kasey gasped. "How did you—"

"Know about your little fling with the baby chef?" he interrupted. "I make it my business to know these things."

"It's just a nickname. It doesn't mean anything,"

Kasey insisted. "I'm just trying to help you. You know Clay isn't going to let you go until you pick someone. Do you have any other options?" She sounded miffed.

"No," Simon sighed. "Fine, I'll screen-test him."

He didn't sound thrilled about it. Mel tried to picture Sam as a television star. She was with Simon on this one. He was a nice guy, but he lacked that indefinable quality that elevated a person to stardom, even if only on the Foodie Channel. She wondered if Kasey was actually having a fling with the young man, then she pushed aside the thought because . . . yuck.

The waitress returned and Mel couldn't hear what was being said while the server put her coffee and dessert on the table. As soon as she left, Mel plugged back into the conversation but it was no good. She glanced over her shoulder and saw that Simon and Kasey were leaving. Damn it.

Mel consoled herself by tucking into the decadent dessert. She lingered over her coffee, thinking about what she'd overheard. Simon and Kasey seemed to be in agreement that Oz was responsible for Miles's murder. Why? They didn't know him well enough to believe that. Mel stabbed the pale green crème brûlée with her fork. She wished she'd turned around and given them a piece of her mind. Oz was innocent. She knew it all the way down to her core. With their unfounded suspicions, were they helping to build a case against him to the police? Mel felt her anxiety spike.

Pushing her plate away, she decided to give her uncle Stan a call and tell him about her concerns.

"Hey, kid," Uncle Stan answered on the second ring. "Everything all right?"

That was so Uncle Stan. A lifelong police officer, he operated on the premise that people only called him if there was a crisis. Never mind that she had called him a million times when there wasn't a crisis.

"Everything is fine," she said.

"Fine, meaning?"

"You're so suspicious," she said.

"Yes."

Mel sighed. This was not going to go as easily as she would have liked.

"I ran into Sarah Lincoln yesterday," she said.

"Ran into her?" he asked. Already his tone was dubious at best.

"I was at the resort, dropping off Mom's seating chart," Mel said. She tried not to sound defensive.

"Right, right," Uncle Stan said. He made it sound like he knew what she was talking about when Mel knew he didn't have a clue. Seating charts were not Uncle Stan's bag.

"Anyway, when I bumped into her, I noticed that her hand was injured," Mel said.

"Line cook, right?" Uncle Stan asked.

"The saucier, yes, she has a bad burn," Mel said.

Mel heard some paper shuffling. "Right, we interviewed her with the others. She said the burn happened that morning."

"Well, you might want to pin that detail down, because when I talked to her, she told me she did it a few days ago, but when I mentioned her to Oz's assistant pastry chef, Sam Whitaker, he told me that she burned herself at the same time that Miles Gallway was murdered."

"Same time?" Uncle Stan grunted. Mel wasn't sure if

that was an indicator that he was interested or a noise he made while he was doing something else to make it sound like he was paying attention.

"So, I was thinking about her burn and the meat tenderizer—you know, the wooden mallet found under Miles Gallway at the time of his death, which was possibly the murder weapon judging by the dent in his head, and I was wondering if the mallet had any burn marks on it?"

"Why would you make that connection?"

"Because if Sarah was the one who clobbered him in the head then maybe she still had the mallet in her hand when she burned herself, and maybe she burned herself trying to hide the fact that she just clobbered a guy," Mel said.

"That's a lot of maybes," Uncle Stan said.

"I know. I get that it's a long shot but it would tie the murder weapon to the murder and the murderer," she said.

"Mel." Uncle Stan said her name in that way he did when he was not happy. There was a moment of silence when she could hear him clicking away on his computer. Then silence. Was he so mad he couldn't even speak?

"Am I in trouble?" she asked. Uncle Stan said nothing, making her anxiety spike. "Because I'm going to be a bride in a matter of days and I have an awful lot going on, which should not include being in trouble with you."

"Do not play the bride card with me, young lady," Uncle Stan said. "And just so you know, I got a call from Ashley Bishop yesterday that you were poking around the resort kitchen. Is that when you 'ran into' Sarah?"

"Actually, yes," Mel said.

Uncle Stan was quiet, taking that in. Obviously, he

hadn't been expecting her to admit it, which made Mel think she might have the advantage here.

"But it was an accident. I was on my way to check on the pastry kitchen for Oz when I ran into her."

"Go on."

"When I noticed her hand, she told me she'd burned herself a few days ago. She didn't mention that it was at the same time that Gallway was killed, which is what Sam told me. But that doesn't add up, because Joe and I walked by the main kitchen right before we found Gallway in the pastry kitchen and there was no activity in the main kitchen. Sam told me that they were all on the loading dock unpacking a delivery truck full of food and that Sarah showed up after Miles was found. She'd clearly burned herself but refused to leave and seek medical treatment until things quieted down."

"Why would she do that?" Uncle Stan asked.

"Maybe she wanted to make sure she wasn't a suspect," Mel said. "Or she didn't want to draw attention to herself or her injury."

"Or maybe she stayed to look out for someone who had helped her out before," he said.

"Like Oz?" Mel was outraged by what he was suggesting.

"Ask yourself this: What possible motive would Sarah Lincoln have to murder Miles Gallway?" he asked. "Was she up for a promotion and he denied it? Did he owe her money? Was she in love with him and he didn't reciprocate?"

"I don't know," Mel said. "It could be any of those things or none of them. I do know that I watched him call her out and humiliate her in front of the entire kitchen staff."

"Interesting," he said. "And a possible motive, especially given that it looks like this was a crime committed in the heat of the moment."

"It doesn't feel right," Mel said. She turned over what she knew about Sarah. "I mean, if she wanted out, why not just quit? Why kill him? And if she burned herself to give herself an alibi, *yikes*, that's nuts, right? I mean, a chef's hands are their livelihood. Sure, we get burns and cuts and all, but you'd never burn yourself on purpose. It could destroy your career."

"You would if your life was at stake," Uncle Stan said. "Maybe her injury was an accident, though; she might have attacked while he was cooking and got burned in the process."

"But if he was cooking, there would have been evidence of it," Mel said. "That kitchen was clean."

"So, we need to know where she was when she burned herself," Uncle Stan said.

Mel glanced up from her seat at the swinging doors that led to the kitchens. The main kitchen had been empty when she and Joe walked by. There was no way Sarah burned herself there. Oz was in the pastry kitchen and found Gallway's body, so it couldn't have been there. Then it hit her. The day that Oz had shown them his kitchen and they tried cupcake samples, he'd mentioned that there was a third kitchen. The banquet kitchen!

"I think I know where it happened," Mel said. "Oz told us there's a third kitchen, the banquet kitchen. It could be she burned herself in there."

"Could be," Uncle Stan said. "At least it gives me another line of questioning for her and the rest of the staff. I'm going to send some crime scene techs over."

"You're welcome," Mel said.

Uncle Stan heaved a sigh. The waitress stopped by the table and asked if Mel wanted anything else. She declined and handed her server enough for her "breakfast" along with a healthy tip.

"Where are you?" Uncle Stan asked.

"Out for breakfast," Mel said.

"Is Joe with you?"

"No, he's trying to clear his desk so we can have an uninterrupted honeymoon," she said.

"What a crazy optimist," Uncle Stan said with a laugh.

Mel relaxed, relieved not to have to say exactly where she was.

"So, exactly where are you having breakfast?" Uncle Stan persisted.

Darn it. Mel grimaced. There was no evading the question. "I'm actually in the restaurant of the Sun Dial."

"What? Why?" he asked.

"I had to drop off the wedding favors," Mel said. "And they have Oz's pistachio crème brûlée, which is to die for, no pun intended."

"Mel, you need to get out of there," he said.

"Why? I mean, our reception is in a few days. It can't be that weird that I'm here," she said.

"Except there is a murderer loose, who is trying to pin it on your pastry chef," he said. "Don't you think they're going to be less than happy to see you hanging around there, possibly chatting up someone who might give you information that would clear your friend?"

"Er . . ." Mel stalled. She hadn't really considered that.

A prickle on the back of her neck caused Mel to turn around. Sitting in the booth Simon and Kasey had vacated was Sarah Lincoln, and she was staring at Mel with an intensity that made Mel's heart pound and her hands sweat.

Fifteen

Sarah twirled a knife, a very sharp, very lethal chef's knife, between the fingers of her uninjured hand. Then she gestured for Mel to hang up. Mel thought about yelling, but Sarah was only a few feet away. The damage she could inflict before Mel got the words out could be fatal.

"Um, Uncle Stan, I have to go," she said.

"What's wrong, Mel? You sound weird," he said. She heard the sound of a chair being pushed back and she knew he was already on his way.

"Sorry, I don't mean to cut you off, but I have to be sharp for my wedding. You know, I don't want to slice it too thin," she said. She hoped he registered the reference to *cut* and *sharp* and *slice* and figured out that she was in trouble. Before she could say another word, Sarah snatched the phone out of her hand and ended the call. Pocketing Mel's phone, she said, "Let's go."

Mel noticed Sarah's hand was shaking. Her eyes were wide and there was a sheen of sweat on her brow. She looked scared but determined. Mel had no doubt that Sarah had overheard her conversation. She scanned her brain, trying to remember exactly what she'd said. She remembered telling Uncle Stan about the burn and how Sarah could have been in the banquet kitchen with Chef Miles and that if there were scorch marks on the mallet they could tie her to his death. So, this was bad.

Mel slid out of her seat. She began to walk to the front of the restaurant, thinking that she could alert the hostess to the situation as she passed. Sarah was onto that trick, however, and stood in front of her, blocking her path.

"No, turn around and go out through the open doors," Sarah ordered. She was wearing her chef whites, so the knife didn't look as out of place as one would hope. She poked Mel in the side with the handle. "Go."

Mel thought about rejecting her instructions but thought better of it. She turned, wondering if Sarah would lose control and stab her in the back in a fit of panic. She quickened her pace, hoping to stay out of reach, but Sarah was hot on her heels. The French doors were propped open and Mel stepped out onto the patio, hoping to find some diners to help her. It was late morning, the sun was hot, and there was no one out here.

"Keep going," Sarah said. "Through the gate."

Mel strode forward, thinking if she pushed through the gate fast enough she could slam it on Sarah and run.

It opened onto a sidewalk that ran along the perimeter of the golf course. The course! Yes! There had to be someone out there on the links.

Mel opened the gate and tried to slip through and slam it behind her. The other woman was too quick for her, however, and caught it with her foot. She looked at Mel as if she'd like to stab her right then and there.

It occurred to Mel that this wasn't going to go her way if she didn't take control of the situation. She decided she needed to try and outmaneuver Sarah. Otherwise, she was likely to be stabbed to death, which would cause her to miss her own wedding in a few days. This was unacceptable for a wide variety of reasons, not the least of which was that her mother would never forgive her, and Mel did not want to have to live or die with that on her head. Oh, hell no!

As Sarah slid through the gate after her, Mel decided to do the unexpected. Instead of docilely continuing to walk, she dropped to the ground and tucked herself into a tight ball, causing Sarah, who was following her too closely, to trip over her and sprawl on the ground. Mel thought about jumping on top of her but Sarah rolled onto her back, still clutching the knife with her good hand and her feet up and ready to kick. Mel did not like the odds of having her legs slashed if she tried to jump on the woman. Instead, she turned and ran.

Her plan on the fly was to sprint down the sidewalk until she found someone, anyone, who could help her. There was no one. How was it that there was no one out and about? It was a beautiful spring day. Argh!

She heard Sarah rising to her feet behind her and she scanned the area. A golf cart with two older gentlemen beside it was parked near the green. Mel ran towards them.

"Help! She has a knife!" she cried.

As she approached she could see the men exchange a confused look. One of them looked at her and frowned.

As she approached, he said, "I did not slice."

"What?" Mel asked. She was already winded, cardio not being her thing and all.

The other man looked at her and said, "Don't mind him, he can't hear a thing." He gestured wide and added, "It is a nice life."

"Huh?"

Mel glanced between them, trying to gauge which one had more on the ball, so to speak. They were well into their eighties, dressed in vibrant lime green and hot pink, and neither one was moving faster than the chow line at an all-you-can-eat prime rib special. She glanced over her shoulder to see Sarah coming at a run.

"Do you have a phone?" she cried.

The first guy cupped his ear and asked, "Eh? What's that? Are we having fun?"

Mel shook her head and the second man patted her shoulder and said, "Of course we're having fun. Now, be a dear, and bring us two more beers." He then slapped a twenty in her open hand.

Oh, geez, they thought she was a waitress. She glanced back again and saw Sarah was closing in fast. She couldn't let these old men be harmed.

"Sorry, I'm on break," she cried. "There's your waitress." She pointed to Sarah, tossed back the twenty, and bolted away. She jumped into their golf cart, unlocked it, stepped on the pedal, and took off.

The men were shouting after her but she didn't care. She floored it. She had to turn around to get back to the resort so she yanked the steering wheel in a sharp left, drove onto the rough, and straightened out the cart to get back on the path.

She almost made it free and clear but just before she accelerated out of her turn, there was a thump on the back of the golf cart. Sarah had made a leaping dive, managing to land on the far backseat that faced away from the driver. Mel jerked the wheel left then right, trying to dislodge her, but no luck. Sarah clung like a particularly persistent stain.

Mel could see the resort up ahead. She knew Uncle Stan was on his way. She just had to get there. She could make it. She jerked the wheel again, keeping Sarah from climbing over the seat. The cart's wheels fell off the path and the vehicle pitched precariously. Both Mel and Sarah yelled, and Mel frantically oversteered, trying to get control of the vehicle, which sent them careening over the path on the other side.

"What is wrong with you?" Sarah yelled. "Do you not know how to drive?"

Mel glanced in the side mirror to see Sarah hanging on with her good hand. In her injured fist, she still clutched the knife. Damn it.

"Look out!" Sarah shrieked.

Coming straight at them was another golf cart. The group of four men, who looked to be young professionals having a meeting while golfing, were all yelling at Mel and one of them, the driver, was calling her some particularly foul names. There would be no help there. Mel cut the wheel onto the grass, sending the cart bouncing on the uneven terrain. Sarah was cursing and muttering.

The resort still looked out of reach, but Mel had no choice; she was going to have to make a run for it. If she could get to the front of the resort, where the parking attendants were, she'd be able to get help and, hopefully, Uncle Stan would already be there.

She took her foot off the pedal and jumped from the cart, giving Sarah no warning as the cart lurched to a stop, knocking her around like a piñata.

Mel dashed for the resort, hoping to make it around the corner. She didn't make it. Sarah took her down in a diving tackle that knocked the wind out of Mel. She lay on her stomach with her face pressed into the dirt. Sarah had a knee in her back. Mel went limp, hoping to convince Sarah that the fight had gone out of her.

"Stop running," Sarah said. "I need to—"

Mel did not want to hear whatever crazy thing Sarah had to say. She sucked in a gulp of air and popped up as high as she could. With a yelp, Sarah fell off her and Mel jumped to her feet and began to run. She wasn't going to make it to the front. She decided to cut through Oz's kitchen garden and his kitchen and get back to the dining room. She could hear Sarah behind her but didn't slow down or look behind her until she got to the garden gate. She yanked on it, but it was locked. She glanced behind her. Sarah was coming at a sprint but was hampered by a bit of a limp. Mel took the opportunity to hop over the fence.

It was not as graceful as it should have been. She was tired and winded and her arms were shaky. Her shoe got stuck in between the iron prongs on the top, and she went splat onto the ground. Her hip took the brunt of the fall. *Ow!* But that was okay. With her wedding in three days, it could have been her face, and Joyce would have been beside herself if Mel turned up with a black eye.

Mel leapt to her feet and tried to grab the shoe that was still wedged in the gate. No luck. Sarah was almost there. Mel abandoned the shoe and ran into the kitchen.

"Help!" she cried. There was no one there. She turned back around to lock the door but it was one of those doors that needed a key turned in the bar that ran across the door. Argh! She saw Sarah leap the gate. She did it in one hop, with a limp, using her uninjured hand, without losing her shoe or dropping the knife. Damn it.

Mel scurried around the main island in the kitchen and dropped to the floor. Maybe Sarah would assume she'd run through the kitchen to the main part of the restaurant. Her heart was beating so loudly; she was certain Sarah would hear her. She was desperate for air, and her breathing was labored, but she tried not to make any noise.

Unfortunately, breathing so shallowly that she made no noise meant she wasn't getting the oxygen her muscles needed and she began to feel woozy.

The door to the kitchen was yanked open, and Mel almost yelped. She heard footsteps pound through the room as Sarah raced through the empty kitchen and out into the hallway. The swinging door shut behind her and Mel sucked in a huge gulp of air. She fully expected Sarah to come back when she didn't see Mel in the other kitchen or the dining room.

Mel glanced at the patio. She could go back out and run around the resort to the front, where there were sure to be other people. Mercy, no more running. Or she could set a trap for Sarah here. She glanced at the walk-in pantry. If she cracked the door open just a bit, Sarah might think she'd ducked in there to hide.

Mel slid across the floor, not risking popping up above the counter. She opened the door just a crack and then stood and checked the top of the doorframe for where Oz had mentioned he kept the key. She felt the metal under her fingers and snatched it, dropping it into her pocket. She scurried back across the kitchen to hide behind the counter, where she wasn't visible from the door. She breathed, she jogged her foot, she tried to think of things besides her desperate need to use a bathroom.

She thought about her wedding and how unhappy Joe would be if she got stabbed before their big day. Of course, this made her think about how much she loved him and how much she wanted to marry him, to become his missus and spend their lives together. Instead, she was running for her life from a crazy knife-wielding saucier. It was as clear as her best Pyrex glassware that she needed to start making better choices. She was about to crawl out from her spot and just slip out the door when the kitchen door banged open.

"Where are you?" Sarah cried. "I know you're in here somewhere. No one saw you leave the dining room and it's the only way out."

Mel started to shake. Sarah was younger than she was and the fact that she had run the same distance as Mel and leapt over the gate and didn't sound the least bit winded, made Mel realize that if she had to fight her, oh, horror, she'd likely get her butt handed to her. Also, not a condition she wanted to be in for her wedding.

She pressed up against the counter, trying to make herself as small as possible. She squeezed her eyes shut. Sarah hadn't moved. She hadn't made a sound. She must be visually scanning the kitchen, and Mel had the crazy notion that it was like being stalked by a velociraptor in *Jurassic Park*. The thought made her almost fear-giggle, meaning of course she was on the brink of hysterics. She bit her lip. That was it, no more late-night scary movies.

She heard Sarah take a step. Was it towards her or away? She couldn't tell. She was consumed with the urge to yell or scream. The suspense was excruciating. She heard another step and then another. They were so soft, Mel fully expected Sarah to appear around the corner of the counter. She glanced around her, looking for a weapon. What the hell? Why hadn't she thought to grab a weapon? She was in a kitchen, for Julia Child's sake! At the very least, she could have grabbed a rolling pin. She was swamped by feeling too stupid to live.

And then she heard a door get yanked open. The pantry! And Sarah yelled, "Aha!"

Holy buttercream! She'd fallen for it. Mel slid out from her spot behind the counter and lunged across the kitchen. She reached the pantry just as Sarah was coming out and slammed the door in her face.

"Ow!" Sarah cried.

Mel didn't care. She reached into her pocket and grabbed the key. Sarah was banging on the door. Mel grabbed the doorknob before she could twist it open. She held it still while she inserted the key and locked the door. Sarah was fighting her for everything she was worth, however. She was full-on slamming her body against the door, trying to break it down. Mel went and got a stool and wedged it up under the doorknob. There was no way Sarah was getting out of there.

Mel collapsed onto the floor. Sarah pounded her fist on the door. She cursed a blue streak. Then she sobbed. Mel was unmoved. Every time she thought about Sarah wielding that knife her resolve hardened. She had caught Miles Gallway's killer. Her work here was done.

Sixteen

Mel was lying on the floor, wondering where her phone was, whether to go get her shoe, and what to do if someone came in and heard Sarah forcibly trying to bust her way out of the pantry.

"Let me out," Sarah demanded. She thumped on the door. "I just want to talk to you."

"Right," Mel said. She was still gasping for breath and the sweat on her skin was beginning to get cold in the room's air-conditioning. "People who want to just talk always do it at knifepoint."

"I'm telling the truth," Sarah said. Her voice sounded wobbly and Mel suspected she was going to start crying. That wasn't going to soften Mel in the least.

"Uh-huh," Mel grunted. She pushed herself up to a

seated position. She needed to find a phone and tell Uncle Stan where she was.

"I know you think I killed Chef," Sarah said. "But I didn't, I swear, I didn't."

"Sure," Mel said. "That's why you chased me all over the resort with a knife."

"I'm sorry, but I needed you to listen," Sarah said.

"Well, a knife is not the way to do that," Mel said. "Unless you're guilty."

"I'm not!" This time Sarah did cry. In fact, she let out a wail that made Mel clap her hands over her ears.

There was a scraping noise and the knife Sarah had been holding was shoved under the narrow gap between the door and the floor. Mel kicked the knife aside with her foot. She wanted Sarah's prints intact, otherwise it proved nothing. The woman could have five more knives on her for all Mel knew. Sarah was still crying, the pitch getting higher and louder.

"All right, all right, stop," Mel said. "Say what you have to say."

"Through the door?"

"I can leave and get someone else to listen to you," Mel said.

There was a barely audible sigh on the other side of the door.

"Time's ticking," Mel said. "I'm calling the police as soon as I catch my breath."

"No, please don't call the police," Sarah begged.

"Give me one good reason why I shouldn't," Mel said.

"Because I didn't kill Chef Miles," Sarah said.

Mel said nothing.

"I didn't," Sarah said. "I didn't mean to hurt him. When I left him, he was alive, I swear."

Mel sat up straighter. Was this a confession?

"Tell me what happened, Sarah."

"I . . ." she began but then paused. She heaved out a huge breath and Mel leaned closer. She could feel Sarah's tension coming through the door.

"You can tell me," she said. "It's all right. What happened that afternoon?"

"I was practicing a sauce that he wanted for dinner that evening," she said. "He told me I had to arrive early and use the banquet kitchen. I had to prove that I could make it to his standards or he was going to pull me off my station."

Her voice quivered and Mel got a sick feeling in the pit of her stomach.

"While I was working at the range, he came up behind me and trapped me against it. He kept touching me even though I told him to stop. I panicked."

Mel heard her gulp back some tears and she suddenly wanted to open the door and hug Sarah tight. Caution made her wait. The saucier had just held a knife on her, after all.

"He'd always been grabby, and I'd complained before," Sarah said. "But Ashley told me that was the price a female chef pays. She said if I made an issue of it, I'd be the one who was fired and out of work. Not him."

Mel nodded. Sadly, she'd heard this story before. Times were changing but cooking had long been a man's domain. "How did you get away?"

"When he wouldn't stop, I grabbed the meat tenderizer

mallet and I swung until I hit something," Sarah said. Her voice broke and she sobbed. "It turned out to be his head. He shoved me hard against the range and my hand landed in the pan. It was seared in the hot oil before I could get it out. I hit him again and then I ran for it. I never meant to hurt him, I was just trying to defend myself."

"I see," Mel said. Now it was all coming into focus. A white-hot fury coursed through her. How dare Miles Gallway use his position of power over this woman? If he wasn't already dead, she'd clobber him with the meat tenderizer herself.

"Sarah, you have to tell all of this to the police," she said.

"No, no, no," Sarah protested. "I don't want to get in trouble. I'm a single mother. I have a son, he's only two. I can't go to prison. I can't. I only wanted to talk to you because I thought you could help me keep the police away. Oz said your uncle is the lead detective in the investigation. Please help me, please."

She began to weep in earnest now and Mel felt like a horrible person for doubting her. Then again, Mel realized she could be getting the biggest con job of her life, but somehow she didn't think so. Gallway was enough of a creep to have used Sarah's single-mother status against her, knowing she couldn't complain about his abuse because she so desperately needed the job to provide for her child.

"Listen, I know someone who can help you," Mel said. "I'm going to let you out."

Sarah's wail downshifted into sniffles and sobs. Mel took the key out of her pocket.

"What is that noise?" Sam strode into the room, wearing his chef's coat and beanie, and looked from Mel to the pantry. "Did you catch a rat?"

Mel blinked at him while she carefully dropped the key back into her pocket. What could she say? "Actually . . ."

"Mel!" Uncle Stan raced into the kitchen with his partner, Tara Martinez, behind him. "Are you all right?"

"I'm fine, Scottsdale police detective who is also my uncle Stan," Mel said. She kicked the pantry door with her heel and the sniffling stopped immediately.

Uncle Stan's head whipped in the direction of the pantry.

"There's a rat in there," Sam said. Mel almost hugged him.

Uncle Stan exchanged a look with Tara and she reluctantly moved forward to grab the chair.

"No!" Mel cried. "It has rabies."

Tara froze and turned her head to look at Uncle Stan. "That is above my pay grade."

"There is no rat," Uncle Stan said. He turned to Mel. "And even if there was, how would you know it had rabies?"

"Um," Mel stalled. She had no idea what a rabid rat would look like.

"Frothing at the mouth," Sam said. He looked at Mel. "Was it frothing?"

"Totally," Mel said. She smiled at her uncle, and said, "So, nothing to see here. In fact, we're just going to call an exterminator and let them take care of the problem before the health department shows up."

Sam frowned. "That would be bad."

"Mel, I know Sarah is in there," Uncle Stan said. "We need to talk to her."

"Sarah?" she asked. She gave him her best confused face.

"Sarah Lincoln?" Sam asked. "The saucier who works here? What's she doing in our pantry with a rat?"

"There is no rat," Tara said. She tossed the chair aside like she was a wrestler in the WWE, and Uncle Stan cringed.

"Easy with the private property there, Detective," he said.

Tara ignored him and tried the door. It was locked. Mel felt a small, tiny, barely even noticeable—really— surge of satisfaction. Detective Martinez had disliked Mel for years for a variety of reasons—the main one, Mel believed, was because Tara had set her sights on Joe and he wasn't interested. Recently, Tara had begun dating Ray DeLaura and Mel had hoped it would mellow her. It had not, and she never missed any opportunity to make Mel feel incompetent, inept, or just plain clueless. So, it gave Mel just a smidge of satisfaction to be the keeper of the key in this moment.

"Where is it?" Tara asked.

"I'm sorry," Mel said. "Where's what?"

"The key, brainless," Tara said.

"Why do you have to talk to me like that?" Mel said. "It's so rude!"

"Is this really the time for this?" Uncle Stan asked.

"She called me brainless," Mel said.

"Fair point," Uncle Stan said. He looked at his partner. "Why are you so hostile towards Mel? I figured once you started dating the other DeLaura, you'd let the past go."

"She jilted my cousin," Tara said.

"No, I didn't," Mel protested. The ridiculous accusation was just maddening. "Manny and I were never a thing."

"He would have stayed in Phoenix for you," Tara said.

"He's happy in Vegas with Holly," Mel argued. "Don't you want him to be happy?"

"I . . . of course I do," Tara said. She looked exasperated. "Listen, not liking you is a hard habit for me to break."

"Clearly."

They stared at each other.

The sound of something crashing came from behind the locked door. Then a very colorful swear word.

"That's quite a vocabulary for a rat," Uncle Stan said.

"Um, why is Sarah in our pantry again?" Sam asked. He looked honestly bewildered. Mel thought about Simon's suggestion that there was something going on between Kasey and Sam. Nah, Sam looked like he didn't even swear, never mind shack up with an older lady.

✶ ✶ ✶

Tara held her hand out and Mel sighed and slapped the key into it.

Tara unlocked the door and out came Sarah. Well, Mel assumed it was Sarah, but it was hard to say, given the dusting of flour that coated her.

Mel jumped in front of her, holding out her arms and shielding the woman. "There's been a huge misunderstanding."

"Yes, there has been," Uncle Stan said. "Ms. Lincoln, if I could have a minute of your time."

Sarah was covered in flour, from head to foot. It even

coated the eyelashes she blinked at Uncle Stan. "Are you going to arrest me?"

"He won't. He can't," Mel said.

Uncle Stan and Tara both looked at Mel in surprise, and she said, "There are extenuating circumstances."

"Such as?" Tara asked.

"Don't answer that," Mel said. She glanced at Sarah, happy to see she had not pulled another knife, as Mel didn't particularly care for the idea of being a hostage. "You shouldn't say anything until you have a lawyer."

"Mel!" Uncle Stan's voice was tight. He was clearly hanging on to his temper by a thread, a very frayed thread.

"What?" she asked. "It's true."

"Ms. Lincoln, while my niece is correct that having an attorney present is a choice you can make—"

Tara let out an exasperated huff of breath. Then she started to cough as she ingested a bit of the cloud of flour floating in the air.

"As I was saying," Uncle Stan said. "I don't believe you're going to need an attorney. I just need you to verify some facts for me."

Mel gave her uncle a suspicious look, which he ignored.

"Such as?" Sarah asked.

"Was Miles Gallway aggressive with you in any way?"

Sarah went very still. "Who told you that?"

"Everyone," Sam said. They all turned to look at where he was busily sweeping up the flour that had been spilled while Sarah was trapped in the pantry. He turned a bright shade of red. "Sorry, I just mean there was some talk."

Sarah hung her head. "I'm doomed, aren't I?"

Before Mel could answer, Sarah said, "All right, I hit

him, okay? He had me up against the range and I couldn't get him off. I grabbed the nearest thing I could and struck out at him."

"Sarah, stop talking!" Mel said. She grabbed her by the shoulders and shook her gently, covering them both in flour.

"What's the point?" Sarah asked. "They know everything. I'm going to lose my son, my life, and my career, all because of that . . ." Her voice trailed off and she burst into tears.

Despite the flour coating the other woman, Mel pulled her in for a hug.

"It was self-defense," Mel said. "She didn't murder Miles Gallway."

Uncle Stan ignored her. He spoke to Sarah. "Tell me what happened after you hit him with the mallet."

Mel let her go and Sarah lifted her head and in a dull voice, she said, "I ran."

"And where were you when you hit him?"

"The banquet kitchen," she said. She pointed to the main kitchen. "You have to go through the main kitchen to get to it. It's on the other side of it."

"And where did you run?" he asked.

"Out the back door to the loading dock," she said.

"It's true," Sam piped up. "She arrived with her hand all burnt and we stopped what we were doing to attempt first aid."

Uncle Stan nodded. "So, you left Gallway in the banquet kitchen?"

"Yes," Sarah said.

"Can you tell me if you noticed whether he was drunk?" She eyed him suspiciously. "Why?"

"Just gathering the facts," he said.

"No, he didn't seem inebriated and I didn't smell any alcohol on him," she said. "And he was certainly close enough for me to tell." She shuddered and Mel was right there with her.

"He was found here in the pastry kitchen," Tara said. Her voice was crisp and no-nonsense but not unkind. "Any idea how he got here?"

Sarah shook her head. "When I left him, he was fine. He was holding a cloth on his head, which was bleeding, and he was yelling, but he was fine. I swear. He called me all sorts of horrible names, but I just wanted to get away from him so I ran and I didn't stop until I found everyone else."

"Understandable," Uncle Stan said. His voice was gentle and Mel watched Sarah visibly relax under his kind regard. She glanced at Tara and saw the same type of empathy on her face, which was unusual for a woman not known for her compassion.

"I assumed he must have stumbled to the other kitchen, looking for help," Sarah said. She caught her breath, closed her eyes, and forced out the words, "Where he died."

Uncle Stan nodded. "He did die there."

Sarah covered her mouth with her hand. She looked wrecked and Mel felt horrible for the woman she had been trying to outrun just a half hour earlier. Sarah was right. This was going to ruin her life. She had to help her.

"We can hire an attorney," Mel said. "I know a guy, Steve Wolfmeier, and he'll help you."

"Ugh." Tara made a face. "The slick guy with the shiny suits?"

"He's an excellent defense attorney," Mel said. Steve did wear shiny suits, but he was very good at what he did.

"That's sound advice," Uncle Stan said.

Mel looked at him like he might have a head injury of his own. Uncle Stan hated Steve.

Sarah nodded and then held out her wrists as if she was waiting for the cuffs to be clipped on.

"Ms. Lincoln, you're not under arrest," Uncle Stan said.

"I figured," she said, "if I could just call my mom. She watches my son and I need to let her know . . . Wait, what?"

"You're not under arrest," Uncle Stan said. "But I would like you to come to the station and give a more detailed statement about the events leading up to the discovery of Miles Gallway's body. Can you do that?" He jerked his head in Mel's direction. "Let her call her friend for you, too. It never hurts to have an attorney present."

Mel felt her mouth slide open. What was happening?

"Can you come with us, Ms. Lincoln?" Uncle Stan asked.

Sarah looked at Mel and she studied her uncle's face. He gave her a small nod.

"Go ahead, he wouldn't lie to you," Mel said. "I'll call my friend and have him meet you."

"Thank you," Sarah said. She looked so lost and sad. "I'm sorry I chased you. I really did just want to talk."

"I'm sorry, too," Mel said. "I might be a little damaged and suspect the worst of people sometimes."

"I'll take her by her house to clean up," Tara said. "Good thing I'm driving a city car and not my own." She looked at Uncle Stan. "Meet you back at the station?"

"Sure," he said.

Mel watched Sarah leave with Tara out the side door through Oz's small garden. The door had just swung shut behind them when Sarah came back in and held up Mel's phone.

"Sorry." She handed it to Mel.

"No problem." Mel said. It was covered in flour but she wasn't going to complain.

As soon as the door shut behind Tara and Sarah, Mel and Stan stepped out of the kitchen, getting out of Sam's way while he cleaned.

"All right, what's going on?" Mel asked.

"What do you mean?"

"Why are you so sure Sarah didn't kill Gallway?"

"Why were you so sure she did?" he countered.

"She tells a compelling story," Mel said. "I think she had a good reason for clobbering him and shouldn't be punished for defending herself."

"Agreed," Stan said. "But why do you *believe* her?"

"She's got a little boy," Mel said. "No mom worth her salt would risk being taken from her child, not if she could help it. But there's something else going on here, isn't there?"

"You can't talk about it to anyone," Uncle Stan said.

"I would never." Mel tried to sound offended. Uncle Stan wasn't buying it. He rolled his eyes.

"Tell me," she demanded.

"All right, but I'm only telling you a tiny bit of it because you'll be away on your honeymoon in a matter of days and won't be able to get any more involved in this case."

"Exactly, I'll be out of your hair, so you should tell me everything," Mel said.

"No." Uncle Stan shook his head. "I'll only tell you this. The wooden mallet found by Gallway's body, the one Sarah used to hit him with, which incidentally does have scorch marks on it, isn't the murder weapon."

Seventeen

"What do you think that means?" Mel demanded of her fiancé later that day. "Uncle Stan wouldn't elaborate at all."

"It means Sarah isn't the killer, or at least she didn't kill him with the mallet," Joe said. They were sitting outside on their wicker loveseat, enjoying the cool evening while Peanut sniffed her way around the yard and Captain Jack lounged on his cat tree in the window behind them.

Mel frowned at the darkening sky.

"What happened after he said that?" Joe asked.

"I called Steve to meet Sarah at the station," Mel said. Joe made a face as if he'd bit into a cupcake made out of brussels sprouts. Steve Wolfmeier was not one of his favorite people. "Then I helped Sam clean up the kitchen

207

before going to the bakery, where I baked a ridiculous amount of cupcakes with Oz, who seemed very relieved that Sarah wasn't the murderer but also worried about what that means for him."

"Rightly so," Joe said. "Without another viable suspect, it pushes Oz front and center again. Does he have any ideas about who might have been in the kitchen at that time?"

"None." Mel shook her head. "But it had to be someone, right? If Sarah is telling the truth, and I believe she is, that she clobbered Miles and ran for it, then someone came upon Miles and finished him off. But who and why?"

"And Uncle Stan said nothing other than the mallet was not the murder weapon?" he asked.

"Nothing," she confirmed. "He told me I need to concentrate on our wedding."

"He does have a point. We're to be married in four days—"

"More like three."

"Three days." He smiled.

It was the same smile that had caused Mel to fall for him when she was just twelve years old. There was a hint of mischief in his warm brown eyes and his lips curved up on one side just a little bit higher than the other. She was going to spend her life looking at that smile, and she couldn't be happier about it, but how could she be happy when Oz might get jailed for a crime he didn't commit? She started to fret.

"All right, what happened there? You were happy and then not. What are you thinking about?" he asked.

"We have two days to figure out who murdered Miles Gallway and clear Oz's name," she said.

"Ugh." Joe tipped his head back in defeat. "And here I thought I'd gotten you to think about us."

"I am thinking about us. How can we be happy if one of our own is wrongly incarcerated for murder?"

Joe took her hand in his. "We'll just have to use all of our resources to help Oz. We won't let him go to jail."

"Promise?"

"Promise."

Mel leaned against Joe. This. This was exactly what she'd hoped her marriage would be. The two of them, in it together, for better or for worse, no matter the obstacles, because as everyone knows, love conquers all.

"Mel, come quick," Marty skidded into the kitchen from the front of the bakery, where he and Oz had been manning the counter.

Mel and Angie were hip-deep in cupcakes and frosting with a huge batch of cupcakes in the oven, the industrial mixer was working up the batter for the next run, and her frosting mixer was churning up a decadent buttercream. Mel was trying to get ahead of things for when she was gone. In short, she was a little busy.

"Is it really important?" she asked, wiping her hands on her apron.

"Only if you care that Oz is going back to the resort and will likely get himself killed or arrested," he said.

Mel jerked upright and then strode into the bakery

with Angie right behind her. There were customers standing there, watching Oz tug off his apron.

"Oz!" Mel said. "What are you doing?"

"I have to go," he said. Freed from his apron, he balled it up in one hand while striding past them and back into the kitchen. Mel glanced at Marty and he raised his hands in the air as if to say, *See?*

Mel followed Oz into the kitchen, again with Angie right behind her and asked, "Where, Oz? Where do you have to go?"

"To get my stuff," he said. "Sam just called me and they're going to break the lock on my locker and toss all of my stuff in the garbage. I have some of my best cookbooks, with my notes in the margins, in there."

Mel put her hand to her chest. She felt exactly the punch to the gut this would be. Oz couldn't lose his notes.

"All right, fine, but I'm coming with you," she said.

"No." He shook his head.

"Yes," Angie said. "She's your cover. She's having her reception there in two days. It would be reasonable for her to be on site, but you not so much unless you're with her."

"Listen to her," Mel said. "It makes sense."

Oz rolled his eyes as if seeking patience.

"What?" Mel insisted. "It just makes sense for me to go." She narrowed her eyes at him. "Why don't you want me to go?"

"Because nothing is ever easy when you're around," he said. "I want to get in and out with my stuff with no drama."

"There won't be any drama," Mel said.

"Riiight," he said.

Mel turned to Angie. "Back me up."

In a shocking display of treachery, Angie said, "He does have a point."

"Ah," Mel gasped.

"I'm just saying that bad things sometimes happen to you that might not happen to other people," Angie said. She hugged her belly. "Sorry."

Mel decided to ignore her. It was clearly the pregnancy hormones making her perception of things wonky.

"Can you handle things here?" Mel gestured to the kitchen.

Angie nodded. "Madison is coming in shortly."

"Perfect." Mel took off her apron and said to Oz, "Let's go. I'll drive."

Looking aggrieved, Oz led the way out of the back door to the small lot where Mel had parked her car.

"Why do you suppose they're tossing your things?" Mel asked on the drive. "I mean, were you officially fired?"

"No, or at least not that I've been told," Oz said. "Sam said it was Ashley's call and she said my stuff had to go to make room for whoever they hired to take my place."

"You think she just wants you out of there because Simon favored you for the television gig?" Mel asked.

Oz shrugged. "I have no idea. This is not exactly how I envisioned the end of my job at the Sun Dial."

"I know," Mel said. "I'm so sorry. But you're crazy talented and there will be other jobs."

Oz shrugged. His expression was blank, as if the current events didn't hurt, but Mel knew that he had to be crushed. He'd really seemed to enjoy having his own kitchen.

She parked in her usual spot, realizing that in two days she and Joe would be arriving in their hired limo for their wedding reception. She was at once full of anticipation but also just the littlest bit nervous. Marriage. It was hard to believe the big day was almost here.

They crossed the parking lot. They smiled at the parking attendant but when Oz made to walk past him, the man, with a name tag that read *Larry*, held out his arm.

"Sorry, Oz," Larry said. "You're not allowed in."

"Since when?" Oz asked.

"Mrs. Perry said that you aren't allowed on the resort premises anymore," Larry said. He looked apologetic, as if it were left to him, he'd let Oz go.

"Well, this is a problem," Oz said. "My stuff is in my locker and I've been told I have to get it before they toss it."

"Who said that?"

"Sa . . . Mr. Perry," Oz lied. Mel glanced at him. She'd never been more proud.

"Oh." Larry scratched his chin where he had a thin coating of beard sprouting. "How long do you think it will take?"

"Not more than fifteen minutes," Oz said.

"Okay, cool," Larry said. He waved his hand at the front door. "Go, but if you run into Mrs. Perry, I never saw you."

"Understood," Oz said.

They headed inside the resort with Mel scanning the area for a glimpse of Mrs. Perry. She was usually hard to miss, a flash of skin, high heels, and a smile. Mel didn't see her.

They hurried through the resort, not slowing down in the dining room but trotting right on through until they got to the hallway where the kitchens were located.

Oz was going to charge right ahead into the staff-only area, but Mel grabbed his arm. "Do you think you should be the one to go in there? What if the other staff have been told to have you removed from the premises, like Larry?"

Oz paused. "I need my stuff."

"I can go in for you," Mel said.

He shook his head. "I don't like it. How are you going to explain being there?"

"I'm your friend and I'm here for your stuff," she said.

"Maybe I can have Sam do it," he said. "Come on, let's see if we can find him."

He turned away from the Staff Only door and pushed through to the pastry kitchen. It was empty. Oz stared around the room and frowned.

"What's wrong?" Mel asked.

"Why is it empty?" he wondered aloud. "Marcus should be here making the dinner rolls, and has nobody fed the Beast?"

Oz bolted for the walk-in cooler. He ducked inside and brought an enormous glass jar over to the counter. He thunked it down and then pried off the lid. Mel peered over his shoulder into the jar.

"Oof, that doesn't smell so good," she said. "It has an alcohol tang. Also, it's not so much a Beast as a house cat that isn't litter box trained."

"Yeah, someone forgot to feed it," Oz said. He went to the pantry to retrieve the flour.

"Tomas, the bread guy, is on vacation. Sam was supposed to keep an eye on it. He's usually more responsible than this."

"Sam, your assistant, the one who was struggling to make a crust for a tart?" Mel asked. "The one who said your locker was getting cleaned out."

"Yeah," Oz said. "I imagine running the show by himself was more work than he bargained on."

Mel stared at the jar. She frowned. "Remind me again, on the day that Miles was murdered, who knew you went back inside to feed the Beast?"

"Sam, Marcus, a few others from my staff," he said. He began to mix equal amounts of flour and water in to the jar. Mel watched him as he added it.

"Just your crew. Anyone else?" she asked.

"No," he said. "We were out on the loading dock helping to unload the supply truck when I got a text from Tomas asking me to feed the Beast. He'd used the starter to prep some loaves of bread that were already on the counter but then forgot to feed the starter. You can't ignore the Beast otherwise . . ."

"You get that," Mel said. She glanced at the jar. Oz frowned.

"Can you walk me through it?" Mel asked. "Not just the moment you found Gallway, but give me an idea of what was happening in here before you all left."

Oz finished mixing the flour and water with the handle of a wooden spoon and secured the lid. He pushed the jar away and washed his hands. He paced while he dried his hands and Mel said nothing, allowing him to gather his thoughts.

"Dylan and Ethan were here, working on a specialty

cake for a retirement party," he said. "I was over there." He pointed to a counter opposite. "I was considering changing one of our dessert specialties on the menu."

"Not the pistachio crème brûlée," Mel said. She tried to keep the horror out of her voice.

"No." He smiled. "Never that."

"Sam was over at the main counter working on filling a batch of cannoli," he said. "We got a call that they needed help unloading a delivery truck. The truck arrived late and they wanted all hands available so it didn't mess up the prep schedule for dinner. I left the menu and went out there with the rest of my guys, but then I got the text from Tomas." He gestured to the door that led out to the loading dock. "I came in through the back door to the kitchen to take care of the starter. I fed the Beast and then checked on the dough Tomas had set out to rise. Two of the loaves were fine but one was a mess. I mixed up a new one and left it in a bowl, figuring it might rise in time."

He frowned and stared at the counter as if trying to remember something that was just slipping out of his grasp.

Mel watched him work through it. He picked up the Beast and took the glass jar back to the walk-in refrigerator. He gestured between it and the pantry and said, "I went back and forth getting supplies, feeding it, fixing the wonky dough, and then I went to the sink to wash my hands so I could go back out to the loading dock." Oz moved to the sink. It was the only spot in the kitchen where a person could see around the counter. "I was here, washing up, when I saw his feet. I dropped the towel and came around the counter, where I found Gallway on the floor."

Oz paled as he stood there, recalling the moment. Mel waited. She knew he was seeing Gallway in his mind's eye and it was not the easiest thing to recall.

"I crouched down beside him and called his name, but he didn't respond," he said. He grimaced. "His eyes were so bloodshot that I thought he'd gotten drunk, slipped, and cracked his head on the counter."

"Did he get drunk often?" Mel asked.

"He seemed to maintain a steady buzz during his shift," Oz said. "It rarely got away from him, but there were a few incidents where Ashley had to step in and finish the night for him."

Mel remembered Uncle Stan asking Sarah if Miles had been drunk when he assaulted her. She'd said no.

"How long do you think you were out on the loading dock before coming back to tend to the Beast?"

"Ten, maybe, fifteen minutes," he said.

Mel nodded. That was definitely long enough for someone to have followed Gallway from the banquet kitchen and have finished him off. But if the murder weapon wasn't the wooden mallet, then how had they done it? She thought about his bloodshot eyes. If he hadn't been drunk, they might mean something else entirely.

"Was anything missing from your kitchen?" Mel asked. "Maybe you didn't notice at the time but its disappearance has left you looking for it."

Oz shook his head. "Not that I can think of, but things were pretty chaotic with everyone running from the loading dock to the larder and back."

Well, that didn't help at all. Mel watched as Oz moved around the kitchen that had been his. He straightened work stations, wiped down a counter, fussed with dish-cloths, and rearranged the pastry bags and specialty tips. He was sorting them when he tossed a handful back into a drawer and slammed it shut.

"Never could get anyone to keep those organized," he muttered. The kitchen remained empty and Oz said, "I have no idea where anyone is. Maybe they're having a meeting. Either way, I need to get my stuff and get out of here."

"Agreed," Mel said. Oz looked reluctant. "You hate leaving."

He ran his hand over the granite countertop. "It was the first kitchen that was all mine."

"I understand," Mel said. And she did. "Having your own kitchen is a chef's dream come true."

"Yeah," he said.

He knocked on the counter twice, as if testing its strength, and then led the way out of the room without looking back.

They went back down the hallway to the door marked Staff Only. Oz didn't hesitate but pushed his way in. This was where the kitchen staff stowed their personal belong-ings while they worked. It was a utilitarian room with a wall of lockers, a bench, and two unisex restrooms at the far end of the room. Oz crossed the black-and-white tile floor to a locker on the upper half of the two rows that lined the wall. He took his key ring out of his pocket and deftly inserted the key. It opened with a *click* and he pulled the round lock off the door handle. He handed it to Mel. It filled her palm and was surprisingly heavy.

He pulled the handle down and with a squeak of pro-test the door swung open. The bottom of the locker looked like a Little Free Library. It was stuffed with cookbooks, notebooks, and miscellaneous papers, all of which filled the bottom half. Two white chef's coats hung on hooks above the mess. In the cubby above was what looked like a white chef's hat, a traditional white toque with many pleats. It was also covered in blood.

Eighteen

At first Mel thought she must be seeing things. It was probably just raspberry stains like she'd gotten on her apron, but no, this was a browner shade and it was on a hat. How would anyone get raspberry stains on their hat? They wouldn't. It was blood. It had to be. Still, just to be sure she nudged Oz.

"Oz," Mel said. She pointed. "What's that?"

Consumed with gathering his precious cookbooks, Oz hadn't noticed the hat. He glanced up, then he reached for it, but Mel smacked his hand away.

"Ow."

"Don't touch it," she said. "In fact, don't touch anything."

Mel reached into her pocket for her phone. "I know who killed Miles."

"What?" Oz asked. "Who?"

"No time," Mel said. "Close your locker. Let's go."

"But my books and notes," he protested.

"They'll keep," she said. She opened her contacts and pressed Uncle Stan's name. The phone started to ring. "Come on, pick up, pick up."

Uncle Stan didn't answer his phone. Mel left a message for him to call her as soon as he could.

"Let's lock it back up," she said.

"But—"

"Do it," Mel said. She was getting a very bad feeling about them being here.

"What's wrong?" Oz asked as he clicked the lock on the door to the locker. "Who are we worried about?"

"I'll tell you in the car," Mel said. She tugged his arm, trying to hustle him along.

They were almost at the door when it opened and in strode Sam.

"Sam, I'm glad you're here," Oz said. "Listen, can you do me a solid and—"

Clay Perry walked into the staff room, interrupting whatever Oz had been about to say.

"Mr. Perry." Oz's eyes went wide. "I'm just here to get my things, sir."

"Are you leaving us then, Oz?" Clay asked, looking surprised.

Oz gave him a side eye. "I was told to clean out my locker."

"By whom?" Mr. Perry asked.

"Ashley," he said.

Clay rocked back on his heels and nodded. "I think there's been a miscommunication here. Ashley does not do any of the hiring or firing here at the resort."

"But—" Sam protested. "She told me—"

"Indeed? Perhaps I should call her and remind her that I'm the boss." Clay Perry stared at the young man. It was an icy-hard look, the sort that could reach into a man's chest and squeeze his heart until it stopped. Sam paled and flop sweat appeared on his forehead, cementing what Mel had begun to suspect.

Sam shook his head, as if he could ward off Mr. Perry's fury so easily, and he pointed at Oz. "But he's a murderer! She's right to get rid of him."

Mr. Perry turned to Oz with one eyebrow raised. "Is this true?"

"What?" Oz cried. "No!" He looked at Sam in bewilderment.

Mr. Perry turned back to Sam. "Explain yourself. Why would you say that?"

Sam looked at Oz and shook his head. "I'm sorry, man, but I can't cover for you anymore. You killed Chef Miles and everyone in your kitchen knows it."

Oz staggered back a step. Mel caught him by the arm. She suspected this was Oz's first betrayal and he would come out of it a changed man, more suspicious and less inclined to trust. In other words, a grown-up.

Oz jerked his head in Mr. Perry's direction. "I didn't. I swear."

Behind Mr. Perry, in strode Uncle Stan and Tara. Mel glanced at Uncle Stan. His face gave away nothing but she knew that he must know. This was a total setup. He frowned at her. Oh, no, did he not know? She glanced at Tara, who looked just as severe. Uh-oh.

Oz opened his mouth to speak, but Mel caught him with an elbow in the ribs. She didn't know if Mr. Perry knew that Uncle Stan was her uncle and she didn't want to enlighten him. Oz looked at her in question and she shook her head ever so slightly. Oz frowned but he said nothing.

"That's quite an allegation, Sam," Mr. Perry said. "Care to back it up?"

Sweat was beading up on Sam's brow now. Mel didn't feel bad for him one little bit. She looked at Uncle Stan, who was watching the young man with interest. Sam's eyes tracked to Oz's locker but he didn't say anything.

"What did Mrs. Perry tell you to say, Sam?" Mel asked. She made her tone friendly.

Everyone turned to look at her but she maintained eye contact with Sam. He swallowed. She looked closely and could see his fingers were trembling.

"No . . . nothing," Sam said. "She didn't say anything. I don't know what you're talking about."

"Really?" Mel asked. "Because she told the parking attendant Larry that Oz wasn't allowed on the premises anymore, but according to Mr. Perry that wasn't true, so it seems there's a lot of misinformation being scattered about."

"She has nothing to do with any of this," Sam said.

Mr. Perry pursed his lips and then turned to Tara. "Detective Martinez, would you be so kind as to go and fetch my wife?"

With a nod Tara slipped from the room. Now Sam looked panicked and he said, "No, that's not necessary. Just open his locker and you'll see. You'll have all the evidence you need."

Oz's eyes went wide and he looked at Uncle Stan, who said, "Go ahead, Oz, open the locker."

Sam blew out a breath of relief. It was short-lived.

As Oz opened the locker, Mel asked, "Oz, where did you get that lock?"

"Sam gave it to me when mine went missing," he said. "He said it was an extra."

"It was," Sam said. "People leave and forget to take them and we have spares. Happens all the time."

"How many keys did it come with?" Mel asked Oz.

"Just one," he said. He used the key on his key ring and unfastened the lock, taking it off.

"Don't locks usually come with two?" she asked her uncle. He nodded.

"So, if someone else had the second key, they could get into Oz's locker," Mr. Perry said.

"There was no second key!" Sam insisted. His voice was shrill and Mel exchanged a look with Uncle Stan.

"Did my husband say why he wanted me?" a woman's voice asked.

They all turned to the door as Kasey Perry was escorted into the room by Tara. She took in the scene at a glance and tightened the belt on her pool cover-up. Her hair was piled high, she was wearing kitten-heeled mules and sunglasses. It was clear she had been poolside. Mel was surprised only that she wasn't carrying a margarita.

"All right, I'm here, what do you want?" Kasey asked.

Her gaze lingered on Oz. Mel fought the urge to stand in front of him and protect him from her. Kasey's attention then moved to Mel. She didn't look happy to see her.

"My dear, so good of you to join us," Clay said. "It seems Sam here believes that Oz has committed murder."

"What does that have to do with me?" Kasey studied her manicure before glancing at him with a bored expression.

No one said anything. Mel felt the tension in the room

thicken as husband and wife stared at each other. Mel glanced at Uncle Stan. He met her gaze and one eyebrow lifted ever so slightly. He wanted her to say something.

"I can answer that question," Mel said.

Every gaze turned towards her, and Oz began to shake his head frantically back and forth. Mel frowned at him.

"Please, don't," he said.

"Relax," she whispered. "I've got this."

"Oh, god," Oz muttered.

"Our story begins—" Mel began but Uncle Stan cleared his throat, interrupting her. "All right, fine. Here's the short version."

Mel paced over to the locker. She pointed up at the bloody hat stuffed in the top of the locker.

"Can either of you fine detectives remove that article of clothing from the top shelf?"

Tara rolled her eyes but proceeded to pull on latex gloves and produced an evidence bag from a pocket inside her jacket. They all watched as she carefully pulled the hat from the locker. The smell was enough to gag even the strongest of stomachs.

Kasey clapped her hand over her nose. "What is that gross smell?"

"At a guess, I'd say the sourdough starter that hasn't been fed and has gone bad. Very bad," Mel said.

Tara opened the hat. It was a traditional chef's hat and, sure enough, inside was a moldy white substance that smelled rancid.

"What the hell?" Oz cried. "Who did that to my hat?"

"Are you sure it's yours?" Mel asked.

"It was in my locker," Oz said. "And why is it bloody?"

"Because whoever murdered Gallway used what they

had at hand," Mel said. "And according to what you've told me about that afternoon, what they had was their hat as you were prepping for the dinner shift and several bowls of sourdough waiting to be made into bread. With Gallway blacked out on the floor of the kitchen, it was a simple matter to scoop some sourdough into the hat, stuff it into his mouth, and pinch off his nose, causing him to suffocate. I bet they found bruising around the nose and mouth and those bloodshot eyes you saw weren't from drinking but rather from being suffocated."

Oz put his fist to his mouth. "I think I might be sick."

Mr. Perry looked a little green as well and he said, "You've given us the how. Any idea on the who or the why?"

Mel strolled forward until she was standing in front of Kasey. She met the woman's gaze and asked, "Do you want to tell him or should I?"

"Tell him what?" she asked. "I have no idea what any of this means."

She held her arms wide as if she couldn't imagine why she was in the staff area to begin with, never mind discussing murder. Mel figured the ingenue thing had probably worked well for her in her youth, but now she was a mature woman and playing the vapid, silly wife just didn't sell as well.

"Mr. Perry, I am sorry to inform you that your wife is having an affair," Mel said.

He frowned, looking displeased. "I know about Gallway. It was over a long time ago."

Mel shook her head. "It isn't Gallway."

His eyes flicked around the room and landed on Oz. He looked grim.

"It isn't Oz, either," Mel said.

"Then who?"

Mel tipped her head to the side. Clay followed the direction.

"Him? Sam?" He barked out a laugh. "He's a boy."

"I'm twenty-two," Sam protested.

"Which makes you half her—"

"Enough!" Kasey interrupted her husband. "I refuse to stand here and listen to these ridiculous accusations. A man suffocated with bread dough, me having an affair with a boy, it's preposterous. And you have no proof."

She turned to leave and Mel let her get almost to the door when she said, "Except I do have proof."

Kasey stopped in her tracks and slowly turned to face Mel. She did not look the least bit nervous, making Mel feel a sliver of doubt. No, no, no. She was positive about this, and she just needed to present it that way.

"You know what they say about a lie?" she asked the room. "They say to keep it as close to the truth as possible so that it's easy to remember."

She felt the weight of Uncle Stan's stare and Clay Perry's, as well. She needed to deliver the answer clearly and concisely. No pressure.

"When Oz asked Mrs. Perry why she said she was having an affair with him, she admitted that she'd lied and explained it away as a joke, that she was really poolside the day Gallway was murdered, as her receipts would show."

"Really?" Kasey asked. "We're doing this again?"

"Yes, because while Oz and I were at the pool, the one thing I noticed was that you refused to sign the receipt for your drink," Mel said. "Your hands were oily, you said.

Your waiter was not surprised so this tells me that you never sign your receipts, which means you don't have any proof that you were poolside at the time of Chef Miles's murder."

Kasey tossed her head. "That's it? A lack of receipts?"

"You told the police you were having an affair with Oz but you weren't," Mel said. "Instead, it was with Sam, another young male chef. Keep it close to the truth." Mel turned to look at Sam. "Right, Tiger?"

He paled. She turned back to Kasey.

"Ridiculous," Kasey muttered. She glanced at her husband and away, as if to gauge his reaction. He looked furious. Kasey never looked at Sam. Mel did. The look on his face was imploring. Mel felt awful but she had to keep going.

"You see, this way she admitted that she was having an affair with a young man, but instead of telling us who it really was, she lied and said it was Oz to keep the suspicion off of Sam," Mel said. "But this keeping it close to the truth is where she really tripped herself up."

Mel paused. Everyone was watching her. Oz looked like he might faint, but he didn't interrupt.

"She said that Oz said he was going to kill Miles Gallway so that he could move up to executive chef and provide for her in the way she was accustomed. Another obvious lie since Oz is a pastry chef and has no interest in being in charge of the main kitchen."

"That's true," Oz chimed in. "I really don't want that job."

Clay nodded as if this was not new news to him. Mel glanced at Uncle Stan, who appeared to have relaxed a little bit, as in maybe he trusted her to bring this home.

"But her lover did make such a vow to her," Mel said. She waited for the protest. There was none. Kasey just watched her with narrowed eyes and Mel knew if looks could kill, she'd be deader than the sourdough in the hat. She decided to shake things up.

Mel whirled on Sam, who was watching everything as if he were a bystander and not a player. "What exactly did you promise her, Sam? That you'd provide for her as well as Mr. Perry? Did you really think you'd be able to step into Miles's job when you don't have anywhere near enough experience and you have Ashley already ahead of you in line for that job? Or was that why Simon was here? To hire Ashley for the Foodie Channel and clear the path for you? Did you really think Kasey would be all right with the paltry salary you'd make as an executive chef? Look at her and look at you—how did you think this was ever going to work? Or did you have your eye on something even bigger? Were you planning to be Simon's discovery, the rock star super chef of the Foodie Channel?"

Sam's eyes went huge and his red face looked as if it had been scalded by boiling water.

"No! I didn't think any of those things," he protested. "That's not what happened at all. Kasey wanted me to kill Mr. Perry, but Chef Miles overheard us and started blackmailing her. She told me I had to kill Chef to keep him from telling Mr. Perry, but I panicked. I couldn't do it. Then I walked into the banquet kitchen and saw Sarah . . ."

Sam's voice broke and Mel had to fight to keep her voice even. "You saw?"

Sam hung his head. "Yeah. I saw her hit Gallway and I called Kasey. She told me to finish him off, but I didn't . . . I couldn't . . ."

"So Kasey arrived in the kitchen and did it herself," Mel said.

The room was dead silent as everyone waited for Sam to confirm or deny.

"Yes, she did. She told me to get him into the pastry kitchen, so I offered to help Gallway with his head wound. He was holding a cloth to his head and he had the meat tenderizer in his other hand. He was ranting and raving about Sarah. He said he was going to kill her when he found her."

Sam paused to swallow. A tear slipped out. Mel could not find it in herself to feel sorry for him.

"Kasey arrived in the kitchen and pretended to help him. Instead, she took the wooden mallet and clobbered him."

"Lies!" Kasey screeched. No one paid her any attention.

"Gallway collapsed on the floor but he was still breathing, so Kasey grabbed Oz's beanie and stuffed it in his mouth, but he could still breathe so she grabbed a fistful of the bread dough that was rising, stuffed it in his hat and stuffed the whole thing back in his mouth, pinching off his nose until he suffocated."

"Shut up, Sam, shut up!" Kasey cried. "I'm telling you this is all lies. Ridiculous lies!"

"Why did you put the hat in Oz's locker?" Mel asked.

"When he found the body . . ." Sam shrugged.

"I was the perfect frame, because Gallway and I had already had a very public argument," Oz said.

"Yeah," Sam agreed. He didn't meet Oz's gaze.

"You gave her the other key to Oz's locker," Mel said. She tipped her head to the side. Then she looked at Uncle

Stan. "You might want to ask how many other people's locks have gone 'missing.'"

Sam hung his head. He mumbled something. Mel could barely make it out and when she did, she was filled with a mixture of contempt and pity for the young man.

"She said she loved me," he said.

"I never!" Kasey snapped. "As if I could ever love you."

"I think we've heard enough," Mr. Perry said. "Detectives, if you'd like to escort my wife off the premises, I'd be obliged."

Tara went to take her arm, but Kasey yanked her elbow out of her grasp and whirled around to face Mel.

"You think you're so clever, don't you?" she asked. She looked Mel up and down, clearly finding her wanting. "Well, this is all speculation and you can't prove anything."

"No, but I'm betting the police lab can," Mel said. "Your DNA is going to be all over that hat and the dough residue and Miles's body. I'll bet your hair and body oil is all tangled up in this."

"You—" Kasey came at Mel with her nails out. Tara stepped forward and grabbed her around the waist, for which Mel was grateful.

"So what if I killed him?" Kasey hissed. She struggled as Tara secured a pair of cuffs around her wrists. "He was trying to blackmail me. *Me!*"

Mel leaned away from Kasey on the off chance she broke Tara's hold and charged her. Still, she knew this was her opportunity to turn Kasey's rage against her.

"You killed Chef Miles when he was already wounded to get out from under the blackmail," she said. "Then you roped your lover, Sam, into helping you frame Oz by hiding the evidence in his locker. Is that about right?"

Kasey answered her with a string of curses that made Mel's ears bleed.

"Keeping it classy, I see," Clay said. He shook his head at his wife and then turned to Tara. "Get her out of here, Detective. I'll follow in my own car shortly."

Tara took Kasey by the arm and hauled her from the staff room. The collective tension level dropped as soon as she was out of sight.

"I'm going to need you to come with me and give a full statement, Sam." Uncle Stan said.

"All right." Sam glanced at Oz. "I'm really sorry, man."

Oz stared at him. "I'll have your locker packed up for you and sent to your home. If you ever step into my kitchen again, I'll break your hands."

"Oz." Uncle Stan's tone was a warning.

Oz ignored him, staring down his sous chef. "Am I clear?"

"Yeah." Sam nodded.

Uncle Stan led him away but paused at the door and said, "I'll need official statements from the two of you."

"Of course, we're right behind you," Mel said.

Uncle Stan stared at her and asked, "When did you figure it all out?"

"The Beast," she said. He looked mystified and she explained, "Oz came back to the kitchen to feed the Beast the day that Miles was murdered, but one of the bowls of dough that his bread guy, Tomas, left out to rise, didn't. Why wouldn't it if it came from the same batch as the other two? Also, Sarah said she didn't smell alcohol on

Miles, but Oz said his eyes were bloodshot. Suffocation does that to the eyes. That's when I suspected someone had used the sourdough to suffocate Chef Miles. The smell coming from the hat in the locker confirmed it. They didn't just murder Miles, they murdered the starter, too."

Stan blinked at her. Then he shook his head and said, "Chefs are weird," leaving Mel and Oz in the staff room with Clay.

"Well, Oz, I don't suppose I can convince you to take your old job back," he said.

Oz shrugged. It was clear he was feeling pretty shell-shocked.

At that moment, Simon Marconi walked into the room. "Oz, my man, I just heard they caught Miles's killer. Do you have a sec? I'd like to talk to you about your future."

Oz turned to Mel. "Save me."

"Always," she said.

Nineteen

"I'm going to cry," Joyce said. "I know it. I'm just going to wail and ruin the whole day."

"Mom, it's okay," Mel said. "You want to cry, cry, no one will judge you."

"It's just that I've waited sooooo long for you to marry dear Joe," Joyce said. She dabbed her nose with a tissue. "I truly never thought it would actually happen."

"Is this your pre-wedding pep talk?" Mel asked. "I have to say it needs work."

"Oh, you." Joyce waved her tissue at Mel, but she stopped crying and smiled before she moved to talk to Judi, the wedding coordinator, who was keeping them all on task.

They were standing in the church's anteroom reserved for brides. Dressed and ready to go, in her wedding gown and veil, Mel had to admit that for the first time in her life, she felt like a princess. Alma had crushed it—not literally—and the dress was perfection, everything Mel had imagined it would be and more. Mel's bouquet was a cluster of soft blue hydrangeas surrounded by sunset roses, pale yellow with deep coral along the edges, and she loved that they were cheerful.

Angie was in a charming empire-waist dress in the same shade of blue as the flowers with silver embroidery along the hem that accentuated her dark hair, which she had in a half-up-half-down style that framed her heart-shaped face becomingly. She was carrying a smaller bouquet that matched Mel's, but at the moment she'd plopped it on top of her tummy while she fussed with a pin in her hair.

"I have to say this is kind of handy," she said. "It's like a built-in shelf."

Mel laughed.

Standing beside Angie, and also laughing, was Mel's brother, Charlie. He and his two sons had worn tuxedos with yellow roses for boutonnieres and acted as ushers for the day. Now that the guests were settled in their seats, the boys were sitting with their mother, Nancy, in the family pew. Mel was still in shock that her oldest nephew was almost the same height as his dad.

"You look beautiful, Sis," Charlie said. "Dad would be so proud."

He had a suspicious glint in his eye and Mel stepped close to hug him tight. Even though he lived in Flagstaff, they'd always been very close, sticking up for each other at school as kids and grieving their father together when he passed. For the past decade, they'd shared the responsibility of looking after Joyce, who had been bereft when Charlie Cooper, Sr., had left them much too soon.

"Thanks, Charlie," she said. "That means a lot."

He nodded. He glanced over her shoulder and jerked his chin at their uncle Stan, who was standing with their mother. He was also in a tuxedo and he looked very dashing next to Joyce in her pale pink, fitted lace dress with a matching silk jacket. She had always been a stunner and she didn't disappoint now. No wonder Uncle Stan was smitten, although Mel knew he'd say it was her meat loaf that had reeled him in.

"Do you think they're next?" Charlie asked.

"I don't know," she said. "How would you feel about it?"

Charlie adjusted his glasses as he considered. "It feels right."

Mel smiled. "I think so, too."

Judi clapped her hands to get their attention. "All right, people, take your places. It's time to begin."

Judi, petite but forceful, lined everyone up, fussing with the men's jackets, the women's dresses, making sure everything was just so.

"Cuz, are you all right?" she asked. She was fluffing Angie's skirt. "You look sweaty. You're not nervous, are you?"

"No," Angie said. She thumped her chest with her fist. "Just a teeny bit of heartburn."

"Gotcha covered." Uncle Stan handed her an antacid tablet from the roll he always carried. She popped it in her mouth and smiled her thanks.

Since Tate was standing up for Joe, it was agreed that Charlie would escort Angie. Given her advanced pregnancy, no one wanted her to walk unescorted down the aisle on the off chance there was a slip, a trip, or a mishap. Angie looped her hand through Charlie's arm as they moved into position in the doorway.

Mel moved to stand behind them with Joyce on one side and Uncle Stan on the other. She put her hand through Uncle Stan's arm and clutched her bouquet with that hand while reaching out and taking her mother's hand in hers.

She took a second to stare at the ceiling. Did he know? Could he see them? Was he happy for her? Mel wished, quite desperately, that she could have just one more moment, a hug, a laugh, or even a smile with her dad.

"Are we ready?" Judi asked.

"Hold up," Uncle Stan said. "I almost forgot."

He reached into his pocket and asked, "Hey, kid, do you already have something old?"

"We forgot!" Angie cried. "You borrowed your mom's dress, your bouquet is blue, and your shoes are new, but—ack!—we don't have anything old. I'm a terrible matron of honor."

"No worries. Again, I've got you covered," Uncle Stan said. He pulled a delicate diamond bracelet out of his pocket.

Mel looked at Joyce, who was staring at the bracelet with wide eyes. "Is that?"

"My mother's?" Uncle Stan asked. "Yes. I got it out of the family vault a few days ago."

"Oh, Stan," Joyce sighed. She watered up, blinking hard and trying not to cry.

"Mel, when your grandmother passed away, your dad and I had to sort her things," Uncle Stan said. "This bracelet was the one our father gave to her for their twentieth anniversary. She never took it off. When Charlie and I packed it away, we agreed that on the day you got married, it would become yours. When you miss your dad, as I know you must be missing him today, look at your wrist and know that he's with you. He's always with you, Mel, and he loves you so very much."

And there it was. The sign. She glanced up at the ceiling, blinking hard, and said, "Thanks, Dad. I love you, too."

She held out her wrist and Uncle Stan fastened the bracelet for her. Her throat was tight and a few tears slipped down her cheeks. She glanced at the others and saw they were equally choked up. Mel let go of her mother's hand and hugged Uncle Stan.

"I'm so glad you're here," she said.

"Me, too, kid," he said. "I know I'm not your dad—"

"No, you're my bonus dad," Mel said. She leaned back to look at him. "You didn't have to step in like you have over the past ten years but you did. You've been more than an uncle to me, and I'm so grateful. I love you, Uncle Stan."

Uncle Stan stared at the ground. He cleared his throat a few times. When he glanced up, a few tears slipped free and he swiped them away.

"I feel the same way, Uncle Stan," Charlie said. He stepped forward and hugged him and they thumped each other on the shoulders in that manly way men do. Then Charlie grinned and asked, "So, can I borrow the car tonight?"

Uncle Stan laughed and the rest of them did, too. The moment passed, and Judi, with an obvious lump in her throat, directed them to their places. Angie glanced over her shoulder at Mel and grinned. "Just think, in a few minutes, we'll actually be sisters!"

Mel returned her smile. She couldn't think of anyone she'd rather have for a sis. With a grunt, Angie turned back around. Mel frowned. Poor Angie—of all the times to have a heartburn attack, this was not ideal.

Judi signaled them to move forward. Mel could hear the organ playing and tightened her grip on Uncle Stan and her mom. This was it. Judi opened the door, the music swelled, and she gestured for Charlie and Angie to go. They exchanged a smile and disappeared into the church. Mel could feel her heart pounding. It took her a moment to realize it wasn't nerves, it was excitement. She was marrying Joe DeLaura. It felt as if she had dreamed of this moment her entire life.

"I love you, baby," Joyce whispered in her ear. Mel turned and looked at the woman who had stood by her side for every success and failure, every heartbreak and dream achieved. She leaned her head against her mother's for just a moment.

"I love you, too, Mom," she said. They took a few seconds to look at each other with love and appreciation, and then Judi was signaling them forward.

Uncle Stan and Joyce matched their steps to Mel's and the three of them entered the church. The guests rose to their feet and Mel looked down the aisle and felt her heart swell. Joe stood there, looking impossibly handsome in his tuxedo. Mel was positively dizzy at the sight of him. When his gaze met hers, it was so full of love, she knew that no one had ever looked at her like Joe DeLaura did, as if she was his everything.

Uncle Stan set a slow and steady pace. So many faces that she held dear surrounded them. As they walked down the aisle, she took a moment to take them all in.

The entire DeLaura family was there. Ray was on the aisle, sobbing quite loudly. Mel looked past him at his date, Tara Martinez, who shrugged. She and Mel exchanged a smile. It was the first time Mel had ever seen the detective smile, and she realized she was quite pretty.

Manny Martinez, Tara's cousin, was there with Holly Hartzmark and her daughter, Sidney. Manny looked happy, and Mel was delighted to have them here. He winked at her when she walked by and Mel grinned. Oz sat right behind the family pew with Marty and his girlfriend, Olivia. Mel was relieved to see that Oz looked well rested, as if he'd finally gotten some sleep. Marty was dabbing at his eyes with a handkerchief while Olivia gently patted his back. Maybe Angie's softening towards Olivia had caused a cosmic shift in their relationship. Mel didn't know, but she realized it would have felt odd not to have Olivia in attendance. Weird.

When they reached the altar, the music faded and all Mel could see was Joe.

"Who gives this woman to this man?"

"Her uncle and I do," Joyce answered.

Mel hugged them both and Uncle Stan escorted Joyce to their pew, where they sat with Charlie and his family. Mel handed her bouquet to Angie, who smiled at her, and then Mel clasped hands with Joe. Father Francis, whom Mel had known for years through the DeLaura family, beamed down at them. He was always smiling, and Mel couldn't think of a better man to perform their celebration of matrimony.

The words poured over them in a swirl of hopeful blessings and prayer. Mel stole glances at Joe every now and then, and each time she found him looking at her with an expression of wonder that she knew was reflected in her own eyes. They were finally really doing this.

With Father Francis guiding them, Mel and Joe declared their consent. Mel heard a small noise behind her, something between a groan and a gasp, and she glanced over her shoulder at Angie, who held both bouquets cradled in one arm, while holding a tissue to her nose. Poor thing, her pregnancy was probably making her overly emotional. Mel smiled at her and Angie gave her a weak one in return.

Mel turned back to Joe for the vows. He stated his with warmth and affection, but Mel, feeling a bit overwhelmed by her feelings for him, found that her voice quavered as she was a bit undone by how much she loved him and how happy she was to be marrying him. It was too much. When a tear slipped down her cheek, Joe tenderly reached up and brushed it away. He held her gaze and suddenly it was just the two of them. Mel spoke directly to him and her voice was sure and strong, just as she knew their marriage would be.

Then it was time for the blessing of the rings. Father Francis took the rings from Tate and Angie. Mel glanced at Angie's face and noticed that she looked a bit pale and rather sweaty. She probably needed to sit down.

"Go ahead and sit down if you need to," Mel whispered.

"I can have someone bring you a chair," Father Francis offered.

"No," Angie said. Her voice was tight and she smiled through gritted teeth. "I'm fine. Please, continue."

Tate peered around Mel and Joe at his wife, his face creased with worry. She waved him off and Mel looked at Joe. Something was going on with Angie. They needed to move this along.

They slid the rings on, and just as Father Francis was about to pronounce them husband and wife, Angie let loose a howl and doubled over.

"Oh, dear," Father Francis said.

Tate abandoned his post to go to his wife.

"I'm fine, really," Angie panted. Her face was red, she was sweating. She reached out for Tate and hissed, "Give me your jacket."

Mel turned to help, but Joe tugged her back around. Angie let out another moan and there was the sound of running water. Angie's water had broken. Right now!

Joe looked at the priest and said, "'Man and wife. Say man and wife.'"

"*Princess Bride*," Marty identified the movie quote from his seat. Oz hushed him.

"I now pronounce you husband and wife," Father Francis said.

Joe kissed Mel and then spun her around so they were facing Tate and Angie. Angie was standing over Tate's jacket, which she had strategically dropped on the floor below her.

"You okay, Ange?" Joe asked. She nodded, clearly lying as she leaned back against Tate, obviously in so much pain she couldn't speak. Joe looked at Tate. "The limo is waiting right outside. Let's use it to take her to the hospital."

Tate leapt into action, scooping Angie up in his arms and hurrying down the aisle with her.

"I can walk," Angie insisted.

"Not on my watch," Tate said. Mel and Joe fell in behind them, and Joe called back over his shoulder, "Change of plans, everyone, we're going to the hospital."

Father Francis called the final blessing over them as they bustled from the church with their wedding guests following in their wake.

The limo driver's eyes were huge when Tate arrived with Angie in his arms. Joe and Mel opened the doors and Tate assisted Angie into the vehicle, helping her to lie down on one of the long seats, using his lap as a pillow. He tenderly brushed the hair from her face and said, "I'm here. I've got you. It's going to be all right."

"My water broke in the sanctuary," Angie said. "That's bad form, isn't it?"

"Or it's the most blessed birth ever," Tate said.

"Let's go with that," she said. Her face scrunched up as a contraction hit.

Joe told the driver which hospital to go to and they were off. Angie started to pant, her face went an alarming shade of gray, and her dress became soaked in sweat. When the contraction passed, she turned to look at Mel and then she started to cry.

"I ruined your wedding."

Mel left her seat with Joe and knelt on the floor in front of Angie and clutched her hand in hers. "No, you didn't," she said. "You are the very best matron of honor and I'm so glad you're mine."

"You have to just dump us off at the hospital and then go on to your reception," Angie said. Her grip on Mel's hand was fierce. "Promise me."

"I promise we'll go on to the reception," Mel said.

Thankfully, another contraction hit before Angie caught on that Mel had not said where or when they were going on to the reception. As far as she was concerned, the reception was dusted and done. There was absolutely no way she was leaving her best friend while she gave birth to her first child.

Tate looked about as frazzled as Mel had ever seen him. He called their doctor and she promised to meet them at the hospital. The drive was mercifully short as the hospital was in the neighborhood. Still, it gave them an opportunity to time Angie's contractions, which seemed to be getting stronger and closer together. Once they arrived, Joe rushed into the hospital to get a wheelchair while Mel and Tate assisted Angie out of the limousine. The driver said he'd park and wait.

Angie's doctor, a middle-aged woman with short hair and glasses and dressed in tennis clothes, met them at the door as she was just arriving. She took in their clothes at a glance and said, "Congratulations."

"Thanks," Joe said. "My sister—"

He seemed to run out of words, and the doctor said, "Don't worry. I will make sure she has the very best care." She looked at Angie and Tate and said, "All right, parents, let's meet our baby. Yes?"

Tate and Angie exchanged a look and then nodded. There was fear and excitement on their faces. Mel hugged Angie tight, and then Tate wheeled her away. As the doors closed behind them, Mel slumped against Joe.

"I'm scared," she said.

"I know, but this is Angie," he said. "She's the feistiest person I know."

"You're right," Mel said. "It'll be fine."

They rode up the elevator to the maternity ward and found the small family waiting room, where Joe called his parents to let them know what was happening. His mother promised to tell the others, including Mel's family, which was great because Mel had run out of the church and didn't have her phone or anything. Mel sat down, expecting the family to start pouring in. Thirty minutes passed. Then an hour.

"Aren't they coming?" she asked. "I mean, they didn't just go ahead to the reception at the Sun Dial, did they?"

Joe shrugged. "They said they're on their way."

He laced his fingers with hers and looked at the wedding ring on her finger. "Hey, you're my wife."

Mel reached over and took his free hand in hers and ran her index finger over his wedding ring. "And you're my husband."

The words made something warm bloom inside her chest. This feeling right here, of loving someone with every breath she took and knowing he felt the same way, this was what the songwriters and poets meant when they wrote about true love. She smiled at him and he pulled her close and kissed her.

"Excuse me."

They broke apart to find a nurse peering around the doorway at them. She was smiling. "The doctor said to tell you that she expects the delivery will take a couple of hours yet. She suggested you go get something to eat. The father said he'll call you if anything changes."

"Thank you," Joe and Mel said together.

The nurse nodded and turned to leave, then she popped back in the doorway and said, "Congratulations!"

Mel and Joe grinned and thanked her again.

"What do you think?" he asked. "Should we go see what the dessert menu looks like?"

"I hope they have something more than toxic-colored gelatin," Mel said. "All this stress makes me want to eat an entire chocolate cake by myself."

"I'm sure they must have donuts at the very least," he said.

They rode down the elevator and Mel pretended not to notice the hospital staff and patients staring at them as they passed. Was she overdressed for the occasion? Yes, but what was a girl to do? Her best friend was having a baby, and she wasn't going to miss it.

The cafeteria at the hospital sounded crowded. She hesitated for a moment, wondering if she really wanted to wear her wedding gown into a room full of people eating off trays.

"There's a big outdoor courtyard beyond the main dining room," Joe said. "We can sit out there. I'll double back and get us some food."

"Okay, but let's find a corner where I can hide myself," she said. "We probably should have ditched the wedding duds and changed into scrubs or hospital johnnies. People probably think we're escaped mental patients."

Joe led her across the cafeteria. Sure enough, everyone stared. Mel smiled and waved, pretending this was all perfectly normal. When they stepped outside, music began to play.

Mel's jaw hit the ground. Her gaze swept across the courtyard, which had several big trees and large tables, at which the guests from their wedding were seated in all of their finery. As she stood there, taking it all in, Ray DeLaura stood up and started clapping. The rest of the guests joined in. Mel turned to Joe.

"What? How?" she asked.

"The DeLaura brothers to the rescue," he said.

Mel glanced around the courtyard again. Everyone was here: their parents, families, and friends. She felt her throat get tight. She and Joe couldn't make it to the reception, so their people had brought the party here. She glanced around the space until she saw her mother. Joyce greeted Mel with a hug and handed her the purse Mel had left in the church.

"This space will do nicely," Joyce said with a smile and Mel laughed. Joyce was going to have her mother-of-the-bride day after all.

Oz's amazing cupcake tower was set up on a table. The floral centerpieces that she'd ordered for the resort tables had been brought here, too. Joe led her through the tables and they greeted their friends while she took it all in. It was then that Mel noticed Sarah Lincoln arrive in her chef whites with carts of food that had been boxed. She paused beside Mel and Joe.

"The banquet chef and I agreed that the food for your wedding shouldn't go to waste, so we boxed it and I brought it over," she said. "Consider it my thank-you."

Before Mel could say a word, Sarah wheeled the cart across the courtyard and began to set up a serving station next to Oz's cupcake tower.

"Mrs. DeLaura, may I have this dance?" Joe asked.

Then he held out his arms and Mel stepped into them. The small band that they'd hired for the resort was playing on one side of the courtyard and an area in front of them had been cleared for dancing. As Joe twirled her around the stone floor, Mel couldn't think of any place that could be better than this.

She danced with Uncle Stan and then worked her way through the DeLaura brothers and her new father-in-law. She was enjoying a glass of lemonade when she noted Oz standing off by himself. Knowing how he felt about her, she wondered if she should just let him be, but that wasn't who they were.

She sidled up next to him where he was monitoring the cupcake tower and asked, "Dance?"

Oz looked painfully uncomfortable but nodded and followed Mel out to the crowded dance floor. As they danced, she looked up at him and asked, "How are you?"

He gave her a closed-lip smile and said, "I'm happy for you and Joe."

Mel grinned. "Thank you. I'm sorry about you and Lupe, but I know you'll find your someone out there someday."

"Maybe," Oz said. He sounded doubtful, but Mel let it go.

They worked their way around the floor, passing Uncle Stan and Joyce, Ray and Tara, as well as Manny and Holly. Mel felt a surge of joy. It was pretty great to have the gang all together.

"Have you figured out what you're going to do?" she asked Oz.

He hesitated for a second and then said, "Yes."

Mel stared at him. She wanted to support whatever he chose, but she really didn't want him to go too far from home.

"I've signed a contract with Simon to do twelve shows, to be filmed at the Sun Dial, featuring me as a pastry chef, making my specialties," he said.

Mel stumbled but he caught her before she fell. She stared at him, trying to grasp what he'd just said. "You're going to be on the Foodie Channel?"

"Yes," Oz confirmed. Then he laughed. "It's crazy, right?"

"It's amazing," Mel said. She hugged him tight and then pulled back to look him in the eye. "If you're happy, I'm happy."

"I'm happy," he assured her, and Mel believed him.

Marty appeared at Oz's side and cut in. Mel told Oz they would talk more later and he seemed okay with that. Wow, Oz was going to be a star—of that she had no doubt. Mel made it around the floor only once with Marty when Olivia cut in, which was fine, because Mel was getting tired and she wanted to be with her husband. She checked her phone for the thousandth time. There was no word from Tate. She tried not to worry.

The band downshifted to background music while everyone ate their meals out of the brown paper boxes with utensils borrowed from the hospital. There was laughter and chatter and they all waved to the hospital staff, patients, and visitors who watched them through the windows that looked onto the courtyard. Tony De-Laura took it upon himself to pass out some of the extra Jordan almond wedding favors to the onlookers.

When Joyce saw him, she turned to Mel and said, "See? It always helps to have extra."

Joe checked his phone about every ten minutes while the DeLaura family took turns going up to the delivery floor to pace the waiting room while they waited for word.

Mel saw Emily Harper and Maria DeLaura, grandmothers-to-be, reach out and hold hands every now and then, as if reassuring each other that all would be well. Mel and Joe bit into the delectable bride and groom cupcakes Oz had created while the rest of the cupcakes were passed out to the delight of the guests. Oz's creations had serious wow factor, and Mel knew that the response was exactly what his battered chef soul needed right now.

And then it came. All at once it seemed every cell phone at the party chimed with an incoming text. It read. *She's here! Mother and baby are doing fine!* A video was attached, and everyone scrambled to open the file. Joe held up his phone so he and Mel could watch it together.

A wizened little face peeked out of a blue-and-pink-striped baby blanket. As they watched, she let out a howl that could have peeled paint. The camera panned up to Angie, who gave the baby an exhausted smile. In a gentle mama voice, she said, "Oh, you're mine, all right." Then she kissed the baby's head and waved to the camera.

Tate's face appeared and it was clear from his red nose and damp cheeks that he'd been crying. In a voice that was hoarse, he said, "My incredible, amazing, courageous, brave, and beautiful wife and I would like to introduce you to our daughter." He paused, clearly too choked up to speak. He glanced away then gathered himself after a moment and said, "Welcome, Emari, named for her grandmothers, Emily Harper and Maria DeLaura. Isn't she beautiful?"

He panned back to the baby, who squinted at them through puffy eyes, then opened her mouth and let out another bellow. Tate grinned like a fool in love and Angie laughed. The video ended on the three of them, huddled together on the bed, a happy little family.

Mel hugged Joe and he kissed her head and the rest of the wedding guests hugged and cheered and cried and clapped. The grandparents all headed to the elevator to see their new granddaughter while Marty took up a glass and toasted the newest member of the Fairy Tale Cupcakes bakery crew.

They toasted the baby, the parents, and everything else they could think of, from Ray's shiny suit to Oz's amazing cupcakes. While everyone was occupied toasting and cheering, Joe pulled Mel aside and said, "Let's get out of here, Mrs. Cupcake."

"Okay, Mr. Cupcake," she said. And she knew as she followed him out the door to their waiting limousine that she was stepping into a brand-new life, and she couldn't wait to get started.

Acknowledgments

There are always so many people to thank, but I want to begin with the readers. This series has succeeded because of all of you who have championed every book and enjoyed being in the Fairy Tale Cupcakes bakery with me and the crew. I can't thank you enough for loving the books as much as you do, and I'm looking forward to many more adventures together! Extra high fives and love to the Fans of Jenn McKinlay and McKinlays Mavens on Facebook. Your encouragement and enthusiasm makes this writing gig even more fun.

Special thanks to my editor, Kate Seaver, and my agent, Christina Hogrebe. Your encouragement keeps me excited about my work and on track when I get distracted, your input is always fantastic, and I'd be lost without either of you. Many thanks to Mary Geren, who keeps me on task, and to Jessica Mangicaro and Brittanie Black, who enthusiastically shine a light on all of my books. You two are aces! Also, a shout-out to the art department. You are amazing and I am thrilled to have such talent grace my covers.

And here's more thanks to the many folks behind the scenes. I am so fortunate to have the support and wisdom of my plot group buddies, Kate Carlisle and Paige Shelton.

They make me a better writer. Huge thanks to my author assistant, Christie Conlee, aka my magical dancing unicorn. She really is magical and since we have entire conversations in gif, I can say unequivocally that "she gets me."

Lastly, much love and appreciation to my families—the McKinlays and the Orfs—and my friends. I know I am always on deadline, forget things, have no idea what day it is, and am ridiculously consumed by my plots and subplots and assorted writing nonsense, but none of you have dumped me yet and for that I am ever grateful. I love you all.

Recipes

Chocolate Orange Cupcakes

A chocolate cake with a chocolate orange truffle
center and orange buttercream.

Chocolate Cupcakes

1⅓ cups flour
¼ teaspoon baking soda
2 teaspoons baking powder
¾ cup unsweetened cocoa powder
¼ teaspoon salt
4 tablespoons butter, softened
1½ cups sugar
2 eggs

1 teaspoon vanilla extract
1 cup milk

Preheat the oven to 350 degrees. Line two cupcake pans with paper liners. In a medium bowl, sift together the flour, baking soda, baking powder, cocoa, and salt and set aside. In a large bowl, cream the butter and sugar, adding the eggs one at a time. Mix in the vanilla. Add in the flour mixture alternately with the milk until well blended. Scoop the batter into paper liners just covering the bottom, place one frozen chocolate orange truffle in the center, then add more batter until each liner is two-thirds full. Bake for 18 to 22 minutes. Cool completely before frosting. Makes 14 cupcakes.

Chocolate Orange Truffles

1 can sweetened condensed milk
3 cups chocolate chips, melted
2 teaspoons orange extract

Line a pan with parchment paper. Whisk the condensed milk into the melted chocolate chips, the add the extract. Mixture will begin to get solid and hard to stir. Use a melon baller to scoop balls onto the prepared pan, and chill in the freezer for 1 hour.

Orange Buttercream Frosting

½ cup unsalted butter, softened
1 teaspoon vanilla extract

3 cups powdered sugar
1 teaspoon grated orange zest
2–3 tablespoons orange juice

In a large bowl, cream the butter and vanilla. Gradually add the sugar, 1 cup at a time, beating well on medium speed, adding the orange zest. Add the orange juice as needed. Scrape the sides of bowl often. Beat at medium speed until light and fluffy. Makes 2½ cups of icing.

Vanilla Sprinkle Cupcakes

A vanilla cake with a sprinkles surprise inside
topped with vanilla buttercream.

Vanilla Cupcakes

2½ teaspoons baking powder
¼ teaspoon salt
2½ cups flour
¾ cup butter, softened
1½ cups sugar
2 eggs
1½ teaspoons vanilla extract
1¼ cups milk
Sprinkles

Preheat the oven to 350 degrees. Line 24 muffin tins with paper liners. In a medium bowl, sift together the baking powder, salt, and flour. Set aside. In another bowl, cream the butter and sugar at medium speed, add the eggs, and beat until smooth. Beat in vanilla extract. Alternately add the dry ingredients and the milk, beating until smooth. Fill cupcake liners two-thirds full. Bake until golden brown, about 20 minutes. Once cool, use a melon baller to carve out the middle of each cupcake, and fill with sprinkles. Makes 24 cupcakes.

Vanilla Buttercream Frosting

½ cup (1 stick) salted butter, softened
½ cup (1 stick) unsalted butter, softened
1 teaspoon vanilla extract
4 cups sifted confectioners' sugar
2 tablespoons milk

In a large bowl, cream the butters. Add vanilla. Gradually add sugar, 1 cup at a time, beating well on medium speed, adding the milk as needed. Scrape the sides of bowl often. Beat at medium speed until light and fluffy. Keep bowl covered with a damp cloth until ready to use. Makes 3 cups of rosting.

Frost the tops of the cupcakes however you like and either roll the edges of the frosted cupcake in sprinkles, scatter them on top, or make a thick circle of sprinkles in the center of the frosting. Sprinkles will spill out of the middle when cupcake is cut or bitten into.

Chocolate Lava Cake Cupcakes

Chocolate cake with melted chocolate in the middle, can be frosted with buttercream or ganache—for this recipe, ganache was used.

Lava Center

¾ cup whipping cream
1½ cups semisweet chocolate chips

In a medium saucepan, heat the whipping cream on medium-high heat. Slowly add in the chocolate chips, stirring until the chips are melted and the mixture is smooth. Refrigerate for 1 hour, stirring occasionally. Mixture should thicken.

Chocolate Cupcakes

1⅓ cups all-purpose flour
¼ teaspoon baking soda
2 teaspoons baking powder
¾ cup unsweetened cocoa powder
⅛ teaspoon salt
3 tablespoons butter, softened
1½ cups sugar
2 eggs
¾ teaspoon vanilla extract
1 cup milk

Preheat the oven to 350 degrees. Line 12 muffin cups with paper liners. Sift together the flour, baking soda, baking powder, cocoa, and salt. Set aside. In a large bowl, cream together the butter and sugar until well blended. Add the eggs, one at a time, beating well after each addition, then stir in the vanilla. Add the flour mixture alternately with the milk; beat well. Scoop the batter into the cupcake liners until each is one-fourth full. Spoon the chilled lava center onto the batter and cover with remaining batter until the liners are two-thirds full. Bake for 18 to 20 minutes. Makes 12 cupcakes.

Ganache Frosting

¾ cup heavy cream
8 ounces dark chocolate chips
1 teaspoon vanilla extract
Pinch of sea salt

In a medium saucepan, bring the cream to a boil then remove it from the heat. Stir in the chocolate until it is melted and smooth, then stir in the vanilla and salt. Let the ganache stand at room temperature for 5 minutes, then move the ganache to the refrigerator and chill until it thickens and becomes shiny and spreadable. This could take anywhere from 15 to 30 minutes, depending on the temperature of your refrigerator.

Limoncello Cupcakes

Lemon-vanilla cupcakes with lemon curd in the
center and frosted with vanilla buttercream.

Lemon Vanilla Cupcakes

1 cup unsalted butter, softened
2 cups sugar
4 large eggs, room temperature
1/3 cup grated lemon zest
3 cups flour
1/2 teaspoon baking powder
1/2 teaspoon baking soda
1 teaspoon salt
1/4 cup fresh-squeezed lemon juice
3/4 cup buttermilk, room temperature
1 teaspoon vanilla extract

Preheat the oven to 350 degrees. Line 24 muffin cups with
paper liners. In a large bowl, cream the butter and sugar
until fluffy. With the mixer on medium speed, add the
eggs and lemon zest. Sift together the flour, baking powder, baking soda, and salt. In another bowl, combine the
lemon juice, buttermilk, and vanilla. Add the flour and
buttermilk mixtures alternately to the batter until batter
is smooth. Fill the cupcake liners two-thirds full. Bake
until golden brown, about 20 minutes. Let cool completely. Use a melon baller to scoop out the center. Spoon
or pipe in the lemon curd into the center. Frost with vanilla
buttercream. Makes 24 cupcakes.

Lemon Curd

¾ cup fresh lemon juice
1 tablespoon grated lemon zest
¾ cup sugar
3 large eggs
½ cup unsalted butter, cubed

In a medium saucepan, combine the lemon juice, lemon zest, sugar, eggs, and butter and cook over medium-low heat, stirring constantly, until the mixture thickens. Once the curd is solid, remove from heat and allow to cool.

Vanilla Buttercream Frosting

½ cup (1 stick) salted butter, softened
½ cup (1 stick) unsalted butter, softened
1 teaspoon vanilla extract
4 cups sifted confectioners' sugar
2 tablespoons milk

In a large bowl, cream the butter. Add the vanilla. Gradually add the sugar, 1 cup at a time, beating well on medium speed, adding milk as needed. Scrape the sides of bowl often. Beat at medium speed until light and fluffy. Keep the bowl covered with a damp cloth until ready to use. Makes 3 cups of frosting.

Look for the next Cupcake Bakery mystery in Spring 2022! In the meantime, turn the page to read a preview of Jenn McKinlay's new rom-com

WAIT FOR IT

Coming from Berkley in Summer 2021.

Annabelle

"Annabelle, please tell me you are not meeting Jeremy at the Top of the Hub for your annual un-anniversary celebration," Sophie Vasquez—my former college roommate, life partner in all shenanigans, and best friend forever—said.

"Fine, I won't tell you," I muttered into my cell phone. My breath came out in a plume of steam in the freezing February air.

I was walk-jogging because I was late. Little known fact: I, Annabelle Martin, am always late. As my father liked to say, "Sunshine, you were born late." He's not even joking. According to my mother, I was two weeks late and wouldn't leave the womb without an eviction notice. Having since learned that life is hard, I think in utero me was on to something.

In my defense, my lateness is not on purpose. I'm not trying to be rude, it's just that my comprehension of the human construct of time is marginal at best. Like, I know that it takes at least twenty minutes to walk to the Prudential Center from my studio apartment on Marlborough Street and while I had every intention of leaving twenty-five minutes ahead of time, I got sidelined by an idea for a sketch because of the way the moonlight shone through my windowpane, making patterns on the floor.

As an artist, I'm constantly distracted by the details that most people can filter out. Shapes, light, shadows, the subtle nuances that make up the world around me, I'm in their thrall. Naturally, my quick sketch made me late and now it was fifteen minutes until I was supposed to be at the restaurant, and I was running through Back Bay in the frigid winter cold, in high-heeled boots, with my thick wool coat flapping behind me, no doubt looking like a crazy person.

"Belle, this is such a bad idea," Sophie said.

"Why? We do it every year. It's tradition." My tone was defensive because I knew how Sophie felt about my relationship with my first ex-husband.

Yes, you read that right. *First* ex-husband. And yes, I am only twenty-eight and have two ex-husbands. I've had a few people give me side-eye over this fact, and I even had one woman accuse me of taking all the men. Yes, she did! I told her she owed me a thank-you for vetting them for the rest of womankind. Honestly.

I mean, it's not like I wanted to be a twice-divorced twenty-something. It's just that life stuff happened—big, bad life stuff—and my coping skills in my early twenties had not been awesome. Besides, I'm impulsive and when

I'm in love, I'm sooooo in love I lose all sense of reason. Clearly.

Considering her tone, I supposed I should have let Sophie's call go to voice mail but when your bestie calls from Arizona, you answer even when you know she's going to challenge your life choices. I heard the distinct sound of water in the background.

"Soph, if you're calling me from a swimming pool, I'm hanging up on you," I said.

Laughter greeted me. "I'm not," she said. "I swear I'm not."

A suspicious splash punctuated her words.

"You are such a liar," I accused. I hurried down the sidewalk, feeling the bitter wind sweep in from Boston Harbor.

"Technically, it's a hot tub. What gave it away?"

"Splashing."

"Sorry," she said. She didn't sound a bit sorry. "How's the weather there? Another blizzard on the way?"

"It's Boston in February," I said. "Cold, gray, and sad. It's just horribly sad. In fact, I think I have a case of seasonal affective disorder brewing."

"Aw, that is SAD, poor Belle," she said. "You should come visit me in Phoenix. It's a delicious eighty-two degrees without a cloud in the sky."

It was two hours earlier in Phoenix. While she enjoyed daylight, I was navigating the early dark on one of those painful thirteen degree days where your snot freezes solid before you can blow it out your nostrils.

"Why, yes, I'll have another margarita," Sophie said, obviously not to me. "Thank you."

"I hate you. You know that, right?" I asked. I adjusted

the purse strap on my shoulder as I jogged the final stretch to the Prudential Center, known locally as The Pru.

"Well, I think you'll hate me less when you hear why I called," she said.

I stepped on a patch of ice and my heel slid out from under me. I fought to keep my balance, pulling a hamstring in the process. "Ow! Shit!"

"How about I explain before you start swearing?"

"Sorry, that wasn't meant for you. I slipped," I said. Now I was limping, which I'm sure was a fabulous look for me. "I'm almost at the building. I might lose you in the elevator."

"Then I'll be quick," she said. "I'm calling to offer you a job as the creative director in our company."

"But your company's in Phoenix," I said. Sophie and her husband, Miguel, owned a graphic design firm that was quickly gaining national attention. This was no small offer.

"Yes."

"You want me to move to Phoenix?" I stopped walking. The bitter wind pushed me up against the side of the building.

"Yes."

"Phoenix, Arizona?"

"Yes."

"But . . ."

"Just hear me out," Sophie said. "You're the most talented graphic designer I've ever known, and we desperately need you here. Phoenix is in a boom and we can top the money you're currently making as a freelancer. Think of it as an opportunity to shake up your life a little bit."

"I wasn't aware that my life needed shaking," I said. It did, but I didn't want to admit it because . . . pride.

"Oh, come on, Belly, come to Phoenix."

For the record, Sophie is the only person on the planet allowed to call me "Belly" because when we were roommates at the Savannah College of Art and Design, she held my hand when I got my belly button pierced. We shared a bond of bad decisions that was stronger than steel.

I tried to picture myself in the southwest. Couldn't do it. She used my stunned silence to press her point.

"You've been freelancing for six years," she said. "Don't you want more stability?"

"No." *Yes.*

"A pay raise?"

"Maybe." *Definitely.*

"Retirement? Benefits? Paid vacation?" *Check, check, check.*

I sighed. It came out as a limp jet of hot breath in cold air. She was making solid points. I had no rebuttal. I went for avoidance. I pulled my phone away from my ear to check the time. "I have to go. I'm going to be sooo late."

"You're always late."

"I'm trying to be better," I protested. "It was my New Year's resolution."

"And how's that going?"

"Shush," I said. "You're not helping here."

"I am helping. You just don't want to hear it. Are you going to get back together with Jeremy?" she asked.

"No!" I cried. "Why would you even think that?"

"Because he's your social fallback plan and you spend an awful lot of time together for people who are no longer married," she said.

"We're friends with benefits," I said.

"You don't need him as a friend and you're not doing him any favors by offering him benefits. You're keeping each other dangling. It's not healthy for either of you."

"We're not dangling," I said. "We agreed that we can date whoever we want."

"And yet, neither of you do," she said.

"You don't know that," I protested.

"Please," she said. "I've been on this ride before. Neither of you is seeing anyone else, but you don't belong together and you know it. You need to stop picking the lowest hanging fruit."

"Did you just call Jeremy an apple?" I asked.

"I think of him as more of a peach, easily bruised," she said. "Your entire relationship was spent with you protecting him by doing everything for him because he's so anxiety ridden and fragile, albeit lovable. You were like a lawnmower wife, moving every obstacle out of his way. Do you really want that for the rest of your life?"

"I didn't—I'm not—" I protested but she interrupted.

"Yes, you did and you are," she declared. "You've run interference for him his entire adult life, even when you were married to the big disappointment, who also used you to prop himself up. And then what did the BD do? He left you—just like Jeremy did when his mother stamped her foot hard enough. Time to break the pattern, my friend."

"I . . ." I slumped against the wall. Is that how she saw it? How she saw me? I didn't know what to say.

"Come to Phoenix," Sophie insisted. Then she made a weird burbling noise. "Do you hear that? That's me gulping down a margarita as big as my head. Come. To. Phoenix."

I heard another splash and decided, since I could no longer feel my toes, the tips of my ears, or my fingers, that I really did hate her.

"I love that you're asking me," I said. "But—"

"Don't say no!" she ordered. So bossy! "Promise me, you'll at least think about it."

"Fine, I'll think about it." I wasn't going to think about it. "Now I *have* to go. Miss you. Love you."

"Miss you. Love you, too," she echoed. "Say hi to Jeremy, you know, before you tell him you're leaving him for me."

"Will do." I said. I wasn't leaving him for her. I mean, creative director? That sounded like I'd have to supervise, which was not my gift and Soph knew it. I couldn't even supervise a house plant. I ended the call and ran into the building, realizing I was entering the danger zone of lateness where Jeremy was going to be peeved with me for causing his anxiety to spike, especially given that it was our un-anniversary and all. Damn it!

\~\~\~

The Top of the Hub sits on the fifty-second floor of The Pru. It's a white tablecloth, fine china, heavy silverware sort of restaurant, which boasts outstanding views of the Charles River, Boston Harbor, and the surrounding city. Jeremy and I had been coming here to celebrate our un-anniversary ever since he landed in Boston a few years ago, shortly after I divorced Greg

DeVane, aka the big disappointment or the BD for short. Yes, he was a disappointing husband, but that's a story for another day preferably accompanied by a shot of three wise men with an IPA chaser.

Jeremy Pettit and I met in Georgia when I was attending the Savannah College of Art and Design and he was at Savannah State studying engineering. I spotted him at a coffee shop on Broughton Street and had been a smitten kitten on sight. He was everything a college girl looked for in a boyfriend—shy, sweet, attentive, as snuggable as an oversized teddy bear, and it certainly helped that he looked like he'd just walked out of the Patagonia catalog wearing their fjord flannel.

Jeremy had the distracted air of a guy with one foot in childhood and the other in adulthood, uncertain of which direction he wanted to go. I figured he just needed a good woman—i.e. me—to give him a solid shove in the right direction. I had not accounted for the realities that I was no readier to be an adult than he was, his mother hated me, and he had a host of issues that didn't even start to appear until after we were married, which was a month after graduation.

If I closed my eyes and listened, I could still hear my older sister Chelsea's shriek of outrage echoing on the airwaves to this day. Our mother had passed away six months before I met Jeremy, and, in hindsight, I could see that our relationship and subsequent marriage was an attempt to fill the gaping hole left by my mother's passing, but what twenty-one-year-old has that sort of insight? Not me.

I'd thought Jeremy was my soul mate sent to comfort and keep me just when I needed him most. I truly believed we'd be together forever and ever. Amen. We didn't last two years. By the time he was finishing his master's degree in biomedical engineering, the ink was drying on our divorce papers, which had been drawn up by his mother's attorney. The only time she ever smiled at me was the day she came to collect Jeremy and his things from our apartment.

Now five years later, we were in the same city, celebrating our un-anniversary at the Top of the Hub, while enjoying an "exes with benefits" relationship of which absolutely no one in my life approved. You'd think that would be more of a deterrent for me. Nope.

The elevator opened and I strode into the lobby, pretending I wasn't panting for breath and trying not to look sweaty. Jeremy, in a navy suit with his hair cut high and tight and sporting a blonde beard, was standing beside the hostess station waiting for me. He looked mildly panicked so it appeared dinner was going to start with tension. I decided to sink that battleship right away.

I dashed across the lobby and threw myself at him. He caught me and I kissed him full on the lips, knowing it would melt his brain and make him forget he was mad.

"Sorry, sorry, sorry," I panted when we came up for air. Then I shrugged and said, "Artist."

To my relief, his shoulders dropped from around his ears, the tight lines around his mouth eased and he laughed. Then he hugged me. "I suppose I should be used to it by now."

Well, yeah, you should, I thought. After all, my tardiness was one of the many reasons we'd divorced. Wisely, I did not say this out loud. Instead, I checked my coat and then curled my hand around his elbow while we followed the hostess to our table.

She led us through the rows, to a table tucked beside a tall window. To my surprise, it was strewn with pink rose petals and a bottle of champagne was in a bucket with two glasses already poured and waiting for us. I gave Jeremy a look.

"You went all out this year," I said.

He shrugged. "It seems like a special un-anniversary, doesn't it?"

His pale green eyes met mine and I felt a prickle of alarm. Had I missed a memo? What did he mean by "special"? My heart started to pound in my chest like warning shots being fired. I could feel my flight or fight response, okay, mostly flight, kick in.

Jeremy and I had celebrated our un-anniversary at the Top of the Hub, ever since he moved to Boston three years ago. It was always low-key and fun right up until last year, when, in a bout of deep loneliness, I invited him to spend the night. He'd been "spending the night," if you get my drift, a couple of times a month ever since.

I knew Sophie was right that the relationship wasn't doing either one of us any good rather like glazed doughnuts, the occasional cigarette, or three-day long video game–playing binges, but I didn't want to give it up because then I'd have to go out there and find a real relationship, which felt like entirely too much work.

He pulled out my chair and I slid into my seat. I felt out of step, like I was clapping on the down beat, and couldn't quite get the rhythm of the room. I noticed that people at surrounding tables were covertly watching us. This was bad.

The hostess put our menus on the corner of the table and stepped back. She was younger than me by a couple of years. She had that fresh-faced enthusiasm that could only be found on a person who hadn't been paying their own rent for very long.

She glanced between us and then with a soft squeak, she stepped back, turned on her heel and hurried away. The early warning system inside me grew insistently louder.

Jeremy picked up the two champagne glasses and handed me one. I debated downing it, sensing that liquid courage was going to be required. He lifted his in a toast. I wished he'd sit down. It felt as if he was looming over me.

"Annabelle, you're my best friend," he said. Oh, dear, this sounded like the opening of a speech. That couldn't be good. Usually we just said, "Look at us," clinked glasses and down the hatch the beverage went. We didn't do speeches.

"And you're mine," I said. I lifted my glass, indicating the toast was over. But he didn't get the message. In fact, he looked as if he was just warming up.

"I know," he said. "Despite the fact that we got married too young and you had that episode with what's his name, we're still each other's plus one."

I stared at Jeremy. That "episode" was my second marriage. Jeremy knew the BD's name, but even now, three years after my divorce, he still refused to say it. I knew he'd been in denial about the whole thing but it seemed significant at the moment that he couldn't say his name or mention my marriage.

"You mean my marriage to Greg?" I asked. I blinked innocently.

He made a face as if a fly had just flown into his mouth. He waved his hand dismissively and continued.

"Yeah, even then I always felt like we were meant to be together, you know."

I didn't know. I had thought we were done except for the friendship and fringe benefits. The cold feeling in the pit of my stomach began to harden into a block of ice. If he was headed where I feared, we were not going to come out of this as friends, never mind friends with benefits.

"I always believed we'd grow old together and end up on a porch somewhere in matching rocking chairs," he said. His smile was adoring when he tilted his head and stared into my eyes. He was going to propose. I could see it coming as if it had the bright blaze of a meteor breaking through the atmosphere.

I had to stop him. I didn't want to marry him again and I didn't really believe he wanted to marry me. It would ruin everything if he asked because I'd have to say no and he'd be so terribly hurt. He did bruise easily just as Sophie had said. I jumped to my feet. I clinked my glass with his and said, "Are you about to congratulate me?"

He paused. He looked confused. I forged ahead, taking advantage of his surprise.

"Sophie told you, didn't she?" I asked.

"Sophie?" He shook his head. "Told me what?"

"She offered me a job as creative director for her company, and I accepted," I said. "Isn't it amazing? I'm moving to Phoenix. Promise you'll come and visit."

His mouth hung open for a moment, then he cleared his throat and said, "Actually, I didn't know. This was—"

"So incredibly thoughtful of you," I said. My voice was high-pitched, a little manic, and my smile brittle. I felt as if I were throwing a drowning man a life preserver and he was refusing to take it. "Here's to new beginnings!" I cried, hoping he'd get with the program and let go of his misguided plan to propose. "Bottoms up."

His eyes went wide as I put my glass to my lips and upended the champagne into my mouth. The stress of the moment had me chugging the fizzy beverage, hoping to ease the tension, but something hard hit the back of my throat and got lodged in my windpipe. Just like that, I couldn't breathe. I dropped my glass and clutched the front of my neck, trying to get some air. I made horrible gasping noises and staggered. Everything went gray and I started to see spots.

"Annabelle!" Jeremy cried. "Oh, my god, you're choking on the ring!"

Ring? I would have asked for more details but instead, I blacked out.

Ready to find
your next great read?

Let us help.

Visit prh.com/nextread